P9-CFP-438

Kitty Hitter

A FRANK PAVLICEK NOVEL

KITTY HITTER

ANDY STRAKA

FIVE STAR
A part of Gale, Cengage Learning

Detroit • New York • San Francisco • New Haven, Conn • Waterville, Maine • London

Five Star Publishing, a part of Gale, Cengage Learning.

Set in 11 pt. Plantin.

Printed on permanent paper.

LIBRARY OF CONGRESS CATALOGING-IN-PUBLICATION DATA

Straka, Andy.
Kitty hitter : a Frank Pavlicek novel / Andy Straka. — 1st ed.
p. cm.
ISBN-13: 978-1-59414-812-5 (alk. paper)
ISBN-10: 1-59414-812-0 (alk. paper)
1. Pavlicek, Frank (Fictitious character)—Fiction. 2. Private investigators—Fiction. 3. Ex-police officers—Fiction. 4. Birds of prey—Fiction. 5. New York (N.Y.)—Fiction. I. Title.
PS3619.T733K58 2009
813′.6—dc22 2009013827

First Edition. First Printing: August 2009.
Published in 2009 in conjunction with Tekno Books and Ed Gorman.

Printed in the United States of America
1 2 3 4 5 6 7 13 12 11 10 09

Kitty Hitter

1

The war between birds and cats began when Dr. Korva Lonigan, a respected physician and animal rights activist, discovered a feather from a Great Horned Owl with what she took to be the remains of her missing tabby Groucho along the curb in front of her apartment building on Central Park West. I'm not making this up.

I never expected to become involved in a war between species. Or between their human campaign managers, at any rate. I never expected to return to New York City, either, except as a tourist. And if I had known that steamy Virginia afternoon about the depths of survival and the spun-off fragments of a real war we would end up unearthing, I might never have answered the cell phone I'd stupidly left tucked in my shorts pocket while balancing two pounds of fidgety Harris' hawk on the back of my left hand.

I fished out the offending instrument with my free, ungloved mitt. New York City area code on the display. Maybe it was Pale Male, the famous red-tailed hawk, calling to be rescued from his unwanted celebrity status in Central Park. No such luck.

"Guess who," a female voice said.

My brain shifted into high-speed reverse, flashing back nearly a decade and a half to a New York courtroom and a dark blue transit cop's uniform. The composed, coffee-colored face of a character witness standing in for Jake Toronto and me, her arms crossed as she stared down the plaintiff's attorney in the thousand-dollar suit who had helped engineer the wrongful death lawsuit against us.

"Darla Barnes," I said.

"Very good, Franco. I see you haven't lost your edge."

"I also have caller ID."

"Strange world these days, isn't it?" she said. "No such thing as privacy anymore. Just bought a new cell phone. Gotta remember to get this number blocked."

Darla Barnes was the only person in the world who had ever and would ever call me Franco. She'd earned that right one misty spring night in the Bronx when I was a newly minted NYPD detective and she, a mere transit rookie, had been instrumental in preventing me from being put under the knife by an overzealous group of bikers at a dumpy watering hole near Yankee Stadium. For reasons different than my own, she'd been working the PI beat almost as long as I had.

"It's been a while," I said.

"Yes, it has. How's that little girl of yours?"

"Not so little anymore. She graduated from college a couple of months ago and is in the process of making the biggest mistake of her life."

"What's that?"

"Working for her old man."

Darla chuckled. "Pee-eyeing with you, you mean."

"You got it. How's your family doing?"

"Not as aged as yours, of course, on account of my youthful grace and vigor. But my youngest, Sweetness, is the cutest little thing you could imagine and my ten-year-old, Marcos, is at the top of his class in school."

"Great to hear it."

"Am I catching you at a bad time? You busy?"

"Not really. Nicky's got some programmer running a security audit on our network, so we're out of business for the afternoon.

I'm just out here messing around with one of my birds."

It was late on a Friday, Fourth of July weekend. For the third day in a row, the mercury in Charlottesville had topped ninety-five degrees. We already seemed to be stuck in that interminable summer pattern of heat building through the day, followed by the break, somewhere in the afternoon, of a thunder-clapping downpour. Today's edition of cloudburst was running a little on the late side, however. The sun still did its thing. Inside my hawk's enclosure the air was as thick as oatmeal. My T-shirt felt like it had been superglued to my back. Bits of fluffy down, cream and black, drifted through the chain-link fence while Torch's talons danced nervously around my gloved fist.

"You mean to tell me you're flying one of your falcons right this second?"

"Not exactly. But I am holding onto a hawk in my other hand as we speak."

"Perfect."

"What do you mean?"

"You'll see . . . Got a job for you, Franco, if you're interested."

"Okay," I said.

In fact, it was very okay. Eagle Eye Investigations was sometimes flush with cash, sometimes not. Since our contract with a Northern Virginia security firm for post 9/11 background checks on federal hires had expired a couple of months before, "not" was beginning to creep more into the equation.

"The client's name is Dr. Korva Lonigan. I'm calling you from her apartment in Manhattan."

"All right." The doctor was most likely having a problem with a piece of property or something she owned down here in central Virginia. Or maybe the issue involved a relative or an ex-husband, or an accident that had occurred in the area.

"I should warn you, though, Frank. This deal's probably a

little different from the kind of work you're used to."

"How so?"

The last time I'd had work like that, six months before, I'd almost drowned at the bottom of a river while trying to figure out how to avoid getting blown to bits.

Darla was silent on the other end of the line for a moment. I adjusted my grip on the jesses and eyed Torch, who was now staring at me warily. Harris' hawks are native to the Southwest. Unlike me, my bird seemed to be doing just fine with the heat. He probably wouldn't even have minded had God decided to crank up the temperature another twenty degrees. There was no hunting for him this time of year, at least while he was in my care. He was too busy molting. All he basically had to do right now was sail around inside his enclosure to keep himself in some semblance of flying condition, eat, defecate, and make new feathers. Call it a wild hawk day spa. With the exception of deigning to interact with me for regular feeding and the occasional weigh-in, of course.

I decided I better tie him back on his ring leash. Torch squawked while I secured the line with a one-hand knot and cast him off to fly up the wire onto his perch again.

"You still there, Frank?" Darla must have wondered if I was experiencing a medical emergency.

"Yeah, sorry, I'm listening." I backed away to lean against the fence, turning my head again into the phone.

"You want to know how this is different, so let me ask you a question. Since you're so into birds and everything, people ever come to you with other animal issues?"

"I've dealt with a few animals who call themselves humans, if that's what you mean."

"I know that. But I'm talking about real live animals here. Criminal actions involving pets. Neglect, abuse, mutilation, killings—that sort of thing."

"Oh, no, can't say that I have. If I ever did, I'd refer it out to the SPCA, or if it were a wild animal, to Virginia DGIF or the feds at Fish and Wildlife."

"I see."

"Unless there was something more than just an animal problem going on, of course."

"Of course."

"What, does this Dr. Lonigan have some kind of problem like that?"

"Possibly," she said. "Not exactly . . ."

I waited, but she said nothing more, so I added, "A lot of times, you know, when you see animal abuse, it's just the tip of the iceberg. Intentionally inflicting harm on a domestic creature can be indicative of a whole host of issues."

"You mean like serial killers."

"That's one possibility."

"Okay, but look, hey, I don't think we're dealing with that kind of an issue here."

"Good. Because I'm out of the serial killer business."

She lowered her voice a little as if she were cupping her hand around the receiver. "This Dr. Lonigan comes from some very serious money. Prestigious job at Columbia. Hoity new place on Central Park West. You get the picture?"

"What kind of doctor is she?"

"Pediatric oncologist."

"Must not be easy work," I said.

"I'm sure it isn't."

"She married?"

"No."

"Children?"

"No."

"You said she's having some kind of problem with an animal, though."

"Yeah. Hear me out, Franco. I don't want you to think I'm

wasting your time here."

"It's all right," I said. "Spill it."

She breathed out a sigh, every bit as audible through our digital connection as if she'd been standing on the other side of the chain-link across from me. "Dr. Lonigan wants . . . well. She wants me to hire you to help me find out what's happened to her missing cat."

Neither one of us spoke while I considered the possibility that a minor earthquake had just struck central Virginia, rendering some kind of momentary breach in the space-time continuum.

"I'm sorry," I said. "Did you say find her missing cat?"

"Yup."

"As in feline, alley cat, pet god or goddess?"

"You got it."

This was not exactly what I'd envisioned when Darla had mentioned a job. But presuming the missing kitty was still somewhere in New York State, at least I had an easy out.

Darla and I may both have been former NYPD and known New York, but in my case that had been so long ago Rudy Giuliani was still working as a US Attorney. And as Darla must have very well known, I was only licensed to take on cases that initiated in the veritable Commonwealth of Virginia, or in neighboring states maintaining a reciprocal agreement with the Department of Criminal Justice Services in Richmond. New York was most definitely not on the list. Heck, for that matter, neither was Washington, D.C.

"Darla, you know I just can't—"

"Hang on a minute. This is my case. You'll be working with me as a consultant."

I thought about that for a moment. Consultant did have a nice ring to it.

"And the client's authorized me to offer you double your

usual rate, plus expenses," she said. "She's even got a vacant furnished apartment in her building for you to stay in and I can have a plane ticket waiting for you at the airport first thing in the morning."

"What, no corporate jet?"

"Hey, I've seen people do a lot worse with their money, haven't you? And besides, there's a lot more to this than just a missing cat."

"Such as?"

"This woman is no flake. She thinks someone may have purposely killed her cat."

"Well, I'm . . . I'm sorry to hear that."

There is something particularly tragic about a dead domesticated animal. Death in the wild happens every second of every day—just look at my buddy Torch here, who knew without question what it was to have to kill in order to survive. But death actively brought inside the protective bubble of your home was another matter altogether. Still, I was having a hard time seeing myself as the next Ace Ventura.

Darla said nothing.

"I agree it's tragic, Darla. I just don't know if it's my kind of case."

"You said yourself if someone did this kind of thing to an animal it could be indicative of much bigger problems."

"Yes, I know, but—"

"It's the only pet the woman has ever owned."

"What kind of cat are we talking about?"

"Angora. Named Groucho."

Cute.

"But she's already hired you. Why does she need me?"

"Okay, here's what's been going on . . . At least two cats, one hamster, one guinea pig, and one puppy are now missing from her apartment building on Central Park West. The tenants have discovered what they think are fur remains for two of them, both of which were accompanied by the feathers."

"Feathers? What feathers?"

"Feathers from the tail of a Great Horned Owl. Dr. Lonigan's had it verified by an ornithologist."

I was beginning to see where this was going. "Are you trying to tell me this group of people believes a wild Great Horned Owl has somehow managed to take their pets from their building in the middle of New York City?"

"No, of course not. It's a newly renovated historic property, by the way. Grayland Tower. Did you see the pictures last month in the *New York Times Magazine*?"

"Sorry, no."

"Anyway, that's not the point. The issue here is the developer of the building. His name is Dominic Watisi."

"What about him?"

"Dr. Lonigan and some of the other apartment owners have been complaining for months about cost overruns with the construction and some other issues. Watisi refuses to even discuss the matter. The dispute escalated a few weeks ago when the tenants filed a lawsuit."

"Okay."

"Now it's made the tabloids, and Watisi isn't happy, you see? His company has another project on hold pending an upcoming bond referendum. There have been a couple of nasty public exchanges between Watisi and the tenants."

"You're saying Dr. Lonigan thinks this Watisi character had her Groucho whacked?"

"Looks that way. She's convinced he's hired a hit man who somehow got hold of an owl. They think this guy gets the pets out of the building, either at night or while people are away at work during the day, has the owl dismember them under the cover of darkness, and attempts to make the killings look like natural occurrences."

"Sounds pretty far-fetched if you ask me."

"C'mon, Frank. You've been around long enough to know that stranger things have happened."

"Maybe. But not very often. Big birds of prey have been known to kill cats once in a while. But it happens pretty rarely, and do you know how difficult it would be for even an experienced falconer, assuming he or she did have an owl, to purposely hunt with that bird in the middle of a city?"

"What about in Central Park in the middle of the night?"

"Anywhere, especially after dark. The whole thing sounds like the figment of someone's overworked imagination, if you ask me."

"Overworked or not, we're talking about burglary, murder, and cruelty to animals here."

"Does this Dr. Lonigan know I used to work in New York?"

"Yes, and she knows a little bit of your history."

"Then she must know some people up there may still think I'm damaged goods."

"She says she doesn't care about any of that."

"I assume someone's already tried contacting Humane Law Enforcement at the ASPCA?"

"Of course. They came out and investigated. Lonigan says they're concerned about the missing pets, naturally, but they refuse to take the idea about Watisi seriously. She even claims it wouldn't surprise her if Watisi's got some of the officials in his pocket."

"I doubt that. All these missing pets belong to people who are party to the lawsuit?"

"Almost. Four out of the five."

"Where did she come up with the falconry angle on the owl? I mean, besides there being the feathers and all."

"This is where it gets really interesting."

"I can hardly wait."

"They've had at least two confirmed sightings so far."

"Sightings?"

"One of the tenants in the building says he saw someone across the street in the park late at night from his balcony. Claims it looked like a small man swinging a rope over his head and a large shape swooping down at him from the shadows. Doesn't that sound like a falconer to you, Franco?"

"With a lure . . . maybe. Not exactly a prime witness though. In the dark, from that distance. He credible?"

"He swears that's what he saw . . . not only that, a security guard from the building now says she saw something, too. She can't say whether it was a man or a woman, but the person was running away, wearing a long glove and carrying something big and gray and brown like an owl on it."

"Might just be some yahoo who happened to get hold of a bird."

"I need to let Dr. Lonigan know. Are you interested in consulting on this case, or not?"

"Maybe. Who'll be doing most of the legwork?"

"You, I'm afraid. It's still my case, but I've got a few other things on my plate at the moment."

"So you're turfing this one to me, huh?"

"If it helps, think of yourself as the outside expert."

"Right."

"So should I tell Dr. Lonigan you're good to go then?"

I'd done worse to pay the rent. From the information given, I didn't believe the theory about the owl; but the sightings of what looked like a falconer, if credible, sounded intriguing. Some kind of nutcase maybe, one who'd gotten a little training in how to handle a raptor, a licensed rehabber or falconer or someone who had worked with one.

"Okay," I said. "I'll do it."

"Righteous . . ." I could almost hear Darla beaming through the phone.

"But you'll need to throw in an extra set of plane tickets."

"What for?"

"For Nicky. She's a falconer herself and she may actually have a better feel for dealing with this type of situation than I do. It won't increase the fee."

Darla cleared her throat. "I'll check with Dr. Lonigan. I don't think that will be any problem. But I also need to warn you about a couple of other things. First, in addition to being a physician, Dr. Lonigan has been a longtime animal rights activist."

"Oookay . . . You might have sprung that little ditty on me sooner."

"I know, I know. But listen, the other thing she wants me to tell you . . . you're probably aware of the friction between some bird watchers and cat owners over cats running loose killing songbirds?"

"Some. I suppose."

"Well, a group of birdwatchers up here in the city read about the story and Dr. Lonigan's accusations in the paper. And they've apparently taken an interest in the matter, along with Lonigan's animal rights group. There has already been a small protest, some picketing and counter-picketing, that sort of thing."

Oh, boy. "No going to sea in a pea-green boat then, either, I suppose."

"Huh?"

"Owl and the pussy cat," I said.

2

“Say hi to Darla for me, but you better watch your step,” Jake Toronto said.

He hovered over my kitchen table, poring through plans and sketches for a new barn he was planning to build at his place in the mountains. He’d been staying with me for a week or so, since returning from an overseas assignment, somewhere in the Middle East, that had left him gaunt and drained. He never talked much about what he called his “occasional government contract gigs” and I never pushed him to tell me more. Judging from the gear he’d packed with him, this particular trip appeared to have been even more stressful than usual. His first two days back in the states he’d barely uttered a word. Four-hour daily workouts at the gym were gradually bringing him back to his old self, however.

“I’ll do that,” I told him.

“I thought you were planning to make the big approach to Marcia tonight.”

“Still am.”

“When it rains . . .” He rolled his eyes. “Don’t worry about the birds, though. I’ll be here.”

In addition to Torch, there was Mariah, the red-tailed hawk Nicole had trapped the winter before, and India, Toronto’s beautiful Gyr-Saker falcon we had babysat while he was out of the country.

“I appreciate it,” I said.

"Least I can do."

"What's your take on Darla's story?"

"Pretty weird about the owl in the park. Someone ought to be after whoever's fooling with it. My old gos took a cat once. Wasn't pretty."

"The hawk get hurt?"

"No. Blind luck."

"Ever hear of this character, Watisi?"

He shook his head.

"Could put a new wrinkle on contract killing."

"Sure." He chuckled to himself. "Like I said. Watch yourself."

The idea of going back to New York City to chase around after somebody's missing feline couldn't have come at a more tenuous time for me.

Lately, I'd taken to driving around the countryside to watch the summer sunsets, listening to country music on the radio and feeling sorry for myself. There is an art, I'd come to realize, in juxtaposing sweet mournful songs with the rhythms of one's own life. I was approaching the big five-o and wondering just how much I had to show for it when it came to the most important relationships in my life.

Nicole said she was beginning to worry about me. The pastor at the small Baptist church west of Charlottesville where I'd been attending services must have noticed it, too. He had pulled me aside one Sunday morning, asked if there was anything he could do.

Later that night, I waited in my truck on the street in front of Marcia D'Angelo's house, rehearsing the lines in my head.

"You're back," she might say.

"I missed you," I would reply. But somehow that sounded all wrong.

Why I would choose this night and this occasion to try to

resurrect what had almost eroded into painful apathy, I couldn't say. Marcia wasn't the only woman to have ever meant something to me.

On the other hand, there comes an age in almost every person's life where you begin to appreciate the fragilely fleeting nature of genuine love, the point of new beginnings and the point of nearly no return.

I suppose I had just about used up the last of my excuses with Marcia. Hurt was beginning to form where it shouldn't have to be. A holiday weekend, and I was headed out of town on some new kind of craziness. It was time for me to push the envelope one way or the other.

The tree limbs around University Circle hung motionless, their dark leaves rich with moisture in the humid air. The smell of fresh-cut grass and dew moss rose from the lawns and sidewalks, puddled shadows of rain faintly appearing on the street in the glow from the streetlights.

Marcia's lawn glistened in the hollow light like all the others. Only the otherworldly *thump* of rap music from a teenager's stereo next door disturbed the broken space between houses.

I was still sitting there trying to decide what to do when Marcia's front door opened. She stepped out into the night with a mug of steaming liquid in her hand, her eyes on me. She was still clad in her summer gardening clothes—matching turquoise shorts and blouse with white trim. She came down the steps to the curb and I rolled down my window.

"I thought if you're going to sit out here in front of my house all night you might like some tea," she said.

"You go ahead and drink it." I shook my head and smiled. "I'll be up all night if I do."

"You know they say that can be one of the first signs of aging."

"Oh, they do, do they?"

"How have you been, Frank?"

"Getting by. And you?"

"Getting by."

"What's that mean, anyway, 'getting by'?"

"It means you're depressed, but you're too proud to admit it."

"Oh, so that's what you call it."

"You want to come in?"

"Yes. I'd like that."

She took a sip from the mug. "Maybe I can find some caffeine-free Pepsi in my refrigerator or something."

I rolled my window up, pushed open the door, and climbed out to join her on the sidewalk. We didn't touch, quite.

"You've lost a little weight," she said.

"Counting carbs."

"Good for you."

"I'm inconsistent, but you keep at it long enough, something happens."

"How's Nicky?"

"Keeping me on my toes, as always. She's been bugging me for weeks to stop by and see you."

She nodded. "I bumped into her on the downtown mall last month. She tell you?"

"She told me. I should've come over to see you then."

"Better late than never."

"I suppose. Are you seeing anybody?"

She laughed. "You always get right to the bottom line, don't you?"

I shrugged. "Guess it's in my nature."

"What were you thinking about while sitting out here in the truck for the past twenty minutes?"

"How to tell you how much I missed you."

She smiled again. "Okay, come on. Let's go inside and talk."

"Talk."

"Yeah. You know, it's what two good friends do when they haven't seen each other for a while."

"Is that all we are now, Marcia—good friends?"

"Why don't we have a talk about that."

I followed her up the steps and into the house. The front hall smelled like ginger. We headed toward the kitchen where the aroma grew even stronger. Miles Davis was playing from the stereo in another room.

"I've been baking all day," she explained. "The PTA is having a summer rummage sale this weekend to raise money for the music department, and they're planning to raffle off some pies and bags of cookies."

"Get thee behind me, Satan."

"Oh, don't worry," she laughed. "All the fattening product is sealed up and packed into containers for delivery tomorrow." She set her mug on the counter, opened the refrigerator and leaned inside to have a look. "You know what? I've got a nice chilled bottle of wine in here. You want some? I might even join you."

"No beer?"

She shook her head.

"Wine it is then."

She pulled out a bottle from a local vineyard and handed it to me. "I'll get the glasses. Still remember where the corkscrew is?"

"Unless you've redecorated."

I found the screw tucked neatly beside some cooking utensils in one of her kitchen drawers and worked open the cork. The wine's aroma was earthy and not too sweet. The Charlottesville region was beginning to gain something of a reputation for winemaking, from what I'd read, which would have pleased old Tom Jeff no doubt, were he still holding forth from his mountaintop mansion, Monticello. I'm no expert on wines, mind you, even the local vintages, but this one tasted okay. We sat down next to each other at the kitchen table and toasted ourselves.

"Are you working much this summer?" she asked.

"Some," I said. "Nicky and I are flying up to New York City in the morning."

"Oh?"

"Got a call from an old friend up there who used to be on the force. She works as a PI, too, and needs some help with a client, a doctor at Columbia."

"What's it about?"

"Her cat is missing."

"What?"

"Her cat is missing and she thinks someone's had it killed."

"Not your usual sort of case."

"Nope." I filled her in on the details of the case.

"Sounds like that story I was reading in a magazine last year when Paris Hilton was offering a $5,000 reward for her lost Chihuahua."

"There you go then." I shrugged, took another sip of wine.

"You do lead an interesting life sometimes."

The jazz playing in the other room ended. It was followed by a smooth R&B tune from an artist I didn't recognize.

Marcia took my hand. "Dance with me?"

"You bet."

I'm not much of a dancer. Maybe it's my big feet or maybe I'm just too self-conscious. But here in Marcia's living room seemed safe enough. The mood was slow. The lights were off. We held each other close and swayed. I led. She followed. Simple, really.

Her head was on my shoulder and I could feel the rise and fall of her hips in time with mine.

"Frank," she said.

"Yes."

"Is there hope for us?"

"Yes."

"I've been thinking about you a lot."

"Been thinking about you, too."

"Why does it all have to be so complicated?"

"I don't know."

"We love each other."

"Yes."

"What do we have to do about it?"

"You could marry me, you know."

"I know. But it's summertime, beach weather. I'm off from school."

"So?"

"I don't know if it's the best time to be making commitments."

"I'm here. You're here. I'm leaving in the morning. What more is there to commit to?"

"You know what I mean."

"Yes. I know what you mean."

She slid her fingers around the back of my neck and kissed me. Lightly. Then she shuddered.

"Frank," she said.

"I'm here."

"I think we should go to bed now."

"Really?"

"I think we should go to bed and I think I should marry you in the morning."

"But I told you, I'm leaving first thing in the morning."

"As soon as you get back then."

"I thought you wanted a big church wedding."

"I know a pastor who will marry us. We don't need a crowd."

"You're serious," I said.

"Absolutely."

"What have we been waiting for?"

"Time. Each other. I've been doing a lot of praying. I know it's right—now." She kissed me softly once again.

"Can you do something for me then?" I asked.

"What?"

I reached into my pocket, felt the smooth touch of white gold. "I bought this six months ago. Basically been too chicken to do anything with it until now. I don't know why, but something made me slip it into my pocket on the way out the door tonight."

I pulled out the ring. Tears began streaming down her face.

"It's a holiday weekend," she said. "Do you really have to leave?"

"I'm sorry, yes."

She slipped the ring over her finger. The music went on as we kissed.

"What time did you say your plane leaves in the morning?" she asked.

3

"Bad memories?"

Nicole caught me staring out the window as our commuter flight began to bank on approach into LaGuardia. The sun had risen over Long Island and was angling its rays into the gray spires of Midtown, which looked almost peaceful at this hour on a Saturday. Haze draped the Verazzano, the East River, and the rest of the city like steam settling over a cauldron. Marcia D'Angelo's house back in Charlottesville was suddenly a distant memory.

"A few. Some good ones, too. How many times does this make it you've been to New York?"

"Must be the fifth or sixth. After you and Mom broke up, back when she was married to the schmuck and had tons of money, she brought me up here a few times to see Broadway plays and go shopping."

"You miss it?"

"Miss what?"

"The money."

"Sometimes," she admitted.

"Yet here we are."

"Yup. Here we are."

Marcia and I had decided not to inform anyone else of our engagement. We'd tell Nicole, of course. And we'd tell Jake, who was still my best friend despite being my former partner and probable best man, and maybe a few other close friends a couple of days before the ceremony. Nicole, however, sensed something was up.

"So how'd it go last night?"

"How'd what go last night?"

"You know what I mean . . . with Marcia."

"I thought things went rather well."

"Rather well? You don't talk like that, Dad. What happened?"

"We talked. We danced. It was a nice evening."

She rolled her eyes in mock exasperation. "You're not going to tell me, are you?"

"Tell you what?"

"Anything," she said. "About what really happened."

"I thought I just told you."

"I need details, Dad. Details . . ."

"Look, I don't quiz you, even though I'm your father, about your romantic escapades, do I?"

"Uggh!" She sucker punched me in the deltoid.

"Hey, watch it. That's my old pitching arm."

As if there'd ever been any doubt, my daughter had grown into a beautiful young woman. Petite, composed, possessed of an innate ability to read others' emotions, like her mother once upon a time. She'd let her dark hair grow out some, but still kept it stylishly trimmed in a French twist. She was neatly decked out for the city in black jeans and a plain white tee.

Why she chose to work with her Neanderthal of a dad was a mystery to me, but not one I chose to try to solve at the moment. The headphones pinched around her neck were plugged into a portable CD player. Anyone looking at her might have concluded she was listening to music, but in fact she was boning up on her Spanish. Four years and a B.S. in computer science had apparently only whetted her intellectual curiosity.

"So you're old buds with this PI who's meeting us?" she asked.

I'd told her most of the story already. "Yeah. I owe her."

"She a good detective?"

"Far as I know. Streetwise. A pro."

"So like I'm learning from you, I can learn a lot by watching her then."

"I suppose. Where are you going with this?"

"I just thought, well, since this seems like a pretty straightforward, low-risk kind of case, you maybe wouldn't mind me doing some of the work on my own."

The engines flared as we touched down.

"We'll see," I said. "New York's not Virginia."

"A chance to relive your glory days," she said with a mischievous smile.

The flight was crowded with people traveling to New York for the fireworks and the holiday, so we had to wait our turn to deplane. Dragging our carry-ons, we entered the gate through a glass doorway. We climbed a set of stairs to the concourse and headed for the main terminal.

At the security checkpoint, which wasn't busy at the moment, a heavyset black woman in a dark green pantsuit leaned against a table, talking and laughing with the two baggage screeners. She turned to examine the line of people exiting the ramp. Her gaze settled quickly on Nicole and me.

"There they finally are," she said as we approached.

"Hey, Darla," I said.

"Get on over here and give this woman a hug, you big fool." She held out a hand, bigger than most of the men I knew, shook mine with it and pulled me into an embrace. There was an easy frankness about her manner, and a world-weary look to her, a combination that commanded a certain respect.

"And this must be Nicky. Last time I saw you, girl, you were barely up to your daddy's knee."

She and Nicole exchanged handshakes and hugs as well. Nicole was smiling.

"You two have any checked bags?"

"Nope," I said. "This is it."

Nicole carried her laptop case and roll-on suitcase. I was wearing my sport coat, so all I toted was a shoulder bag. In Virginia, of course, we might've also toted our legally concealed handguns, but not here in the litigation and gun-control-happy Big Apple. I didn't figure we'd need them. And if it turned out we did, it wouldn't be too difficult to find whatever was required.

"Good," Darla said. "My car's right out back of the terminal here. Not too far at all. One of the bennies of being ex–Port Authority."

She nodded and gave a wave to the screeners, then turned to the side to pull open a large metal door emblazoned with the words *Authorized Personnel Only*. We followed her through the opening and began to descend a flight of stairs.

"Where are we headed?" Nicole asked.

"Thought we'd stop someplace and grab a cup of coffee before I take you across the river to meet Dr. Lonigan."

"Sure," I said.

She cupped her hand to her mouth and stifled a yawn. "I need something to get my motor started this morning."

"Late night?"

She nodded. "Decided to try some surveillance in the park."

"Central Park?"

"Where else?"

"Trying to catch this guy with the owl."

"You got it. Which—me being clueless about the bird thing—makes me glad you two are here."

We were at the bottom of the steps at a junction with more doors and an entrance to a tunnel that seemed to run between the terminals. We started down the tunnel. Long fluorescent fixtures ran the length of it. The floor was smooth cement and the walls were made of concrete block. A couple of guys wearing airline maintenance uniforms approached and passed us, headed in the opposite direction. They didn't even give us a second glance.

"Looks like you're pretty well known around here," I said.

"You might say that."

"How long have you been looking for these missing pets?"

"Couple of days is all. And with other business, I haven't had much time to spend on this."

I nodded.

"Oh, don't get me wrong. Like I told Dr. Lonigan, I'm for sure gonna catch this idiot with the bird, whoever he is. But when I told her about you, Franco, she thought maybe you could help speed up the process."

"I take it money's not an issue with this client."

She offered me fish eyes. "You really never heard of this building where she's living?"

"No."

"Don't get out much anymore, do you?"

"Not to Manhattan anyway." Maybe that would change once Marcia and I were married. I pictured taking her on a romantic weekend to the city. Broadway show. Carriage ride. Lunch at Tavern on the Green. Expensive, but it would be worth it.

Darla grunted an affirmation.

"I read about the Grayland Tower renovation in an architecture course I audited my last semester," Nicole said. "Art deco preservation with a modern twist."

"Now here's a woman who's up to speed." Darla smiled.

"Modern twist, huh?" I said.

Nicole shrugged.

"You agree with Lonigan then?" I asked Darla. "You like the developer for whatever's going on with her cat and these other pets?"

"I don't know." She paused for a moment. "I managed to get in to see the man, but didn't get very far with him."

"He hiding something?"

"Could be. He's no rosy, cooperative type, I'll tell you that."

"What about the other pet owners? You think they're playing straight?"

"Far as I can tell. I haven't had a chance to talk to most of them yet."

"It still seems like a lot of trouble to go through, putting all of us to work on this, don't you think?" Nicole said.

"Probably," Darla said. "But hey, if it was one of your precious falcons or whatever missing like that, you'd be going all out, too, wouldn't you?"

Nicole looked at me and nodded. Hard to disagree with that.

"So Lonigan strikes you as a straight shooter," I said.

"Absolutely. And besides," Darla said, "there's been some creepy stuff going on with this whole deal."

"What do you mean, creepy stuff?"

"I'll tell you all about it when I get my hands on that coffee," she said.

We'd come to another junction with multiple doors and a new flight of stairs. After climbing the steps, she led us through another door, this time back outdoors.

The morning air shook with the roar of an airliner taking off on a nearby runway. It didn't feel much cooler than Virginia. The slight breeze off the bay was already full of humidity and the smell of jet fuel. A late-model Dodge minivan with New York plates stood parked on the blacktop between the terminal wall and a row of maintenance vehicles.

"Your van?" Nicole asked.

"I've got three kids. Two still in school," Darla explained as we approached the vehicle.

Her gaze locked on something in front of us for a moment.

"Hold up," she said, pulling up short and reaching out her big paw to block us from passing. We stopped in our tracks. I followed Darla's line of sight through the glass into the back seat of the van. "Weird . . . Don't touch anything."

"What is it?" Nicole asked.

"Wait one second," I whispered. "Don't move."

Darla reached inside the jacket of her pantsuit and came out with a mini-Glock. She pointed the gun at the van with both hands, knees flexed in a shooter's position as she made a slow, shuffling circle around the vehicle, taking her time. Finally, she ended up back next to us, her lip quivering a little, but her fingers gripped around the Glock as firm as stone.

"Okay. Clear," she said.

"What's gong on?" Nicole wanted to know.

Darla didn't answer. She reholstered and secured her gun, then whipped out her cell phone, and punched in a number.

"That's what's going on," I said, pointing toward the back of the Dodge.

A child's booster seat was strapped into one of the captain's chairs in back. Which wasn't an unusual sight for such a van. What was unusual was the shape of the K-bar knife someone had plunged into the base of the child's seat, the exposed portion of its serrated blade winking out at us like a set of jagged teeth.

Something moved in the corner of my eye. A door in the terminal wall behind one of the other vehicles was closing softly.

"Hey!"

I dropped my bag and sprinted toward the gap. Managed to get there just before the door shut and flung it open with a bang against the outside wall. Footsteps pounding down metal stairs, flash of green, a dark shape moving below. Nicole behind me yelling.

I leapt down the first short flight of steps and landed with a hollow crash against a metal screen wall. Kept going.

Vapor rose from somewhere. Gargantuan air-conditioning units pounding. The stairs terminated in the middle of a dim tunnel. Had the runner gone left or right? I waited, listening. Nothing—impossible to tell.

Behind me, Nicole and Darla *pounded* down the steps, Nicole hauling both our bags, Darla with her gun drawn again.

"You see anybody?" Darla asked.

"Not really. Just a glimpse," I said.

"Is this the kind of creepy stuff you were talking about?" Nicole asked.

Darla nodded, looking at me. "Welcome to the big apple again, Franco," she said.

Back beside the van, I moved carefully around the side to have a better look at the damage with Nicole looking over my shoulder. Darla positioned herself in front of the vehicle, her phone welded to her ear and cursing under her breath, talking to someone from the airport police.

The entire glass panel from the Dodge's rear sliding door had been shattered. This was no routine smash and grab, where thieves went after the stereo or anything else of value. Even though there was no security on the private lot, someone had gone to great lengths to pull this off in broad daylight, not to mention the strength required to drive the blade so deeply into the seat.

Darla finished talking on the phone and stepped around to join us. I stared with her into the back seat at the image of the blade buried in the Graco Turbobooster.

"Looks like you've got yourself some nasty new friends, Darla."

"Shoot. More like the Terminator on speed, you ask me. Cops'll be down here in a minute."

"They catch anything on their surveillance system?"

"There's no camera on these parking spaces."

"Figures. Our Terminator must have known that, too."

"Yup. My guess is, it was someone posing as a baggage handler or a maintenance worker."

"Remind me not to hang with you next time I fly."

"I guess I should've said something to you folks earlier about the threat." Darla shielded her eyes and looked past me into the glare of the early morning sun as a LaGuardia patrol car, its beacons spinning, whipped into the lot.

"Threat?" I said. "What threat?"

4

Half an hour later, after working through the intricacies of dealing with the airport cops and Darla's insurance company, Nicole and I were standing by a rental car counter with Darla, waiting for the agent to process the paperwork on the new van Darla had rented.

The knife was being checked for prints and any other trace evidence, and so was the Dodge, before they towed it to a body shop. The cops were treating the incident as a routine B&E, figuring we'd been lucky to scare away the person responsible. The knife was simply the idiot's twisted calling card, left when he realized he'd have to bolt empty handed. If Darla weren't ex-NYPD and who she was, they would simply have written up their report and wouldn't even have messed with the van any further.

"I'm sorry you two had to walk right into this mess," Darla said.

"No apology needed," I said.

"Mmmmm."

I was beginning to wonder what else she might not be telling us as she took the keys and the paperwork from the agent. I knew I could trust her with my back, but not if we were only dealing in partial truths. There was a bench outside on the curb where the three of us sat down to wait for the rental car shuttle.

"You said something earlier about a threat," I said.

"Yeah," she said. "It's like this. Yesterday, I got a message on my service. A voice says to stay away from the cat thing with Dr. Lonigan or there might be consequences. That was the word they used—consequences."

"All right. So?"

She reached inside her jacket pocket and pulled out a folded slip of white paper. "So—when I was pulling my stuff out of the van before leaving the lot with you all, I found this under the front seat. Perp you chased must have dropped it. Probably got wind of us coming and had to bug out in a hurry."

She handed the paper to me and I unfolded it. In bold black magic marker someone had written out the word *CONSAQUENSES*. I showed it to Nicole.

"Butchered the spelling," Nicole said. "Your caller specifically named Lonigan?"

"Uh-huh," Darla said.

"Was the voice male or female?" I asked.

"Male—definitely male. Had some kind of accent, too, but I couldn't really tell what kind."

I looked across at Nicole then back at Darla. "Is there some reason you didn't tell me about this before offering me the job?"

"No. I should have."

"You try to trace the call?"

"Tried to, but it turns out they were using a stolen wireless phone from an international carrier."

"Where?"

"Africa. The Sudan."

"Pretty volatile place."

"I didn't even know they had cell phone service in places like Sudan," Nicole said.

Darla turned toward my daughter. "Learn something every day. There ain't many countries left on this planet don't have some kind of cellular."

"Hey, Dad, Sudan's next to Egypt, isn't it? Isn't Dominic Watisi Egyptian?"

"Egyptian-American," I corrected. The info Nicole had dug up online the night before about the prolific developer showed that he'd actually been an American citizen for most of his life. He'd emigrated from Egypt with his parents when he was eight years old.

"Yeah, but he could still have some ties there. Maybe he even does business over there."

I glanced hopefully at Darla.

The big woman shrugged. "He could be doing business overseas. Watisi's about as red-blooded American as they come. Man keeps a giant American flag in the corner of his office. Got a framed picture on the wall of himself shaking hands with President Bush."

"Sounds like a politician," Nicole said.

"No, just a businessman."

"One who's not very cooperative when it comes to talking to private investigators," I added.

"There is that."

"Okay, he's visit numero uno after we meet and greet with the good doctor. How are we going to get around, by the way, if you're not with us all the time?"

"Oh, I almost forgot. Dr. Lonigan said you can use her car. She keeps it garaged and hardly ever drives it. A Porsche, I think."

"Cool," Nicole muttered under her breath.

"So we can be inconspicuous," I said.

"What, you'd rather take the subway?"

"Depending on where we're going, yes. But we're not looking a gift horse in the mouth."

"That would be my advice," Darla said.

"Hey, I know. We can make what just happened work in our

favor, let whoever did the knife work think they've scared you off the case," Nicole suggested.

"Not a bad idea," Darla said. "But you're forgetting one thing."

"What's that?"

"You don't make threats against me or my kids and expect me to just go away and stop paying attention."

"And if they—whoever *they* is—are paying any attention at all, they're going to figure out we're working with you," I said. "Which means the threat will be coming down on us next."

Verbalizing it made me second guess my insisting that Nicole accompany me on the trip. I glanced at her, but not too long for fear that Darla might pick up my apprehension.

"You two didn't bring any personal firearms, I take it," Darla said.

I shook my head. "Didn't think we'd have the need."

"Have to see about remedying that."

"What's the word on Watisi? He been known to use strong-arm tactics before?"

"Not for public consumption at least. But like almost any big developer in this town, I've heard some rumblings. Maybe it's part of the cost of doing business."

The rental car shuttle arrived. We climbed aboard and took seats in the back. Fortunately, we were the only riders at the moment. I looked at Darla, whose expression carried a weary glaze. Neither one of us was the eager-beaver cop we once were.

"You must have rattled Watisi's cage when you tried to talk with him yesterday," I said.

"I suppose."

"Anything else about him suspicious?"

"Just that he's a big game hunter. You should see the trophies mounted on his wall."

"May not be anything wrong with that."

"Maybe not. But what if the man hates cats?"

"The man hates cats?"

"That's what his wife let slip—she's his secretary—when I asked about the stuffed lion and tiger heads he's got in his office."

"Maybe we should check his taxidermist for Groucho."

"Somehow I don't think it's going to be so easy to pin this rap on him."

"So I take it your stakeout in the park last night was a waste of time."

"Pretty much. I sat watching both the building and the park across the street for more than five hours. Seen the usual—homeless types, teenaged hookers, young folks sneaking off together into the woods to do whatever. Bunches of bats. Even a few pigeons."

"But no owls. And no mysterious man wearing a big glove around, either."

"Right. But don't forget. We've got people saying they've seen this dude with the bird. I figured it was worth a shot."

"Did you call and talk to Dr. Lonigan while we were standing around dealing with the cops?"

"Yes."

"You tell her why we were running late?"

"I just said there'd been some complications and I'd explain when we got there. She said she'd wait for us. Already did her weekend rounds at the hospital."

"Early riser."

"I don't know if the woman ever sleeps."

"Tell me some more about your kids."

"Sweetness is five and in kindergarten. Cute as a button. That's her booster seat in the van. My middle boy, Marco, is nine. The quiet type, but sharp. Doesn't miss a trick."

"You must be proud."

"I am."

"They well protected?"

"They will be now. First thing when I get home, I'm shipping them out to stay with my sister in Pennsylvania."

"Depending on how our meeting goes with Watisi, I'd like to start looking more deeply into his affairs."

"Go for it. One thing I haven't had time to do yet is follow the money trail," Darla said. "Could be some kind of connection between Watisi's dispute with Dr. Lonigan and some of his other developments."

"I thought we already knew that," Nicole said. "Isn't there a public referendum or something coming up?"

Darla said, "There is, but developers like Watisi get into disputes all the time with their tenants. That wouldn't be enough for Watisi to risk causing a stir by killing a bunch of pets."

"Maybe," I said. "Unless you're trying to keep a really low profile because you've got something to hide and you don't like all the publicity the dispute with Lonigan and the other tenants is raising . . ."

"But you start killing people's pets, that sends a very personal message."

"Bodies of other pets have been found?" I asked.

"No. None."

"Seems to me if you want to send a message, you make sure the bodies are found."

"Yeah. Maybe."

Our shuttle had arrived at the lot where rows of shiny new cars sat parked in the sun, somewhere among them our new ride.

"Hey," I said to Darla. "You never did get that coffee you wanted."

"Don't matter," she said, rising to depart as the van pulled to a stop and the driver *swish*ed open the doors. "I'm awake enough now."

5

The ride in from the airport to Manhattan with Darla and Nicole was a silent affair, each of us lost in our own thoughts.

Through the rental van window I watched a teenager jog along Frederick Douglas Avenue. His spotless Air Nikes contradicted the rest of his outfit—greasy blue jean cutoffs, cheap yellow T-shirt, and a red and blue mesh baseball cap advertising some sort of lobster house over on Broadway. His hollow cheekbones and purposeful eyes made him look much older than he probably was. A couple of blocks from Morningside Park, he turned into an alleyway between 115th and 116th Streets, disappearing from view. Just another kid on a city street.

By now, the sun had risen high overhead. In the heat the city moved with an urgent cadence. Air conditioners roared, tempers flared, and cab drivers swerved across lanes. Darla calmly steered the van through traffic, as if she barely noticed. We had to leave the van in a garage a few blocks from Doctor Lonigan's building. Except for the Porsche Darla had mentioned earlier, apparently working for Dr. Lonigan as an investigator didn't come with parking privileges.

Grayland Tower blended snugly into the star-studded array of apartment buildings running along Central Park West. These places are the jewels in the crown, architecturally speaking, of Manhattan's Upper West Side. Unless there is real trouble or they're moonlighting as security guards, cops rarely, if ever, make it inside.

Dominic Watisi, whatever his predilection to intimidation, petnapping, and other threats might be, had built a first-class, swank-looking edifice to the good life. Having hoofed it with our bags, however, the ambiance was lost. The collared shirt I wore under my sport coat was ringed with sweat.

At least inside the air was cool and dry. Behind the security desk the aforementioned guards, one a Latino male and the other an African-American female, were decked out in expensive dark suits and sported little black ear buds. If things ever failed to be challenging enough at Grayland Tower, they looked capable of securing whole nations. They probably made three times what I did. I bet none of them drove old Ford pickups, either.

" 'Morning, folks," Darla said.

They nodded, nearly in unison.

"These are two private investigators from Virginia who are going to be working with me. We have an appointment with Dr. Lonigan."

"Yes, she called and gave us the word," the female guard said. "May we see IDs, please?"

Barnes showed hers, and Nicole and I produced our Virginia PI cards. The guard, whose name badge read simply *MILLER*, took our identification and examined it and us carefully. "Okay," she finally said.

"Jayani," Barnes said to her, "Mr. Pavlicek and his daughter, in addition to being private investigators, are also licensed falconers."

"Is that right?" Jayani Miller, whose light brown eyes and sculpted hair served to accent her chiseled face, gave little indication of interest.

"Frank, Jayani is one of the witnesses I was telling you about who saw the person with the owl."

I nodded.

"Maybe later, when you're done with your shift, you could sit down and go over what you saw again with Frank in more detail," she said to the guard.

"No problem," Jayani said. "You turn up anything on the missing pets yet? Mrs. Halverson, the lady missing the puppy she thinks was stolen, too, came by on her way out a little earlier. She was asking if we knew anything."

Barnes' eyes turned toward me for a second then back to the guard. "Let's just say we've had, uh, an interesting morning."

"Sure."

"Are you on all day?" I asked.

She glanced at her partner. "I'm off at five."

"Perfect. I'll meet you down here then."

The high-speed elevator rose efficiently and with a minimum of sound. Obviously, a lot of money had been spent to renovate this grand structure. The mahogany wainscoting and other decorative touches had been skillfully preserved and blended in with the new.

"You want me to go with you to meet the guard, Dad?" Nicole asked.

"Let's see how our meeting goes with the client and if we make any progress with Watisi. There might be other things to do."

"Okay." She turned to Darla. "Who's the puppy lady?"

Darla twisted her mouth. "Name is Veronica Halverson. She's the ex-wife of some big oil company executive. She has two grown poodles, too, but they're both fine. She's watching her grandchildren for part of the summer and the puppy was for them."

"She find feathers or fur, too?"

"Uh-uh. Nothing. She's fully on board with the owl theory, though. The people I've talked to in the building so far all seem to be, now that it's been in the paper and everything."

"Who is the other person who found a feather?"

"Gwen Farley, Apartment 12D. Lost her cat, too. But I haven't had a chance to talk with her yet. I'll go over the list with you guys later. Besides Watisi, there's enough to keep you busy."

"What about neighboring buildings? There may be more witnesses who saw the guy with the owl."

"Why don't we take it one step at a time," I said. "We've got a lot of apartments out there."

At the seventeenth floor, the elevator doors opened on a carpeted hallway. Only two sets of doors were visible on either side of the hall, with another pair of doors at each end, meaning the apartments must all have been quite large. Sparkling crystal fixtures overhead lit the way.

"How many apartments per floor?" I asked.

"Most have four or five, not including the penthouse, which was supposedly bought by some Russian tycoon who hasn't even moved in yet."

The soft *thud* of a door bouncing against a wall came from the other end of the hall.

"There you are."

The voice belonged to a tall woman wearing blue jeans, a sweatshirt and running shoes. Strikingly thin, her long dark hair was tucked attractively beneath a baseball cap. She stood propping the door open with her hip while she balanced a paint can and roller in her hands.

"Dr. Lonigan," Darla said under her breath.

"Sorry," she said. "I was just doing some base work on a canvas in the living room and thought I'd open the door for some air."

Darla made a beeline in her direction. I followed with Nicole. Lonigan smiled and set the paint brush down in a tray on the floor just inside the door.

She was younger than I'd expected. I guessed mid-thirties. Her eyes were nearly as dark as her hair and although she was thin, her bare arms were ribboned with muscle. I'd been imagining some grim-looking academic type who took everything in life so seriously that her face had begun to contract into a severe scowl. Instead, her grin radiated a hint of mischief. I guessed her young patients loved this about her.

"You must be Frank," she said, extending her slender fingers to shake my hand. "And this must be your daughter, Nicole, right?"

"Yes," Nicole said as they, too, shook hands.

"Well, come on in. The place is a little turned upside down right now with some of my projects, but I'm sure we can find a spot for us all to sit."

She led us into the foyer, where an oblong table coated in black lacquer supported a large glass vase of orange and yellow daylilies. To the right, a doorway offered entrance to the kitchen where a cool tile floor and granite countertops predominated. The air in the apartment was permeated by that faint new-house smell you get with extensive renovations.

The significance of Lonigan's cat in her life became obvious from the two large framed black and white photos in the entryway. There was also a snapshot of the cat in a frame on the end of the kitchen counter that I could see through the door.

Lonigan's taste in décor tended toward the eclectic, some modern mixed with old. It said, but didn't scream, expensive. Her projects apparently included not only her painting but refinishing what looked like a valuable antique sideboard stationed in another side hallway between the kitchen and the dining room.

But all that paled in comparison to what we encountered as we entered the heart of the apartment, a high-ceilinged great room with huge plate glass windows looking out on the city and the park below.

Three large easels stood in front of the windows. Canvases were scattered in a semi-organized fashion throughout the room. Watercolors. Oils. Portraits, landscapes, and still lifes.

"Dr. Lonigan's an artist, too," Darla said. "I guess I should have mentioned that."

"Rank amateur," Lonigan said. "But I do love it. Keeps me sane when I'm not at the hospital."

"This is very good," Nicole said, stepping right up to the work in progress on the largest of the easels. It was an impressionistic rendering of the view from the windows.

"Are you interested in art?" Dr. Lonigan moved to stand alongside her.

"Some. I'm into computers mostly. But I took an art history class my sophomore year at UVA, and I really liked it."

"Surrealism and magic realism and all that."

"Twentieth century, yes. But we also spent a lot of time on ancient art and older forms."

"Wonderful. Good for you."

"Nicole's also a licensed investigator," I said, not wanting to interrupt a discussion about art but figuring we had higher priorities at the moment.

"Of course." Dr. Lonigan turned to Darla. "So you had some difficulty getting together at the airport?"

"Not quite," Darla said. "A lot worse than that, I'm afraid."

"Oh?"

An air conditioner rumbled on somewhere and a blanket of cool air floated down on us from vents in the high ceiling above.

"Should we get down to business then?" Darla asked.

"Absolutely," our hostess said. The long white sectional in the center of the room seemed like the most obvious place to sit. We took seats on the leather sofa with the exception of Dr. Lonigan, who perched comfortably on an artist's stool before us. She wore open-toed sandals, and her toenails were painted gold. "Please. Tell me what happened."

Darla laid it out for her. She told her all about the van and the knife and the threat with the note. The doctor seemed frozen to her stool. She drank in every word without moving a muscle until Darla was finished.

"I'm almost too stunned to respond. First they kill our pets, now more threats. What's going on here?"

"Somebody obviously doesn't want us poking into this situation," Darla said.

"What did the police say?"

"We haven't told them about the threat yet. They're treating the incident at the airport as a robbery with a pissed-off thief."

Lonigan turned to me. "I hope this isn't more than you bargained for, Mr. Pavlicek."

"It's got my attention, that's for sure."

"What do you think about the situation?"

"I haven't seen enough yet to form an opinion one way or another," I said.

She searched my face for a moment. "Of course."

"Last night's surveillance in the park came up empty," Darla added.

"Question," I said. "What does the building security video show about the nights the pets disappeared?"

"That's easy," Darla said. "I asked to see the saved feeds and checked all of the dates when the pets were taken and when the witnesses reported seeing the guy with the owl. The tapes show nothing out of the ordinary."

"Nothing? Where's the video kept?"

"There's a computer network housed in the basement that helps monitor all the systems in the building. One of the servers is designated to hold the video. It gets archived to external storage once a week. The room is locked up tight. Only the building super and the guards have access."

"Okay," I said. "We can check that out later. I'm on board that something major is happening here, especially after seeing the knife. But from everything you folks have told me so far, I don't think we can come to any firm conclusions yet about what may or may not have happened to Groucho."

"Really," Lonigan said. "Why is that?"

"We don't even really know for certain your cat is dead yet."

"But he's gone, isn't he?" She seemed to take offense at my contradicting her basic assumption. "He didn't just hop on the elevator, walk out the front door, and catch a cab across town. And I found the fur and the feather. Someone must have taken him."

"Tell us more about that, about how Groucho went missing and how you found the remains."

She smoothed out a wrinkle in her jeans. "All right. He went missing last Friday night. I'd been working late at the hospital. I had a meeting, then a couple of difficult in-patient cases to follow up on."

"What time did you get home?"

"It was after eleven."

"Anyone see you?"

"Sure. The guards downstairs."

"What happened then?"

"Well, I rode the elevator up as usual. There was no one else around since it was so late. I unlocked my door and came into the foyer, expecting . . ." She paused for a moment and raised her hand to her mouth, then put it back down. "I'm sorry."

"It's okay. Take your time."

She sniffled and drew in a deep breath before going on. "Expecting . . . expecting to see Groucho greet me at the door like always. He always did. I'd usually scoop him up and rub his belly, and we'd go into the kitchen. I'd let him sit up on the counter while I read the mail."

"But not that night," I said.

"No," she said. "He wasn't there at the door."

"Had that ever happened before?"

"A few times. I'd usually find him curled up on my bed or in the den. But when I checked through the apartment . . ." Her hand shot to her mouth again for a moment. "He was gone."

"Any sign of a forced entry, broken lock, anything like that?"

She shook her head. "That's why I thought of Watisi. He would have access to all the apartments in the building. He still owns the overall property and his company hires the security."

"Okay. Had your cat, Groucho I mean, been outdoors much before?"

She thought for a moment. "Not really," she said. "Not here in the city anyway. I took him with me once or twice on a picnic in the park, but that didn't work out because he liked to run off. A couple times a year, for the holidays, mostly, Groucho and I would head up to Vermont where my parents have a place. We always let him outside there and he was fine. I think he quickly got used to it."

"Cats are natural hunters," I said.

"Just like owls," she said.

"Tell me about the remains you found."

"I was coming back in from jogging the night after Groucho disappeared. I was walking up the sidewalk in front of the building when I thought I noticed something strange in the gutter by the curb."

"Was it hard to spot?"

"What do you mean?"

"Was it really obvious? Were you looking for something like that?"

"No, I wasn't looking for something like that at all. And yes, it was right out there in plain view. The feather was sticking up at an angle. It was wedged into a grate."

"What time of day was this?"

"It was late again, but not that late. It wasn't quite dark yet. I'd say about 8:45 P.M."

"But you didn't notice the feather or the fur when you left the building to go jogging?"

"No, I didn't, but I was in a hurry to get my run in. They could've been there. Even though they were right out in the open, most people would've probably passed them by. Later, when the streetlights had come on, the color of the fur caught my eye."

"Have you or anyone else found any more substantial remains from your cat or from any of the other missing pets?"

"Well . . . no."

"I understand you sent some material off to a lab. Do you still have any of the evidence you discovered?"

"I do. I have it locked up in my study."

"May we see it?"

"Of course."

She stood abruptly and disappeared down a back hall. She returned carrying a couple of sealed clear plastic bags.

"Here," she said, handing them both to me. "Have a look for yourself."

Inside one bag was a moderate-sized feather. I could readily believe, even at first glance, that it might have come from an owl. Inside the other was something far less definite. An amorphous tuft of fur, basically.

"And you feel certain this fur came from your cat?" I asked.

"Yes. You see the swirling streaks of white running through the brown? That fur came from Groucho, I'm sure of it."

I said nothing. I noticed the pattern she had described but wasn't convinced that the fur might not have come from any number of similarly colored animals.

As if reading my mind, Darla added, "Like I told you, it'll be at least a couple of months before we get back any kind of DNA analysis."

"A couple more questions, if you don't mind," I said.

"Of course," Lonigan said.

"Did you see any other evidence, such as splattered blood, where you found the remains?"

"No. But I do have this." Dr. Lonigan reached behind her and produced another baggie that had been sitting on a bookshelf. There was no mistaking what it contained. A cat's collar, gold leather with a chrome buckle.

"Groucho's?" I asked.

She nodded. No one had mentioned this before, either.

"You found it with these other two items?"

"Yes." She handed it over so I could take a closer look.

"It looks spotless. Have you cleaned it since you got it back?"

"No."

"Had it stained with Luminol, anything to check for faint or aged blood?" I looked at Darla.

"I asked one of my old buddies who works forensics now to take a look at it yesterday. He said he couldn't find anything on it," she said. "And, before you ask, I had the area around the gutter and the curb where this stuff was found checked, too, and there was nothing. But the feather does have invisible traces of blood on it."

"May I see the feather?" I asked Dr. Lonigan.

She handed me the bag.

I slipped open the seal, removed the feather, and ran my fingers along its edge. Owl feathers are soft. They also have serrated edges, like the k-bar stuck in Darla's car seat, which helps the owl fly silently at night. The original stealth bomber.

"You want to know what I think?" I asked.

Dr. Lonigan, who had sat back down on her stool, crossed

her legs again. "Yes. I do."

"I don't think your cat, Groucho, was killed by an owl. If he's truly dead, that is."

"What?"

"Sorry if I have to get too explicit here, but you're a doctor and you should understand."

She nodded.

"Owls are sloppy eaters. There is no way, if that big a bird of prey had somehow managed to pick the collar off of your cat, that there wouldn't be blood on it."

Lonigan didn't miss a beat. "But what if this person, this falconer or whomever, took the collar off first and left it there with the remains as a ghoulish statement."

I thought about it. "It's possible, I suppose."

"Look," Nicole, who'd been silent all along finally said, "if someone is actually hunting with an owl at night in the city, then they're doing so illegally. No falconer in their right mind—one who cares about their bird anyway—would send their bird after a cat, especially a good-sized tomcat. A Great Horned Owl could kill a cat that big, it's true. But not without a battle that could easily injure the owl."

"Which only compounds the horror Watisi has brought on us, if it's true," Lonigan said.

"I agree with that, at least," I said.

"We need to talk to Dominic Watisi," Nicole said.

Darla cleared her throat. " 'Cause if this dude is operating on the sly like you say, maybe he not only steals the pets, he gets off on the owl and cat fights, too."

"Then what are we screwing around for?" I said. "Why don't Nicky and I go have a chat with the man and see what we can shake loose?"

As promised, the good doctor was only too happy to let us take her rarely used sports car. She gave us the keys and an entry card and told us we'd find it parked in a private space beneath the building next door. (Apparently, even Grayland Tower's costly renovation hadn't included parking.) Lonigan also promised she'd be available later to answer more questions about the circumstances surrounding Groucho's disappearance and the evidence she'd found.

Before we split up with Darla, however, in the elevator on the way back downstairs, my old friend looked me in the eye and said, "I want to get real serious with you for a minute, Franco. I want both of you to understand something."

We waited.

"I know this case started out as some kind of crazy bird thing. Dr. Lonigan thought it was a good idea and I thought it was cool to bring you in. But the situation's changed since this morning, and I think you know that."

"Sure," I said. "But it's not that surprising. If someone was willing to steal pets, then it stands to reason their next step would be making more direct threats."

"No matter. I want you to know you can just walk away right now and say screw it, if you want to. No problems, no worries. You'll get paid for your time. I'll put you back on a plane to Virginia tonight."

No one spoke for a moment.

"Why would we want to do that?" Nicole asked.

"Because," Darla said, "Dr. Lonigan and I started this deal and I don't know what kind of shit storm we may be stirring up. That's why."

The question had been on the tip of my tongue, too, but since Nicole had been the one to speak first, I let her go on.

"I'm not worried," Nicole said. I could see in her eyes it was true. Maybe bravado had some sort of genetic component, but I could never take credit for such a thing.

"Umm-hmmmm." Darla turned to me. "Frank, no offense, but it's been a long time since you worked up here. Players change. The game has changed. As bad as it was then, in some ways it's better. But in a lot of others, it's even worse now. You guys have moved on. You have another life in another place."

She obviously smelled the fear in me, the father's desire to shield his daughter from harm. I might not be able to put Nicole out on the front lines, even if the situation called for it. I wasn't the only one who recognized that could be a problem.

"You need to get us those handguns," I said.

"I'll take care of it," she said. "But that's not the issue."

Nicole asked, "What are you trying to say?"

"She means we could be in some danger," I said. "And I'm your Dad, and she knows a big part of me is always going to be looking out for you."

"I can take of myself," Nicole said. "You don't need to be concerned about me."

I looked again at Darla. "I think what Nicole's trying to say is that we have a special history. We've been through some things. She and her mom and I, well, we didn't exactly grow up as a family together like Ozzie and Harriet."

Darla's face broke out in a grin. "Nicole, honey, do you even know who Ozzie and Harriet were?"

"Haven't got a clue," she said.

"Beautiful, Franco. Do you even know your own daughter?"

"I've taught her to use a gun." Defensive.

"Oh, well that helps. Question is, what are you going to do if she has to use it?"

"I don't care," Nicole said. She turned to look Darla dead in the eyes.

"Say what?" Darla look half amused.

"Dad and I can do the job. You'll see."

6

Dominic Watisi's office was on a side street off of Malcolm X Boulevard uptown.

Two white faces cruising through Harlem in a red Porsche Boxster drew a bit too much unwanted attention, but there was no helping that. The car felt taut and shifted smoothly. Very few, if any, offices were open on a late Saturday afternoon, especially before a major holiday. But Darla assured us the developer would be working. Apparently, Watisi stuck to a rigorous schedule: six days a week, virtually fifty-two weeks a year. I guess luck alone couldn't earn you the kind of wealth he possessed.

I would have expected the developer to keep a suite of offices somewhere in Midtown, but as Darla explained, Watisi's operation was a little different. His headquarters occupied the first floor of a brownstone he had under renovation. The neighborhood was what the development trade liked to call "transitional." Which meant that most of the pimps and dope dealers had moved on to greener pastures while children and grandmothers did their best to reclaim the streets from the homeless and assorted vagrants.

Someone had opened up a fire hydrant around 130th Street. Three or four dozen smiling, laughing kids were running in and out of the stream, some in swimsuits, some in their underwear, trying to beat the heat.

"What's Watisi's deal?" Nicole asked. "I mean, with all his

money, he could afford a ritzier address."

"Man's probably no fool. He goes where the development action is."

"And Harlem is happening right now."

"You bet."

"He doesn't know we're coming, though."

I shook my head. "I prefer the element of surprise."

"Me, too," she said.

Half a block down from the address, we actually found a legal parking space. The stoop in front of Watisi's brownstone was festooned with paint-speckled drop cloths and makeshift sawhorses. An elegant-looking brass and glass sign did, however, proclaim it the home of Watisi Enterprises, Watisi Partners, and Watisi Capital Development Corporation.

Two workmen wrestled with a heavy metal grate in the foyer. We simply ignored them and marched into the place as if we already had an appointment or belonged there.

A center hallway with a marble floor opened to a carpeted reception area where a tiny Middle-Eastern woman with dark eyes and beautiful olive skin worked away at a computer. She was wearing a telephone headset under a white head scarf.

"Yes," the woman said. "May I help you?" She gazed at us with more than a hint of suspicion.

"My name's Frank Pavlicek," I said, producing a card and handing it over. "And this is my associate, Nicole."

She read the card, but said nothing.

"I was hoping we might have a chance to speak with Mr. Watisi. Is he in?"

The woman's expression remained unchanged.

"He's in a meeting at the moment. He said he's not to be disturbed."

"I understand. But something very important has come up in regards to his dispute with some of the apartment owners at

Grayland Tower."

The woman crossed her arms and regarded us for a moment. "Why are you here from Virginia?" she asked.

"That's one of the things we were hoping to talk to him about."

She punched a button on a console to her left, waited, then turned and spoke softly in Arabic into her headset.

After listening to the reply, she said something else unintelligible and pushed the button on the console again.

"I'm sorry. Mr. Watisi is very busy now. He cannot talk to you."

"He cannot, huh?"

She blinked at me and nodded. If I didn't figure out how to get past her stonewalling—tomorrow being the Fourth of July—we'd be spending at least another thirty-six hours without even having a chance to talk to our primary suspect.

"Maybe I didn't make myself clear," I said in my best apologetic tone. "He's involved in a dispute with some apartment owners and there have been allegations in the press, and—"

"There's no misunderstanding. I'm telling you the same thing I told the black woman yesterday. Mr. Watisi has nothing to say to you. If you'd like to speak with his lawyer . . ." She began reaching for the Rolodex next to her phone.

"I don't want to speak with his lawyer, thank you. I want to talk to the man himself."

Behind the woman, a chime sounded and a door clicked open from a darkened corner of the room. A bald, twenty-something-year-old man with flat green eyes to go with about two hundred and eighty pounds of muscle appeared out of the shadows.

"Is there a problem, Mrs. Watisi?"

So it was the Mrs. with whom we were dealing. "I don't know," the woman said, not turning but keeping her gaze fixed on us. The green-eyed monster blinked an instant appraisal. I must not have measured up.

"Sorry, buddy, but you've been asked to leave."

I must admit, I have never responded well to intimidation. Maybe it's a faulty gene somewhere, a throwback to some primordial past.

"Really," I said. "I don't recall hearing that request."

"Well, you're hearing it now." The big stiff advanced around the side of the woman's desk.

Nicole brought her diplomatic charms to bear. "No big deal," she said, stepping between us. "We'll be more than happy to go."

"That's more like it," the man said, crossing his arms.

"But we still would like to talk to your boss. Maybe Monday?"

The man said nothing. Mrs. Watisi shook her head.

"Must be something you people don't like talking about," I said.

Mrs. Watisi said, "My husband is a very busy man, Mr. Pavlicek. He has more important things to worry about than a few spoiled apartment owners who have nothing better to do than to try to create a public spectacle over nothing."

"Like sending Ivan here to jam a Jim Bowie blade into 'that black woman' friend of mine's child booster seat, I suppose."

Actually, the glimpse of the dark head in green I'd caught flashing down the stairs at the airport looked nothing like the top of this goon's bald head, though he could have been wearing a ski cap, I suppose.

Mrs. Watisi glared at me. "Please leave these premises immediately," she demanded.

"Okay. But you may want to keep that lawyer's number handy," I said. "We'll be back."

Or, I forgot to add, we might never leave.

Out on the street, we took in the scene around the Porsche.

"Be a shame to give up this parking space," I said. The block was quiet, peaceful. Nothing happening.

Nicole asked, "You want to sit on him then?"

"There might be a back entrance in the alley. You have your cell?"

"Always."

"Okay. You go ahead and slide into the car. I'll take the alleyway."

Nicole looked around us at the row houses and newly gentrified residences. From somewhere not too far away, notes of Latin music drifted down the sidewalk. The air was stickier than ever and smelled of charcoal. "Do you have any idea what normal people are doing this afternoon?" she asked.

"A weekend holiday? Pushing their kids' swings in the park. Headed out to a ball game. Grilling hamburgers. Why?"

"I was just thinking, that's all."

"Why did you step in like that, I mean between me and the lug?"

"Because I didn't think it was a good idea, before we've even talked to Watisi, having two mounds of testosterone go toe to toe. Plus, the guy had almost twenty years and a hundred pounds on you. I didn't know if you stood much of a chance."

"You're right," I said. "About the first part, at least."

I left her tuning the Porsche's stereo, her eyes locked on the front of the brownstone, and walked down the street to a convenience store on the corner, where I bought a newspaper and a chocolate bar, before heading back to the alley. A gray Dumpster full of construction debris offered just enough space for a car to pass and me enough cover between the building to move a stray cinder block into position, sit down, and keep an eye on things without being obvious. The nose of a dark blue Mercedes was visible in a parking slot at the rear of the brownstone. The heat in the alley was stifling but not so bad down low against the cool wall of the building.

I, too, began to wonder where "regular" people were this afternoon. What was Marcia doing back in Charlottesville? Tending to her garden? Visiting an elderly acquaintance? Famous in her neighborhood for keeping track of everyone's troubles, Marcia always found the time. Who tended to such needs here in the city where the enormity of human heartbreak and the riotous pace made even knowing your neighbors difficult?

I finished the candy and the sports section, and had just started in on the national and international news when my cell phone vibrated in my pocket.

"They're coming out the front door," Nicole said.

The Mercedes' engine burst to life at the back of the building. I hadn't seen a driver come out of the building or down the alley. Maybe the chauffeur had been sleeping in the car. As the car slid down the alleyway, however, I noticed it was the young man we'd met inside driving. There must have been another exit back where the car was parked, not visible from the alley.

"I'm out of the car and moving to intercept them," Nicole said.

The Mercedes roared past my observation post, obviously in a hurry.

"I see a car coming out of the alley," Nicole said.

"I'm right behind him." I tossed my newspaper and candy wrapper over the rim of the Dumpster and hustled it down the wall as he turned the corner onto the street.

"Okay, I'm on them," she said and hung up.

A few seconds later, I rounded the end of the building to find Nicole at the curb in conversation with Dominic Watisi and his wife, who were standing next to the Mercedes. The bodyguard was out of the car, trying unsuccessfully to use his body to shield them from talking.

Physically, Watisi was not a large man. But he gave the impression of being one. Of average weight and a head shorter than I, he wore a tan silk coat and tie. His brown wrists and hands contrasted with the ends of the white cuffs of his shirt showing from beneath his jacket. His dark eyes looked almost luminous.

"You people certainly are persistent," he was saying as I approached. The bodyguard frowned and stiffened at my presence.

"That's because you make it hard to talk to you," I said.

"I've no interest in discussing the Grayland Tower situation with anyone but my legal counsel," he said, prodding his wife toward the car, the back door of which was now being held open by the younger man, who glared at me with a murder-one stare.

"That why you're threatening the other private investigator working the case?" Nicole asked.

Watisi paused for a moment, his hand on the door. "I'm doing no such thing."

"Well, someone is," I said. "They're trying to stick a knife into her business."

Watisi looked perplexed. "I don't understand."

He listened for a moment while I told him about the threat and the incident at the airport.

"These things are linked then, you believe, this problem with the animals at Grayland, the phone threat, and the airport crime?" he asked.

"Looks that way, yes."

He looked over at Nicole then back at me. "What do you people have to do with any of this?"

"We're both falconers. Ms. Barnes and her client thought we might be able to help find this man with the owl."

Watisi's brow narrowed at the mention of Dr. Lonigan. "Yes,

I read about the supposed sightings in the paper, too. You say you are a falconer?"

"Yes."

"I am a hunter, you know. But with a rifle. Not with birds."

"So I've heard. We saw the big cats on the wall inside."

"I've seen this falconry, of course. It is a popular sport in Egypt where I grew up. For centuries, a pastime for princes."

"Yes."

"And ruled by a code of chivalry."

"It carries that association."

"For knights and noblemen and those who would stay true." He nodded. "Would an owl be worthy of a falconer?"

"That depends," I said. "A better question might be, if it were the right bird, would a falconer be worthy of the owl?"

The developer looked at his watch. "I'm very sorry to hear of the threats against Ms. Barnes. But the idea I would have anything to do with knives or barn owls or whatever happened to the poor creatures from the doctor's building is ridiculous."

"A Great Horned Owl," I said.

"Yes, whatever. I pay for top security at Grayland, as I do at all of my properties. I'm sorry that Dr. Lonigan and some of her fellow owners have decided to turn our small dispute into a public spectacle. I'm sorry all of you have to get so involved and waste so much time on the matter as well."

"We're not wasting time if it turns out we find someone who is making threats and murdering animals," Nicole said.

"I assure you, young lady, neither is the case with me. Now, if you'll please excuse us."

Watisi climbed in the back of the Mercedes.

Nicole put her hand on the edge of the car for a moment. "Just one more question," she said. "You have any pets yourself, Mr. Watisi?"

"What?"

"You know. Dogs, cats, hamsters."

He ignored the question, but Mrs. Watisi smiled from across the seat. "Our nine-year-old daughter, Alvina, is a budding zoologist, I'm afraid," she said. "We have two dogs—Pomeranians—three hamsters, a turtle, and eight species of aquarium fish at last count, I think."

"But no cats."

"No cats."

Igor, or whatever his name was, almost slammed the door on Nicole's hand with a disgusted look on his face. He climbed in front and they sped off, leaving nothing but a trail of carbon monoxide.

"That was fruitful," I said.

"So much for animal-torturing serial killers," Nicole said.

7

"I deduce they're hiding something," I said as I wheeled the Boxster back downtown.

"You think?" Nicole rolled her eyes, reaching over the seat and pulling her laptop out of her bag. "Places are starting to close down for the holiday. I need to find a fast Internet connection so I can really start looking into this guy's finances and other dealings. Something that isn't wireless."

"Hopefully we can get you set up back in the apartment where we're supposed to be staying."

"What are you going to be doing?"

"Darla wants to meet me at the Central Park precinct before the shift changes. There's a detective there she wants me to meet. Later on, I've got the guard in the lobby to talk to. After that, we'll see what you find out about Watisi, and if I think the guard makes any sense at all, we can take over Darla's stakeout duty in the park. If we can find this idiot with the owl, we might save ourselves a lot of trouble."

"What about asking a few more questions of our client?"

"Why? Don't you trust her?"

"I'm not sure."

"Me, either. But she's not going anywhere for the time being."

"You want me to run a check on her, too? See what I can find?"

"Go for it," I said.

NYPD's old Central Park Precinct building on Eighty-Sixth and Transverse Road looks like a cross between a gingerbread house and a brick and stone fortress. I'd never visited the tired-looking edifice during my years on the force. No occasion to.

I wouldn't be visiting today, either. The building was supposed to be undergoing renovations and the word was they might go on forever. The precinct was now being housed next door in a big red structure that looked more like a Broadway theater, complete with marquee sign, than a police station.

Ruminate all you want about the ironies of the park itself, eight hundred acres of nature wedged in the middle of the metropolis—a manufactured wilderness. If I had it to do over again, working as patrol officer, I'd have applied to work here.

The reception area and waiting room were surprisingly empty. A lull in the busy weekend crime blotter, no doubt. I knew I was in trouble, though, when the desk sergeant, a burly mound of a man with a shock of red hair, turned to look up at us as Darla and I entered.

Warren Fitzhugh had been working the streets back when Toronto and I were still detectives. A grin spread across his face as soon as our eyes met.

"Hey, hey, hey. Would you look who's here."

Darla had already told me about her visit to the precinct a couple of days before to talk about the Lonigan case. I didn't expect to be running into a ghost from my past like Fitzhugh.

"Don't I know this guy?" He cocked his head, shifting his gaze between me and Barnes. "Frank Pavlicek. Didn't you used to be a real cop?"

"Some people used to think so."

He lumbered off his stool behind the bulletproof glass, depressing a switch that clicked open a heavily fortified door.

Stepped out to greet me and pumped my hand so long I thought I might develop arthritis before he gave it back to me. "Hey, you lost a few pounds since I last saw you."

"Blame it on the country air."

"Sure. You're where now, North Carolina? Charlotte or something like that?"

"Charlottesville, Virgina."

"Right. The wife wants us to retire down to Carolina. Get out of this friggin' cold. What, you working with Ms. Barnes here now?"

"Just lending her a hand on a case."

He glanced at Darla, who was watching both of us with a bemused half smile on her face. "Bringing in some old-school talent, huh, Barnesy? I'm impressed."

She shrugged. "You know I just lie awake nights, Sergeant, trying to figure out ways to impress you."

"Don't I wish. Hey . . ." He looked back at me. "You're not talking about this Kitty Hitter deal, are you?"

Word had obviously gotten around.

"Kitty Hitter?"

"Yeah. That's what Marbush, the lieutenant who took the report, dubbed Barnesy here's case involving some woman doctor who claims a guy with a bird killed her cat and a bunch of other pets."

"Cute," Darla said.

"Yeah, but at least the doc went and hired you, so now the NYPD can rest easy." He turned back to me. "That's not the case you're talking about, though, right, Frank?"

"That would be it," I said.

Fitzhugh stared at me. "I'll be damned."

Darla added, "Actually, Frank's a falconer. Works with big birds and stuff. Doctor Lonigan thought his expertise might be useful in our investigation. And we stopped by because we've got an important development to report," she said.

"Yeah?" The big cop eyed her for a moment. Then he motioned toward the squad room in back. "Why don't you two come on back."

He punched a combination into a keypad by the door. It clicked open and we followed him into a large, brightly lit hallway that opened up to a great room full of desks, some of which were sectioned off by partitions.

"You guys want something to drink?"

We both declined.

"Smart," he said. "Last time I tried to drink the battery acid they call coffee around here, I thought my ulcer was going to explode."

We rounded a corner and passed a room where four or five other cops were meeting. The space was filled with desks, phones, and computer terminals, all snaked together by what appeared to be miles of cable taped and bundled into walk-overs on the floor.

"Looks like a hacker's convention," I said.

Fitzhugh addressed the room, "Hey everybody, look what the cat dragged in." He tried not to break out laughing.

"Stop," Darla said.

"Ms. Barnes has a new partner on the Kitty Hitter thing. Mr. Frank Pavlicek, also formerly of the NYPD."

A few mildly curious looks. A muscular Latino man in dark pants and a white-collared shirt stared in our direction.

"Hey, Pavlicek, ain't you heard? Jim Carey already done the movie."

Guffaws rippled across the room.

Fitzhugh waved his hand. "You guys are hopeless," he said. Turning back to us, "C'mon, I'll take you to meet Marbush."

We moved on down the corridor toward the back of the building.

"You just get into town, Frank?" Fitzhugh asked.

"First thing this morning."

"This doctor must be getting real serious about her missing feline."

"Something happened out at the airport," Darla offered. "That's why we're here."

"Okay."

"I went to pick up Frank and his daughter, who works with him. When we got back to my van, someone had broken the glass and stuck a Bowie knife through my kid's car seat."

Fitzhugh stopped and gave us both a hard stare. "You must have really pissed somebody off."

"Maybe." She told him about the threat she'd received and the note she'd found in the car.

"Kind of moves us a little ways beyond the pet detective scenario, doesn't it," he said.

We all looked up as a tall woman with short red hair came out of a doorway ahead.

"Hey, Lieutenant," Fitzhugh said. "We got visitors."

The woman glanced up from the file she was holding. "Yes?"

"You remember Darla Barnes. And this is Frank Pavlicek. Also ex-NYPD, living in Virginia now. Folks, Lieutenant Stacy Marbush."

She stepped forward and shook our hands. There was a blankness to her face, the mask of one who had been on the job so many years she'd learned to bury her emotions. Her fingers were pale and gripped mine firmly.

"Got a new case? Not more cat stuff I hope."

Darla smiled. "No. Still working the kitty thing."

"Jesus." Appraising me. "What, you've gone and brought in more talent?"

"I'm afraid so."

"Look, people, I'd really like to help with this, um, matter.

You're welcome to look at my report. But right now I've got a lead on a couple of rape cases."

"There's been a more serious development," Fitzhugh said.

"Oh?" She raised an eyebrow.

Fitzhugh excused himself to return to his post in front.

Darla began telling the lieutenant about our discovery at the airport. About halfway through, Marbush motioned us into her office. We sat in chairs beside a metal table she was using as a desk.

"So you're trying to tell me you think these two things are related? Some doctor with a crazy bird story in Manhattan and your knife thrower in Queens?"

"Yeah. We think they may be related."

"Okay. What else, exactly, do you expect me to do about this?"

"I don't know," Darla said. "Maybe nothing. We just wanted to keep you informed. Frank here and his daughter, who's also a private investigator, may be mounting some surveillance in the park, hoping to spot this falconer people claim to have seen."

"All right," Marbush said. "I'll let patrol know about it. Anything else?"

"You still think this whole thing is some kind of fool's errand."

Marbush scratched the back of her head. "I don't know, Darla. And no disrespect to either of you. But it's the middle of summer. Kids are off school. The homeless don't have as much need for the shelters. Right now, I've got a caseload that would break your heart. A lot of minor stuff, but several bigger offenses, too. So if you're asking me do I have time to go chasing down some woman's lost cat or searching for some phantom birdman, the answer is no.

"Even if there might be a link to what happened out at LaGuardia, all you've really got are vague threats and some missing pets. Why don't you touch base with me again after the holiday. That's about the best I can offer you right now."

"Fair enough," Darla said.

Marbush turned her quizzical gaze on me. "Pavlicek, your reputation precedes you. What's your interest in all this?"

"Help out an old friend," I said, nodding at Darla. "Maybe rein in some guy with a big bird who's gone off the reservation. That was about as far as it went until the knife thing."

"You think there's something more here?"

"I do. What do you know about this developer, Watisi?"

She shrugged. "Whatever I read in the papers, same as everybody else."

"He's clean then."

"Far as the NYPD is concerned. There may be tenant complaints and such. You can talk to the housing authority. But nothing criminal that I've ever heard of."

"What a guy," I said. "So much money and he's probably never even been audited."

"That, I wouldn't know."

Darla shifted in her seat. "Frank and I have both tried to talk with this guy, but he's stiff-arming us. Can't you give us any help at all?"

"If we start finding solid ties to Watisi or his building regarding these threats," Marbush said, "then we can start bringing some heat."

Phones rang almost simultaneously somewhere across the building, and for a moment I was back in my own precinct fifteen years before.

It had been different then, of course. Different time and place. The Forty-Fifth Precinct had been housed in a much older building in the Bronx. But a similar uncertainty hung in the air; a stale, institutional shabbiness that went beyond the dust in the corners, the smell of gun leather, or the urine stink of a drunk. As a cop, you had to learn to keep a lid on your feelings, had to learn to listen impassively and with grave attention, because somebody had to wade knee deep into the garbage and attempt to sort it all out.

"You still with us, Frank?" Darla asked. She and Lt. Marbush were staring at me.

"Yeah, I'm here," I said. "You know what?"

"What?"

"Watisi thinks of himself as being noble."

"So?" Darla shrugged. "Don't we all?"

"Yeah, but standing by the car earlier, he wanted to talk about falconry and chivalry."

"What are you getting at?"

"I don't know yet," I said. "Just something buzzing around in the back of my brain."

8

Though her shift had ended, Jayani Miller was still working when I returned to the lobby of Grayland Tower. Out through the glass doors, she and her fellow security guard were helping a statuesque blonde fit a feeble old man into the passenger seat of a gray sports car parked in the turnout.

Somehow, their earpieces and finely tailored suits didn't look so impressive when they were playing doormen. I guess every job has its lesser moments.

As the Mercedes slid out into traffic, the two came back inside to assume their posts behind the desk.

Jayani smiled at me. "You made it."

"Promised you, didn't I? You still working? I thought you finished up at five."

"Nah, I'm done. Just helping out until you showed up." She nodded at her partner, who seemed ready to begin shouldering his duties alone. This was not the same man who had been working with her earlier. The other guard must already have left for the day.

"There's a coffee shop two doors down," Jayani said. "You want to buy me a cup?"

"You got it."

A couple of minutes later, she sat across from me sipping a Grande Mocha. I myself made do with a bottle of sparkling water. Figured I'd save the additional caffeine imbibing until later when I might really need it.

Once she was out of range of her place of employment—with her earpiece tucked away in a pocket—Jayani seemed like just one more bright ambitious young person in a city always looking for fresh faces. But for the discreet Grayland Tower insignia on her breast pocket, she might have worked on Wall Street or for a publishing company.

"Okay," I began. "I know you've been through all this before, Jayani. But I'd like you to tell me again exactly what you think you saw the other night."

"Not what I think I saw," she said. "What I know I saw."

"Okay."

"It was three days ago. I was working the graveyard shift that evening, not much happening, a pretty quiet night."

"Alone?" I asked.

"Yeah. Just like you saw now. We only keep one guard on after midnight during the week and after five on the weekends. It's mostly the snooze patrol."

I nodded.

"Anyways, about three o'clock in the morning, I hear this *thud* against the glass out in front. Not real loud or anything, just a thud. So I stepped outside to check on it."

"What did you see?"

"I didn't see anything at first. There's a Japanese Maple between the street and the sidewalk around the corner. I was thinking maybe it was a squirrel or a bat or something that flew out of the tree. Then I saw the guy with the bird running down the sidewalk across the street. They disappeared into the alleyway between the buildings."

"You saw a guy with a bird? You're sure?"

"Absolutely."

"What kind of bird?"

"Well, I'm not very good at identifying birds. It was big. I thought it might be some kind of eagle or something."

"What did you do then?"

"I yelled out, 'Hey! Hold up!' But the guy didn't even turn to look at me, just kept going."

"You see anybody else on the street, anything else unusual?"

"Nope. It was kind of eerie, to tell you the truth. I went back inside and called the cops to report a prowler. A patrol car cruised by a couple of minutes later, but by then he was long gone."

"So you're sure this was a man you saw running?"

"Pretty sure, yeah. But I didn't really get a look at his face. He was wearing, like, a baseball cap."

"Caucasian? African-American?"

"Couldn't really say."

"How was he holding the bird?"

"He had something covering his hand. The bird was sitting on it, and he was holding the bird up and out, almost like you'd hold a torch."

"Could you make out any coloring on the bird?"

She shrugged. "Not really."

"Was the bird still or moving? Did it spread its wings?"

"No, sir. That thing was as still as a stuffed animal."

"Maybe it was a stuffed animal."

"No. That was it, you see? Just before they hit the alley, the bird turned its head around and looked at me. Like it was spinning on a swivel or something. I saw its eyes."

"What kind of eyes?"

"Big yellow ones. It creeped me out."

"What about the profile of the bird's head when it turned. Was the back of the head tapered or squared?"

"I don't know what you mean."

"What shape was the bird's head?"

She thought for a moment. "I don't know, I was focused on

those eyes."

"Sure."

"So hey, you think this guy's out at night hunting with that bird?"

"Possibly," I said.

"Some kind of weirdo. Are you going to try to catch him?"

"We might."

"Mind if I tag along? That would be something to see."

I thought about it for a moment. An extra set of eyes might be useful, especially at night. But I decided we better not. "Thanks," I said. "I think we've got enough hands on deck at the moment."

"Oh. Okay."

"Have you read the newspaper article about the missing pets?"

"Sure. Everybody's talking about it."

"If this man with the bird is responsible, how do you think he got the pets out of the building?"

She shrugged. "They didn't come by me or anyone else working the security desk, unless . . ."

"Unless what?"

"Unless it was someone who already lives here. They could've smuggled them out. People come by carrying all sorts of stuff, and it's not like we search them when they're going out or anything."

"Okay. That's good. Anything else you remember that might be helpful?"

She thought for a minute then shook her head. "No, not really." She tapped her extra-long fingernails on the table, clearly ready to end the interview. The nails seemed out of sync with the rest of her, almost as if they were the remnants of a different kind of past.

"Okay, just one more quick thing," I said. "What's it like working for Dominic Watisi?"

"Mr. Watisi?" Her demeanor became all business again. "Well, you know, I don't really have any direct contact with Mr. Watisi himself. I'm the senior guard here, but my supervisor's up at Mr. Watisi's office in Harlem. He reports to a vice-president who reports to Mr. Watisi."

"You've met the man, though?"

"Sure. A couple of times."

"How long have you been working for the company?"

"Three years."

"Most of the people who work for the organization happy?"

"I think so. The pay's good and the hours aren't bad. I'm taking classes toward my bachelor's two nights a week."

"What do you know about the lawsuit between Grayland Tower apartment owners and Watisi?"

She hesitated for a moment. "Nothing, really. My boss says we're not supposed to talk about it. We're supposed to just go on with business as usual. The lawsuit is for the lawyers and newspapers to get all worked up about."

I said nothing.

"I've got to get going." She forced a tight smile.

"This guy you say you saw with the bird could be totally unrelated to Mr. Watisi, you know."

"I don't know," she said. "I'm just telling you what I saw. You people are the detectives—you figure it out. I gotta go." She pushed away from the table and stood to leave.

"Thanks for taking the time to talk with me, Jayani."

"No problem."

She hurried out the door of the coffee shop and disappeared up the sidewalk.

A few seconds later, Nicole appeared on the sidewalk and entered the shop.

"I thought I'd find you here."

"Did you see Jayani go by you just now?" I asked.

"Yeah. I bumped into her. She confirmed my guess."

"She say anything else?"

"No. She seemed in a hurry. Why?"

"Nothing. Just wondering."

"Think she's legit?"

"Near as I can tell."

"She looked worried about something."

"Maybe just her job."

"She saw something then?"

"So it appears."

"An owl?"

"Sounds like it."

"Could the guy really be hunting with a bird like that at three o'clock in the morning, right here in the middle of the city?"

"Or just carrying it around for some other purpose. Maybe for show."

"Harry Potter," she said.

"What?"

"You know, the Harry Potter books. Harry's got a snowy owl named Hedwig."

"Right."

"Except I don't see any witches or warlocks or magic flying brooms around here," she said, looking over her shoulder.

"Well, if you do, you be sure and let me know."

"I can do better than that."

"What do you mean?"

"I've been searching the web," she said. "Wait until you see what I've found."

9

Nicole hunched over her laptop in the kitchen of our temporary apartment. She'd been surfing the Web, she said, for the past couple of hours, trying to find more information about Dominic Watisi and his various enterprises, as well as our client Dr. Lonigan and the Grayland Tower restoration.

One bonus: our apartment was as nice as the finest suite at the Ritz-Carlton. The floors were covered in the plushest, thickest pile carpet I'd ever sunk my toes into. The furniture was top of the line deco modern. The kitchen, like Lonigan's, was enormous and chockfull of the latest super-sized appliances and conveniences. In the bathrooms, heated Mediterranean tile on the floors would keep our bare feet from ever suffering a chill as we stepped from the shower.

"So what do you have?" I asked.

She flexed her fingers and pounded the keyboard. "A lot. First of all, our client isn't all she's cracked up to be."

"What are you talking about?"

"Dr. Lonigan was arrested twice in Oregon in the 1980s on suspicion of vandalism and arson."

"Convicted?"

"No. The charges were eventually dropped."

"Let me guess. Something to do with logging."

"You got it. She was part of the movement that said they were trying to save the spotted owl."

"Woman must have a thing for owls. But so what? She was

probably just out of college then, right?"

"Yup. Vassar, class of '84."

"So she earns her spurs in left-wing activism, grows up a little, and moves back east to go to medical school and enter the real world."

"More or less."

"And she's made no secret that she's still an animal rights activist."

"Not just that, she's listed as a major contributor for about half a dozen different groups, most of which have to do with the environment or animals."

"So what's your point?"

"I just think we should watch ourselves with her, that's all."

"You think she may have more of an agenda here than she's letting on?"

"Maybe."

"What about Watisi?"

"His background's a little bit harder to crack."

"Why am I not surprised?"

"He's been here in the United States since the early 70s, been a citizen for more than twenty years. He's involved in a lot of limited partnerships and various financing deals."

"Who are some of his partners?"

"Big banks. Some Who's Who on Wall Street. All I've been able to come up with so far. And he's got his own activist credentials, in a way."

"How so?"

"Through his church and some other organizations, he and his wife have given lots of money and been very involved in helping new immigrants settle here in America, especially African and Middle Eastern immigrants."

"So what's he hiding?"

"Good question."

"You found all this out online?"

She shrugged. "That and a few phone calls. And, let's just say I might have visited a few people's servers when they weren't looking." She smiled.

"I don't want to know."

"But I've got more."

"What's that?"

"If there really is a guy running around the park playing falconer, whether Watisi has hired him or not, we might be dealing with some kind of reenactor."

"What do you mean?"

"I kind of got sidetracked, but I think you'll find it interesting." She pulled the laptop screen to a better angle for me to read.

"That's the problem with all this Internet stuff. There is so much information out there at your fingertips, you end up spending half the day sifting through minutiae."

"Just read, Dad," she patiently instructed.

I did as she said. "It's a Web site about falconry." No big deal. I'd seen plenty of sites like this before. This one wasn't even particularly high-tech. No flash intro or streaming video of screaming falcons. Nicole was pointing me toward a section of text on the page.

FALCONRY IN AMERICA—AN UNUSUAL TALE.

While a growing metropolis, New York in the 1840s and 1850s was not then the great city it is now. Most of the population still lived toward the southern end of Manhattan island. In the area just above Midtown that would eventually be seized by eminent domain to form Central Park, was a place known as Seneca Village.

It was a mixed-race settlement of around two-hundred and seventy free blacks and whites, with three churches and a school. For a period of time, the village served as a critical junction on the Underground Railroad, helping to ferry escaped slaves pursued by bounty hunters on their journey northward into Canada and freedom.

Obadiah Robertson was a former slave, but not in America. An Ethiopian, he had served in the house of a wealthy Arab, where, owing to his skills with animals, he had been pressed into service as a falconer. There, his formidable talents training the swift hunting birds earned him an honored place and eventually, his freedom.

Robertson (his Americanized name) migrated to the United States and settled for a time in Seneca Village. He trapped and hunted with peregrine falcons, red-tailed hawks, and even owls. Before long, Robertson, who had become a devout Christian, began guiding groups of slaves up the Hudson valley, into the Catskills, and on into Canada. Short in stature, with quick, lithe movements, he was a superior guide, and he frequently traveled with one of his hawks or falcons. His hunting prowess allowed him to provide meat for the starving refugees while they were on the move, without fear of attracting attention by the use of a firearm.

"Pretty wild story," I said.

"Keep going."

Robertson disappeared under questionable circumstances in 1851. Some said he was murdered near Seneca Village. Others claimed that after the dissolution of Seneca Village he had taken a Native American wife and gone to live with the Indians in upstate New York. For years afterward, escaping slaves on the trek North would whisper tales about the mysterious caches of rabbit and squirrel meat that would sometimes appear at their campsites, especially in the dead of winter when they were near starvation and struggling through the bitter cold. These events, it was said, were often precipitated by the distant screaming of a hawk or the hooting of an owl.

"What do you think?" Nicole asked when I looked up from reading.

"Unbelievable."

"I was cross-referencing property listings around the park, got into a bit of the history, and decided to plug in falconry to see what came up."

"Amazing. Nice work."

"Do you think this could be significant for our case?"

"So what, you want to go tell Darla and Dr. Lonigan that now we think we might be chasing a ghost?"

"Wait," she said. "There's even more." Her fingers danced across the mouse pad. She clicked on the cursor and a new Web page came into view. It was a small section of text, part of a larger examination of the architectural archives of Manhattan.

Obadiah Robertson, who could read and write, unlike most former slaves, supposedly kept a journal of his bird-training activities and other exploits. In particular, the book apparently chronicled Robertson's hunting adventures around Manhattan and his use of a rudimentary tunnel system under a section of what is now Central Park. Called Book of the Mews, *a reference to a facility used to house raptors, this leather-bound volume was rumored to have been part of a private collection in New York City but has never been found. If located, it would prove an invaluable primary source document for the history of New York City and Seneca Village, as well as for the ancient sport of falconry. Robertson was said to be fond of hunting with a specially trained Great Horned Owl at dusk or sometimes even after dark.*

I looked up at Nicole. "So you think someone's gotten their

hands on this book?"

"Could be."

"Might be living out some kind of historical fantasy."

"Or even better. Maybe they've found one of his old tunnels and are using it to keep something hidden."

"Have you found out anything else about this Robertson character? Does he have any living descendants, that sort of thing?"

"No. I've found several other references to Seneca Village. There was even a children's book published recently. But nothing about him. And to do a complete genealogical tracing, I'd need to have a wife or a child's name or something else to go on."

"What about the book?"

"I searched all available online databases and came up with nothing. It's not listed for sale anywhere. Not that I expected it to be."

"So for now all we've got is an interesting story."

"With one coincidence—the possible similarity to a falconer hunting in Central Park," she said.

"Right."

"And you've always told me you don't like coincidences during an investigation, Dad," she said.

10

Darla Barnes' office was in the Richmond Hills section of Queens. Nothing garish. A second-floor walkup over a realtor's office in a commercial strip of tired storefronts. We only stopped by for a few minutes on the way to her house so she could check her mail.

While I'd been talking with Jayani and looking over Nicole's Internet find, Darla had been busy on another case, taking pictures with her digital camera of a pickup basketball game on the Upper East Side. The players were impressed, she told us, must have figured her for a scout, especially one six-foot-eight dunking machine whose day job was stacking boxes. The Knicks wouldn't be calling. But the insurance company the phi slamma jammer had scammed out of several thousand dollars in workman's compensation payments just might.

"Nothing but bills," she said, closing the door behind her as we left descending the stairs.

"Tell me about it," I said. "Where's the glamour anymore in the private eye life?"

"Honey," she said. "Ain't no glamour here. Lest you plan to be paying for it."

The sky outside had turned a gentle shade of mauve as the sun in the west ducked beneath a bank of clouds. The air smelled of fried chicken and spices. A group of Asian drummers and dancers were performing on the street a few blocks away, drawing a sizable crowd.

"How far to your house?" I asked.

"It's close. Just a few blocks. Makes for an easier commute than back when I was working Transit, I'll tell you that much."

"Okay."

"So you guys have made some progress," she said.

"Some." I told her about my conversation with Jayani and Nicole told her the story about Obadiah Robertson and what else Nicole found.

"Strange," was all she said. "Where do you go from here?"

"I thought we'd try staking out one section of the park tonight," I said. "Someplace that would be likely for a falconer after game."

"You mean you think this guy with the owl might really be hunting with the thing, not just stealing people's pets?"

"I don't know. But it's what the birds do."

Her house turned out to be a pale blue Cape Cod cottage with a porch. At the end of the street, a cul-de-sac backed up to a reed-filled swamp next to a school playground. Three children were playing in front of the house, one boy of about ten and two little girls on bicycles. A middle-aged black man with gray eyes to match his gray beard sat on the porch shucking ears of corn into a metal bucket and keeping watch over the youngsters.

The kids looked on warily at first, probably confused at the sight of the unfamiliar vehicle. Then they caught sight of Darla as we stepped from the van.

"Mommy!"

One of the little girls hopped off her bike, dropping it on the sidewalk before running into her mother's arms.

"Hey, Sweetness." Darla gathered her daughter up and kissed her on the cheeks. "Marco, you come on, too. There's someone here I want you to meet."

The other little girl waved good-bye to Sweetness like Nicole and I were the bogeyman and pedaled her bike down the sidewalk, up the driveway and into the garage of the house next door. The boy stood a ways off at first—he was busy doing something with a fishing pole—before he came over to accept a hug from his mother as well.

"Did you buy a new car, Mom?" he asked.

"No, I'm afraid not." Darla laughed. "It's a rental. I ran into a little trouble with mine."

She turned the children toward us. "Marco, Sweetness, I'd like you to meet Mr. Pavlicek and his daughter, Nicole. They're detectives working with me on a case."

I stepped forward and reached out to shake the boy's hand. He looked me squarely in the eye, facing things head-on the way his mother must have taught him. Sweetness wanted me to shake her hand, too.

"And on the porch over there is my friend Carl."

The man nodded at us but made no move in our direction.

"Thanks for watching after the kids this afternoon," Darla said to him.

Carl nodded again. He'd finished up his corn and stood with a slight grimace. Against his chair leaned an ornately carved walnut-colored cane. He bent down to pick it up with one hand, and reached over and picked up the bucket of corn with the other, looping the handle over his arm.

"No trouble," he said, limping toward the screen door to the house. He cantilevered the door with his elbow and slipped inside with the bucket tucked against his body. Not exactly the cold shoulder, but a far cry from the welcome wagon.

"Carl was a fireman. Retired on disability."

"He know who I am?" I asked.

She nodded.

"He's uncomfortable with me then."

"Yes," she said. "But don't let it bother you."

"He live with you?"

"No. He's got his own place up in Bayside. A motorboat he likes to take out on the water, too. He and Marco would probably go to sea on the thing if they could get away with it."

"Call of the wild," I said.

"Right. Like we ain't got enough wild happening around here already."

She turned to the children. "Kids, you go on and get washed up now for dinner. Mr. Pavlicek and Nicole and I will be inside in a few minutes."

The two kids followed after Carl and the screen door slammed behind them.

"I just remembered something. Don't know how it slipped my mind," Darla said when they were out of sight.

"What's that?" I asked.

She stared at me for a moment as she pulled her oversized handbag off her shoulder and started walking back toward the van. "Come on, I'll show you."

We followed her around to the rear of the vehicle away from the house where she lifted up the hatch. There in the back was a gray canvas bag. She unzipped the bag and lifted two jet-black mini-Glocks from inside, a couple of clips of ammunition as well.

"How did you—?"

"Called a judge I know. Man owed me a really big favor. I got him to sign the paperwork for an emergency authorization."

"On a weekend no less. All legal and everything. What did you do after that, break into the registration office?"

"Nope. Actually, I took care of the judge and the registration business yesterday before you two ever showed up. After the threat on my voice mail, I had a bad feeling this thing could turn ugly and I didn't know whether you people would be carrying or not."

"So you were just testing me earlier."

She offered me a sheepish grin. "Pretty much."

The plan called for dinner with Darla and her family, then some rest at her place before heading back into the city to spend a few midnight hours in the park. Darla said she'd decided to come with us, at least for the first go round. Carl had volunteered to baby-sit a little while longer until Darla's sister showed up. The sister would take the children back with her to Pennsylvania the following morning.

Marco took the news of the impromptu vacation stoically, but Sweetness made it tearfully clear she didn't want to leave.

"But we'll miss the fireworks, Mommy."

"Oh, they have nice fireworks out at your Aunt Veronica's house, too, darling. You wait and see."

"But you won't be there with us."

"Mommy's got to go to work on an important job. But I'll come out and get you both and bring you back as soon as I'm done. Probably just a few days, that's all."

An hour later, after dessert and coffee, Carl retreated to the family room where he sat alone nursing a Budweiser and watching the news. The kids hung around long enough for dessert, but beat a hasty retreat, too, when the grown-up talk grew too boring. Sounds from a video game echoed down the stairwell.

I raised the issue of the old Underground Railroad falconer again.

"This is really something," Darla said. "Now we're talking about spirit owls and spirit falconers. What would some fruitcake acting out his own version of history have to do with the doctor's missing cats, the threat I received, and that knife in my van this morning?"

"We might need more than some ghost to figure that one out."

"No ghosts here." The voice belonged to Carl who had obviously been eavesdropping while he kept one eye on the TV.

"Something else, though."

"What's up, Carl?" Darla asked.

We followed her into the family room where dark yellow curtains framed the windows and the smell of furniture polish and crayons filled the room. The noise from a window air conditioner forced the TV volume to be turned up higher than usual.

Carl said nothing, simply pointed over the top of his beer can at the screen.

The reporter on the scene, who looked like she couldn't have been out of her twenties—probably a holiday weekend fill-in for one of the usual news people—stood beside a police barricade on the edge of some woods. Shots had been reported earlier and two bodies had been discovered in Central Park. It was still light enough that we could see a crime scene unit setting up behind her in the background.

"There went somebody's weekend," Carl said.

"This day don't seem to want to end." Darla gave me a sardonic look over her shoulder. "You recognize the location?"

I squinted at the screen, but my recollection of park geography was a little rusty. I shook my head. "No."

"It's just a couple of blocks down from Grayland Tower."

"Then I guess we better go see if we can find out what's going on," I said.

11

The dopey-eyed parking garage attendant on Eighty-Eighth Street was still happy to take our money, though if he remembered us from earlier in the afternoon, he didn't show any sign.

Since we'd planned to stop by Grayland Tower to pick up our surveillance gear anyway, Darla decided she'd better leave hers locked up in the van until we got a better feel for the situation. On a normal summer Saturday night at this hour, many spots in the park would be buzzing with people. It would be unlikely that our mysterious falconer would make a sudden appearance. Add to that the heightened police presence, and we might be in for a long night with nothing to show for it.

At the police barrier several yards into the park from Central Park West, we gave our names and asked to speak with Lt. Marbush. We had to wait about ten minutes before we saw her walking toward us from a grove of shaded oaks where an impromptu command post had been set up, klieg lamps backlighting the scene.

She looked a year or two older and tireder than she had in the bright light of day.

"I can only spare a minute or two," she said.

"We were planning to work the park tonight," Darla said. "But we wanted to check out the situation here first."

"I appreciate it. But no way can I have you people working in here tonight. We've got the whole area sealed from the reservoir up to Central Park North."

"Channel 12's reporting there were shots fired and a couple of bodies had been found."

"That's right. And whoever took them out was using heavy artillery. Place looks like a war zone."

"Gang related?"

"What else? One African-American male, one Latino. Major Case Bureau says they both belonged to a particularly nasty crew out of Spanish Harlem known as Los Miembros."

"The members," I said, remembering my high school Spanish.

"Yes."

"Any clue who turned the double play?" Darla asked.

"Not much to go on at this point. Apparently, these guys tend to spread the trade around. Drugs, prostitution, sex-trafficking. So it could have been any number of players. We've closed everything down around here as a precaution. Fortunately, the evening concert up at the Meer had just ended. So it hasn't been too much trouble getting everybody out."

Darla nodded. "How old were the vics?"

"Damon Hicks, nineteen, and Louis Mansuela, eighteen," Marbush said, shaking her head.

"Kids."

"Yes. But not kids anymore on the street. Best information we have is that neither one was a major actor. Part-timers, peripheral to the gang."

Darla said, "Doesn't stop them from being dead."

"No, it doesn't. You people certainly seem to be attracted to trouble today."

"Tell me about it."

"You're going to have to let your cat thing go for at least one night. Sorry." She turned to go.

"Maybe not," I said.

"What?" The lieutenant faced us again.

I pointed toward the grove of trees where another police detective was approaching. "Lieutenant Marbush," he said as he neared. "We made photos and have got the area marked, but I thought you'd want to see this."

He was holding something in his gloved hands. Of all things, it was a medium-sized stuffed animal, a squirrel with a bushy tail. A patch of dried blood covered one portion of the cloth animal's back. A ten- or twelve-foot length of thin rope was fastened to the faux squirrel's head and fixed to its side was a very visible chunk of raw meat.

"What's this," Darla said, "some gang banger's idea of a sick joke?"

"Could be, but I doubt it," Nicole said, our eyes meeting as I nodded.

Marbush looked at her then back at me. "What are you talking about?"

"What she means," I said, "is that what you've got there looks exactly like a makeshift lure for an owl. I have the same kind of thing packed in my bag up in the apartment. Mine's a little more sophisticated, but the same general idea. Fur made to look like a small animal. If I attach some meat to it, throw it out from behind cover, and tug on the rope to get it moving, you get the same result."

The lieutenant glared at me for a moment then looked again at the stuffed animal the man was holding. "This is too much," she said.

"Any witnesses to the shooting?" I asked.

"None we've been able to identify. Except for reporting the shots, no one's come forward, and the bodies are in a pretty thick stand of trees and bushes."

"No one saw anything unusual? Somebody carrying a bird or maybe just wearing a big thick glove on one hand? Or even the owl itself?"

Marbush looked at the other detective, who shook his head.

"Why don't you let us come in and take a look at the crime scene?" Nicole suggested, looking beyond the man to the van and the taped-off area in the distance.

"You people finally have my attention," Marbush said. "But we're talking about two homicides now. In broad daylight, in my park. And, no offense intended, I won't have a couple of PIs poking around in this investigation to muck it up."

"Why not, when we might be able to help?" Nicole asked.

I held up my hand to signal her to back off.

Darla stepped in. "No problem, Lieutenant. Thanks very much for the information. Anything we can do, you just let us know."

"I'll be sure and do that," Marbush said. "Thanks for the tip about the owl thing." She proffered a small wave as she and the other detective strode off into the darkness toward the lights. For a moment I thought I saw a picture of myself years before: the determined but slumping shoulders, the weariness and the ugliness of it all. In her shoes, I knew I would have done and said pretty much the same thing.

We left the park and started walking back downtown toward Dominic Watisi's Grayland Tower. My mind was jumping ahead to a hundred different possibilities. I tried to slow myself down and think.

"There's our best evidence yet that our owl man is no fantasy," Darla said.

"Yeah," I said. "But a couple of things are bothering me. I'm having a hard time picturing someone with an owl on the wing shooting it out in a gunfight."

"Which is why he must have dropped the lure," Nicole said. "The owl could still be in there, too."

"Maybe. But the lure's only used if you need to call your bird down in a hurry or in an emergency."

"If bullets and murder don't constitute an emergency, I don't know what does."

"Sure. But if he gave up the lure, he must have retrieved the bird before bugging out. Otherwise, he would have hung on to the lure as insurance."

"You mean to make sure the bird would come back to him," Darla said.

"Exactly. But there's one other problem. He's only been sighted before in the middle of the night. Now he's out here while it's still light."

"Hunting, you think?" Nicole asked.

"Maybe. Although he can still do that at night, too, if he's good and have a much easier time avoiding detection." I turned to Darla. "What do you know about this gang she was talking about?"

"Los Miembros." Darla shook her head slowly. "I've heard nothing good about them. We start tangling with them, you two are going to be doubly glad I gave you those guns."

"You've got one Hispanic vic, the other black. They working together, you think?"

"Could be. Whoever killed them might have thought so."

"Where do these Los Miembros hang out? They have any cribs around here?"

She shrugged. "Uptown a ways, I think."

"Anywhere near where our friend Watisi keeps his office?"

"Not too far, I suppose."

"I've been meaning to ask, where's he live, by the way?"

"Watisi? He's got a mansion up in Westchester, but you'll never get near the place."

"High security?"

"Like Fort Knox. I checked it out before I went looking for him at his office."

"What do you think these two dead gangsters were doing way

down here in the park?" Nicole asked.

"Drug deal of some sort would be my guess," Darla said. "What else?"

"Marbush going to give it priority?" I asked.

"Sounds like it. But you know how it goes, Frank. What are the numbers now? Something like ninety percent of all murders in the city are drug or gang related, mostly black on black."

"Most unsolved."

She nodded sadly.

"That lure might throw a different wrinkle into the picture, though," I said.

"Maybe."

"It's got to have something to do with our case," Nicole said. "They can't cover the whole park, can they? We could get in there and take a look around, see if we can help find out what's going on. Maybe our guy with the owl is still around."

I looked at Darla who looked back at me with a mixture of frustration and resignation. "Going to have to leave it for tonight, Nicky. If he's still in there, they'll find him."

Darla put her arm around my daughter's shoulder. "There's a time and a place for everything, honey. The last thing we need right now is to be pissing off a police lieutenant. You people just got here. We need the cops now a lot more than they need us."

"You want us to talk to Lonigan about what's happening?" I said.

"No. I'll call her from the car and bring her up to speed."

"I'd still like to have another look at that lure," she said. "In a few hours it'll be the Fourth of July."

"Happy Independence Day," Darla said.

We walked on for another half a block without speaking. The noise from the city seemed to swell from the dark and the heat. Somewhere a few buildings away an illegal firecracker went off, its streamer whistling into the night.

12

Marcia called me a couple of hours later. In addition to its other accoutrements, our apartment was outfitted with its own mini-gym, a room equipped with a treadmill and weight bench, TV and a big picture window that looked out on the park. I was winding down on the treadmill when my cell phone rang.

"You sound out of breath."

I told her what I was doing.

"Sounds more like a vacation than work."

"I wish."

"How was your day?"

"You first," I said, slowing to a walk. She told me about a volunteer picnic she'd attended on the grounds at the university and a movie she'd gone to see with a couple of her girlfriends.

"Your turn," she said.

I stepped off the treadmill, wiped my forehead with a towel, and sat down on the weight bench and gave her most of the blow-by-blow details.

"Wow," she said when I finished. "You think your wealthy developer might be in bed with a street gang?"

"I don't know, but stranger things have happened. Which reminds me, you have your local telephone directory handy?"

"Sure, right here in the drawer."

"Can you look up Jackson Miller's home number for me?"

"Jackson Miller? The bookstore owner?"

"Yeah. I've bought a few books from him in the past. A big

portion of his business is dealing with collectibles. He might know someone up here in New York he can put me in touch with about this long lost *Book of the Mews.*"

"Okay."

I waited while she looked up the number and gave it to me.

"I wouldn't mind finding out more information about that book myself," she said. "Sounds fascinating, and it could be related to my own work."

Marcia's specialty was the role of women in the civil war.

"I'll let you know if anything pans out," I said.

"What's Nicky doing right now?"

"She's in the other room, looking out the window with night vision binoculars."

"At what?"

I glanced over the top of the treadmill through the glass and down to the park below where the spinning lights from police vehicles were still visible in the distance. "Trying to see whatever she thinks she can still see of the murder scene."

"Wonder where she gets that trait from?"

"Ummm."

"This sounds like it could be getting dangerous."

"Possibly."

"What will you do if someone tries to harm her or you?"

"Harm them first."

"You're confident you can do that."

"Yes."

There was a pause on the line. "I wish I were there with you," she said.

"Me, too."

"Maybe I should fly up there, too, and take in some of the sights."

"Would that be professional—to bring my fiancé on the job with me?"

"Since when have you been hung up on being so professional?"

"All right, I'll think about it." I was already thinking about it. The idea of Marcia and me alone in a romantic hotel room together almost caused me to drop the phone. Maybe I could find a justice of the peace to marry us in a hurry.

"You sure you're all right?" She must have detected a note of apprehension in my voice. A little scary to think she knew me so well.

"Sure, everything's fine."

"When you get back, I'd like to talk with you about dates for the wedding. Have you thought about any of the details yet? Are you planning to ask Jake to be your best man?"

Okay, scratch the justice of the peace idea. The reality hit me then that I was about to be married for the second time in my life. It gave me something of a warm glow all over. I guess that's what it was, at any rate.

"Uh, yeah. I was planning on asking him when I give him the news."

"Good," she said. "I miss you, Frank. I'm praying for you."

"Thank you. I miss you, too."

"You didn't say anything to Nicky, did you, about our big plans?"

"Not yet."

"Good. I think it's best."

"Whatever you say."

"I'm looking at the ring right now on my finger," she said. "I was afraid to wear it earlier for fear I'd have to explain it to my friends, but I did have a talk with my pastor. He said he'd be happy to perform the ceremony as soon as we're ready, as long as we wanted to keep things informal."

"Perfect."

"You sure you're ready for this, Frank?"

"I gave you the ring, didn't I?"

"I just wanted to make sure you weren't having second thoughts."

"I've never been so free of second thoughts in my life."

"Good," she said.

We said good-bye and hung up.

Although it was late, I decided to give Jackson Miller a call. It might lead to nothing, but like Nicole said, the similarities between Obadiah Robertson's story and the mystery facing us were too much to pass up without at least checking into it further.

Miller's gruff voice answered the phone after three or four rings.

"Who is this again?" he asked after I'd identified myself.

"Pavlicek. Frank Pavlicek."

"Oh, yeah, yeah. Frank, good to hear from you. What are you calling me at this time of night for?"

"It's about a book."

"A book, huh. What kind of book?"

"An old one. Written before the Civil War."

"Okay, I'm listening."

I told him the story of *The Book of the Mews*.

"I never heard of this book," he said when I was finished. "But I bet I know someone up there who has. Why don't you give me your cell phone number and I'll see what I can find out in the next day or two. It's a holiday weekend, you know. May not be too easy getting hold of people."

"I appreciate it, whatever you can do," I said, and gave him my number before ending the call.

The next morning Nicole decided to sleep in, according to the note she left outside the door to my room, having stayed up too late for nothing, as she put it. I got on the horn and talked Darla into picking me up in the van to go meet someone I'd long wanted to meet.

It was a long shot, but Nixon Deebee was as near a legend as you got, at least in the sport of falconry. A retired game warden, he lived on a small farm near West Point and kept anywhere from five to ten hawks and falcons, depending on the year and the results of his captive breeding operation. From what I'd heard, Deebee had a contract with New York City to help rid the parks of pigeons by bringing his hawk in to fly to the lure. He wasn't the only person performing such services. A much bigger outfit used falcons as part of a comprehensive program to keep the runways at Kennedy Airport clear of migrating birds. And around the world, dozens of other falconers had been hired by various municipalities to deal with similar problems.

Darla was outfitted for battle this morning. She wore a white Polo shirt tucked into blue jeans, which served to reinforce her bulk. Handcuffs and pepper spray hung from her belt, and her Glock was tucked neatly into its holster beneath her seat where she could easily reach it. She had a line on a bail jumper in White Plains, and she was hoping we could take a run at him on the way back from the farm. Not her usual line of work, especially on a holiday, but the call had come in on her service the day before, her kids were gone to her sister's, and money was money.

"You hear any more from Marbush about what they found at the murder scene last night?" I asked as we cruised up the Saw Mill River Parkway.

She shook her head. "Nada."

"Probably keeping us out of the loop."

"Probably."

"You ever work with any PIs back when you were on the force?"

"Never."

"Me, neither."

She said nothing.

"After we finish with Deebee," I said, "since we're up in the area anyway, I thought you might want to take a swing by and show me Watisi's manor."

Darla chuckled. "I figured you might have an ulterior motive in this little wild-goose chase. Like I told you, it'll probably be a waste of time. But we can take a run by there, if you want, on the way to track down my claim jumper."

"What did Lonigan say when you told her about the shootings in the park?"

"She said it makes her more worried than ever about Watisi."

"Obviously something strange is going on here. When we get back to the city, Nicky and I will head uptown, see what more we can find out about Los Miembros and any ties they might have to Watisi. Nothing to stop us from trying to find out whatever we can about the dead men, too."

"Just try to stay out of Marbush's way," she said.

"Will do."

"Tell me some more about this bird guy we're going to see and this raptor fascination you all are into," she said. "You guys all obsessed with eagles, or knights and lords and ladies or something?"

"Not quite," I said.

"So it's a big bird. You take the thing and what, you train it to kill stuff for you?"

"Sort of. More often than not the bird trains you."

"The bird trains you?"

"Birds already have the instinct to chase and hunt game when they come out of the egg."

"No kidding."

"Most birds of prey know more about hunting and survival than any idiot with a rifle will ever know."

"So you're against hunting with a gun? Is that what you've got against Watisi?"

"Not at all. I'm just saying, why have the artificial experience when you can get up close and personal with the real thing?"

She shook her head. "You people are out there, I'll give you that. You think this Deebee character knows anything about our falconer in the park?"

"I have no idea, but he knows more about the parks and falconry than anyone else in the region, and he might have heard something that can help us."

"Okay. If you say so."

We drove on in silence. Half an hour later our tires crunched onto a rock-strewn dirt road that led off the state highway into the woods, the nose of the van bobbing through potholes like the prow of a ship. After a few hundred yards of stomach lurching, Darla was beginning to look at me like I'd lost my mind. The trees finally broke to reveal a quaint nineteenth-century farmhouse with a front porch swing, an old windmill next to a barn, and roses climbing up arbors. There was also a second barn, this one a long, low-slung structure lined with individual stalls framed by barred windows. Deebee's hawk house, no doubt.

A gray Dodge pickup and a dark red Chevy Suburban were parked on a pad between the house and the main barn. The hood of the pickup was raised, and a man was bent over the engine with a wrench in hand. His head popped up when we came into view. Two small dogs, a beagle and a mixed breed that looked like it was part schnauzer, came racing around the side of the barn, barking.

Nixon Deebee looked for all the world like a grizzled sea

captain, complete with white hair and full white beard. Even bent over the truck, he had a commanding presence. When he stood to his full height, he looked to be about six-foot-five.

"I guess this is our guy," Darla said. She stopped the van a few feet behind the parking pad.

I'd seen pictures of Deebee in a falconry magazine. "Looks like it," I said.

The air was still and already thick with humidity. Deebee, with sweat running down the sides of his face, checked us out for a moment, then put his tool down and called off the dogs. He began wiping his hands on a rag as we climbed from the van. "Help you folks?"

"Nixon Deebee?"

"You're talking to him."

"My name's Frank Pavlicek. I'm a falconer from Virginia."

Deebee's face relaxed a little. "You don't say?" He came forward, extending his newly cleaned hand. We shook. "Pleasure to meet you."

"This is Darla Barnes," I said.

Deebee shook hands with her, too. "Happy Fourth of July to you both."

"Same to you."

"How long you been a falconer?"

"This'll be my fifth season," I said.

"From Virginia."

"Yes."

"Who was your sponsor?"

"Jake Toronto."

"Toronto? Wait a minute, I know you guys. The two of you used to be cops, didn't you?"

"You got it."

"Aren't you a private investigator or something?"

"That's right, I am. Darla here is one, too," I said.

The expression on his face hardened a little. "I heard about what happened with Chester Carew last year down in West Virginia."

"It's a long story," I told Darla.

"So how can I help you people this morning?" Deebee asked. "You here to see some birds?"

"Actually, we're here on business."

"No kidding? Must be important to bring you all the way up here on the Fourth of July."

"It is. We may be looking for someone from the area who's a falconer."

"Okay. Why don't you two come on into the kitchen. I'll put on a pot of coffee and we can talk about it."

Ten minutes later, we were seated in the cool of Deebee's kitchen in front of our mugs. While making the coffee, Deebee told us that his wife of thirty years had passed away the year before from brain cancer.

"Now what would you like to know?" he asked. The beagle, named Rosie, jumped up on the chair next to him and watched us expectantly while Deebee scratched her neck and ears.

"I figured you must know a lot about falconry in the greater New York area," I said.

"I've been a member of the New York State Falconry Association since it started—was one of the founders, in fact. So yes, while I might not know everything, I'd say I know pretty much everyone involved with birds of prey in the region," he said.

"You're the man I want to talk to then. Tell me, what are the chances someone has decided to start taking up nighttime poaching down in Central Park?"

He stared at me for a long moment. "In the city? Zip, as far as I'm concerned."

"What if someone were paying them a lot of money?" Darla asked.

He shrugged. "I still wouldn't believe it."

We told him our story. About Lonigan, about the missing pets, the threats, and the shooting in the park with the discovery of the lure the night before.

"That's one of the nuttiest things I've ever heard. You can start calling every member of the association if you want. I can give you the list, but I doubt it's going to get you anywhere."

"What are there, a couple of hundred members?" I asked.

"Something like that. And then there is New Jersey, too. But you'd be wasting your time. I used to be a game warden. Somebody with a hawk or an owl wants to go poaching after dark, they're not going to be registering with the state or the feds. They're in violation of several different state and federal laws."

"But somebody might know somebody," I said. "Maybe a hanger on or a wannabe. Someone who's shown up at the meets before or gone out hunting with a legal falconer."

He scratched his chin and rubbed his dog's ears some more. "Could be," he said.

Something in his demeanor shifted, as if an unpleasant memory had worked its way to the surface.

"You know anybody like that, Mr. Deebee?"

He didn't answer for a moment, maybe marshalling his thoughts. "Now that you bring it up, there is one person I can think of who might bear looking into."

We waited.

"I don't even know if he's still in the city."

Darla took out her pad and pen.

"Anything that might be of help," I said. "You never know."

Deebee took a long sip from his mug of coffee. "I guess it's been maybe six, seven years since I saw the guy. His name is

Raines, Cato Raines."

Darla wrote it down.

"He had a falconry license for a while, but then he stopped showing up at meets and I heard he gave away his last bird."

"It happens," I said.

"Yeah, but this was different. The guy lost it or something. Lost his job, had to declare bankruptcy, divorced his wife. I heard he might even be an addict, hopped up on speed or whatever it is people get juiced on these days."

"Okay."

"You know what? I might even have an old picture of the guy. He was flying a Cooper's hawk for a while. I used to be editor of the newsletter. Someone snapped a photo of him and his bird at one of the meets. Not the best picture so I never used it, but I think I've still got it somewhere. Hang on."

He pushed away from the table and stepped into a small alcove off the kitchen. A beat-up filing cabinet in the corner was covered with various photos of people and birds, families and friends. I wasn't sure where any of this might be going, so I just sat there with Darla and we sipped our coffee for a few minutes while Deebee rummaged through the drawers.

"Here it is," he finally said. He came back into the kitchen and sat down across from us, holding a Polaroid in his hand. "I thought I remembered keeping it." He handed the smudged photo to me. "That's Cato Raines."

The image was of a smiling, round-faced young man with a bird on his glove, standing in a parking lot full of other falconers and birds. The lighting in the photo was poor.

"So if it's been so long since you've seen him, what makes you bring Raines up now?" I asked.

"Okay, here's the thing. I was in the city week before last with a couple of my birds when I ran into Raines."

"Where?"

"North end of Central Park."

I glanced up at Darla, who said nothing.

"What was Raines doing?"

"Nothing. That's just it. He was sitting alone on a curb. He looked awful."

"Homeless?"

"Looked that way. I almost didn't recognize him."

"Did you talk to him?"

"I tried to, but he barely seemed to remember me. I asked if there was anything I could do to help and he said no. So I gave him twenty bucks out of my wallet and went and got in my car and drove home."

"So you're saying this guy Raines may be wandering around the city and in particular Central Park."

"Yeah, that's right." The beagle shifted on the chair, then jumped into Deebee's lap. The white-haired man let her stay.

"He say anything to you about falconry or your birds?"

"Uh-uh." He shook his head. "But when he looked at the Harris' hawk I was holding, he got a funny look on his face."

"What do you mean?"

"I don't know. Just seemed to me he was angry about something."

"You think there's any chance he might be our man with the owl?"

Deebee shrugged. "Stranger things have happened," he said.

13

An hour later, Darla and I were seated in the minivan outside the entrance to Dominic Watisi's Bedford Hills estate. Darla was right. The man had built himself a personal fortress. A ten-foot brick wall ringed the entire acreage. On top was an unbroken row of black, wrought-iron spear tips; and if that weren't enough to keep the curious at bay, discreetly sheltered video cameras monitored every inch of the wall.

"See what I mean," Darla said.

"I do."

Just inside the front gate, a bearded, Middle Eastern man dressed in a security uniform regarded us with suspicion from inside a brick booth.

"You want to try to storm the front gate?"

"Not yet," I said.

"At least now you know where the man lives."

"There is that."

By the time we made it back to the city, the Fourth of July was bursting into full swing. A couple of softball games had heated up in Morningside Park to go with the throngs of morning bikers, joggers, and rollerbladers. The bail jumper in White Plains had turned out to be a bust. There was no sign of him at his residence, despite the tip Darla'd been given.

"So what do you want to do about Raines?" I asked, pulling the photo from my pocket and twirling it in my fingers as we made our way down the Henry Hudson toward Midtown.

"I think it's worth checking out," Darla said.

"We'll start asking around."

"In addition to talking to people about the shooting."

"Exactly."

"What about other people in the building at Grayland Tower?"

"Whoever is home, we'll try to talk to them. And we'll make some copies of this picture and pass them around the park this afternoon with our business cards."

"Have at it. It's a big park and a big town. I spent weeks once looking for a New Jersey runaway before I finally tracked the girl down."

"Everybody's running from something, I guess."

"I suppose. I promised Carl I'd spend the afternoon with him. Maybe tonight after the fireworks I can help you guys case the park."

"Sure," I said.

We passed a black church on Frederick Douglas Boulevard, worshipers spilling out its doors.

"You religious at all, Frank?"

"Sometimes," I said.

"Sometimes? What kind of an answer is that?"

"An honest one, I hope."

As we waited for the light to turn green, a group of well-dressed parishioners—men, women, and children—moved across the street in front of us.

"I used to be religious," she said. "My father was a preacher. I ever tell you that?"

"No. He still alive?"

"No, no." She shook her head. "He died from a stroke four years ago. But Dad was a preacher all right. At one time his church had over three hundred members."

"No kidding."

"Sometimes I think the problem with religion isn't God, it's the people."

"Amen to that."

"Dad used to always say that Jesus was alive and that his holy spirit could come and live inside us if we believed. You think that could be true?"

"Your dad sounds like a very wise man."

"I don't know. After a day like yesterday, it's hard to tell where anything sorts out."

The light turned green and we continued on down the avenue.

Ten minutes later, she dropped me off in front of Grayland Tower, where she'd picked me up just after sunrise.

"See you back here at eight," she said. "I'll keep my cell phone turned on in case anybody needs me."

"You bet."

I nodded to the lone guard at the reception desk—Jayani Miller must have had the day off—and rode the elevator upstairs to find Nicole in the dining room of the apartment. A *Sunday Times* was spread out on the table in front of her, and she was eating a bagel and cream cheese. She didn't look up as I came into the room.

"You get my note?" I asked.

"I got it." She took another nibble of her bagel, her eyes glued to the newspaper.

"You aren't mad, are you?"

"What do you think? Of course I'm pissed off."

"Why?"

"Why didn't you wake me?"

"I thought we agreed you wanted to sleep in."

"I never agreed to that."

"Plus, I thought you could use the sleep more than chasing after some curmudgeonly old falconer who might not even be home."

"Was he home?"

"Yes."

"Was he curmudgeonly?"

"No. Not really."

"There you go, then. You should have woken me up."

I stepped around and kissed her lightly on the forehead. "I'm sorry, sweetie."

"I'm not a teenager anymore. I can do without sleep."

"You're right. How are the bagels?"

"There are some more in the bag in the kitchen if you want one."

"You pick them up down the street?"

"Yeah, and I did a little more than that."

"What?"

"I took the keys to the Porsche and drove uptown."

"You what?"

She flipped to the next page in the newspaper. "Talked to the mother of one of last night's shooting victims and to the sister of the other one. There's a story here in the paper about the killings, but it doesn't really tell us much."

"Now wait just one minute."

"You didn't expect me to sit around here in the apartment while you were out working, did you?"

I glared at her for a moment. Brilliant, at times, she had as much of a nose for this thing as I did. Who was I to try to rein her in? Just her father, trying to keep her from getting her beautiful face shot off.

"Next time you don't go without backup," I said.

"Hey, it was just background work on a Sunday morning. No one there was going to hurt me."

"What did you find out?" I could envision Nicole, in her tactful, feminine way, holding the hand of the aggrieved.

"That these two kids were into some serious goings-on."

"Not just hangers-on with Los Miembros then?"

"Nope. These two were players."

"In what way?"

"Mansuela's mother said her son was flashing around a lot of money lately, and that he always seemed to have a different girl with him. Fraser had just bought a new bullet bike, according to his sister."

"Maybe they hit a major score and someone wanted it back. Were the two of them friends?"

"Not really. The mother said she'd never heard of Damon Hicks before but Louis never really talked much about his friends anymore."

"I don't suppose either the mother or the sister knows anything about our mysterious falconer, either."

"No. I hinted around a little and asked some open-ended questions, but they genuinely didn't seem to know what I was talking about."

"Okay. So where can we go from here with what you've learned?"

"The brother."

"What brother?"

"Hicks has an older brother, too. Never involved in the gangs, the sister said, but he knows stuff."

"Where do we find him?"

"At the sister's place on Lenox Terrace near Harlem Hospital. He was supposed to be coming over there for a big dinner party cookout later, but the plans have been changed with Damon's shooting. Now it's just going to be family."

"A private wake."

"Something like that."

"And the sister's okay with us crashing this intimate get-together?"

Nicole nodded. "I've got an appointment for seven. She says she'll talk to him first, make sure he knows we're okay."

"Nice work."

"One more thing."

"What's that?"

"She hasn't told the cops much of this stuff. Doesn't trust them."

"But she trusts you, after one conversation."

"I'm good, aren't I?" She smiled and gave a bow.

I shook my head. "All right," I said. "We'll keep pursuing what you've got so far on Los Miembros. In the meantime . . ." I casually pulled the photo from the back pocket of my jeans and tossed it so it landed faceup on the table next to her.

"What's this?"

"That," I said. "Is how we're going to spend some of our afternoon."

Even with the holiday, we found a copy center on Fifth Avenue that opened at noon. Nicole charmed the young man behind the counter into letting her tweak the image quality controls on the computerized color copier and we managed to crop the image to eliminate the bird and print out several halfway decent copies of the head shot on plain paper.

At Nicole's insistence, we divided the stack in half and headed off in opposite directions around Grayland Tower and the park, planning to meet up a couple of hours later to compare notes.

The day had become a scorcher. The sun seemed lost in the bright brown haze above. My first stop was the taxi stand on the corner of 110th Street. It being a Sunday and the Fourth of July, business was slower than usual. Several dozen cabs were lined up behind one another in the sun. A group of drivers of varying ethnicities stood beneath the shade of a canopy, talking. A few glanced in my direction as I approached.

"Excuse me," I said. "I'm looking for a man who might be living in this area on the street." I held up a copy of Raines' photo. "His name is Cato Raines. Any of you gentlemen happen to recognize him?"

Shaking heads all around.

"Why don't you check out the Piscataway Hotel on 116th Street?" one man said. "They house some of the homeless over there."

He gave me the exact address and I thanked him.

It wasn't that far away. Since I was on foot, I would have to pass through the projects between 112th and 115th Streets, but it was a good lead.

The brick rectangular high-rises loomed over the sidewalk, where people were milling about. Some kind of festival, probably related to the Fourth, was taking place on the promenade. The only evidence of birds of prey I witnessed were a couple of barrio brothers clearly interested in sizing me up for the taking as I moved around a corner and past their darkened doorway where the crowd had thinned. I would be too much work, they must have decided.

The Piscataway Hotel was an ancient establishment with crumbling stucco outside and crumbling plaster in the lobby. In its heyday ninety years before it might have been a decent place to stay. Now, the city's Department of Homeless Services paid the entrepreneur owners thirty dollars per room per night to temporarily shelter homeless families. Or so I learned from the old copy of a *New York Post* framed on the wall in the lobby.

I really didn't think Raines would be living in such a place. First of all, if my information was correct, he didn't sound like the type to register with the Department of Homeless Services. Second, Raines struck me as a loner. It was the height of summer and the weather was a lot more conducive to sleeping outdoors, where he probably preferred to be anyway.

Still, someone in the Piscataway Hotel might have come across Raines and recognize his picture.

I spent the next half hour canvassing the building, from the sharp-eyed but inarticulate desk clerk in the overcooled lobby to the elderly woman wearing footed pajamas in her sweltering corner room on the top floor. No one remembered seeing Raines. No one seemed to have heard of him.

Okay, by last count there were anywhere from thirty to forty thousand homeless people in and around New York City. Even if I was in Raines' neighborhood, it still made finding him cold like this a gargantuan task.

Outside on the street, the heat was building to a mid-afternoon crescendo. Cars and buses and cabs plied the streets. Diesel smoke perfumed the air. What would I do if I were Cato Raines on a day like today? I wouldn't be sitting in some flea-bag hotel, that was for sure.

I'd be out enjoying the park.

A few minutes later I was walking along 110th Street again across from the Harlem Meer. Nicole was planning to go down as far as the Reservoir and work her way back north along the west edge of the park. I would enter the park from this end and work my way down the eastern side, looking for anyone who might recognize Raines.

The old black man was the fourth homeless person I talked to. He didn't seem inclined to say anything at first, or even look at the photocopy I showed him, but a much higher quality image of Andrew Jackson began to loosen his tongue.

Reed thin, he had a modest crop of curly hair that had turned yellow gray, thick eyebrows, and an unruly tangle of beard the same color and consistency as his hair. A pair of wiry gold hoops pierced through the corner of one of his brows. His old coveralls were torn and dirty, but he looked otherwise presentable.

"Raines, you say?"

He repeated the name and stared at the grainy photo I was flashing.

"Yeah. Cato Raines. You know him?"

"I know him," he said. "But he don't call himself no Cato Raines."

"What does he call himself then?"

"Pock."

"Come again?"

"Pock. Dude calls himself Pock, short for Pocket. 'Cause he's short, I guess, and he's good at relieving people of some of their change, you know what I mean."

"Have you seen him lately?"

"I saw him just last night."

"Where?"

"Down by the boathouse."

"Between Seventy-Fourth and Seventy-Fifth?"

"That'd be the one."

"How many times have you seen him before?"

He shrugged. "A few, maybe."

"You know where else he likes to hang out?"

The man smiled. "Wherever he can find a crowd. You see? He'll clean himself up and blend in so he can do his bidness."

"What's he doing on the streets?"

The man made a circular motion with his index finger around his ear.

"Crazy?"

He coughed. In a hoarse whisper he said, "Ain't we all? But Pock, he's . . . he seems like he may have a few more screws loose than the usual."

"If you wanted to find him right now, where would you look?"

"Right now, this minute?" He thought about it for a few moments. "Today's Sunday, the Fourth of July, ain't it?"

"That's right."

"What time is it?" he asked.

"Almost three-thirty."

"You got Cynthia Scott singing over by the Meer at four. That's where Pock'll probably be working. That woman sure got a voice on her. She'll draw herself a crowd."

"What does Pock wear when he gets himself cleaned up?"

"Blue shirt. Red tie. Red suspenders. You keep an eye out. Betcha he'll be there."

A little while later, Nicole and I were working the crowd on the edge of the park at the Harlem Meer Performance Festival. The place was indeed packed. The crowd consisted of a varied selection of New Yorkers, white, black, and brown; male and female, young and old; uptown, urbane, and sophisticate.

My cell hummed. Nicole said she'd spotted him. She directed me to meet her at the corner of the Dana Discovery Center where she was leaning on the side of a booth chatting up a snow-cone vendor, using the concession as cover while she kept an eye on our wary pickpocket.

We hadn't caught Raines in the act of practicing his trade, however. At least, not at the moment. Like almost everyone else in the crowd, he was focused on the music, his eyes fixed on the stage a few hundred feet away, his smallish body swaying with the beat. Even from the back, though, there was no mistaking who he was.

We edged over to a spot directly flanking him, Nicole on one side and I on the other, just in case he decided to bolt.

I stepped up beside him and said quietly, "Cato Raines?"

He winced and offered me a sidelong glance.

"Been a while since someone called me that."

"You prefer I call you Pock?"

"Yeah. That's my name now."

"All right, Pock. I was wondering if we might have a word."

I pushed a business card in front of his face and watched his expression while he read it. He seemed more annoyed than anything else.

"What for? I ain't doing anything here but listening to the music like everybody else."

Just in front of him, one of a group of three middle-aged women carrying shopping bags looked back at us as he spoke. This was not what he had in mind.

He swore under his breath, turning away from the stage and toward the street behind us. "C'mon," he said. "Let's go."

We began to weave our way through the throng. Nicole stayed close behind us.

"Who's the girl?" Raines asked, without looking at her.

"My partner," I said.

"She looks too much like you to be just that."

"She's also my daughter."

"Cute. You two family types got any ID?"

Whatever else you might say about Cato Raines, he didn't appear to be delusional. I showed him my license and that seemed to satisfy him.

"So what do you want?"

"We've been looking for you. Nixon Deebee gave me your name and said I might find you somewhere here in the city. He says you used to be a licensed falconer."

"Deebee? That old bear. Yeah, man, that's right. I used to fly lots of birds."

"Why'd you give it up?"

He didn't answer right away. He rubbed at his nose, tilted his head almost imperceptibly, and fixed his gaze somewhere in the middle distance. When he spoke, his voice became more measured.

"First," he said. "I lost my job. Then I couldn't find another one. Then my lover died."

"I'm sorry. Had she been ill a long time? Deebee said you were divorced."

"You're talking about my ex-wife. I'm talking about him." He stared at me for a moment. "And yes, we found out later when he tested positive for AIDS."

"I'm doubly sorry then. A crappy way to go."

"Yeah, well, then I had to go into the hospital myself for a while."

"You sick, too?"

He smiled. "I'm clean as far as AIDS. But my mind got a little sick," he said, pointing to his head. "You know what I mean?"

"Sounds like you've been through a lot," Nicole said from behind us.

"You might say that," he said, turning to look at her.

"Ever think about working with a bird again?" I asked.

"You mean a hawk or a falcon?" He looked back at me. "Shoot. I see them all the time out here in the park. But no, I don't want to have to mess around with another one."

"Why's that?"

"No place to keep the thing. Can't feed it if it doesn't catch game. Can't even feed myself half the time."

A kernel of an idea formed in my brain. But it was so outrageous I just about dismissed it as my own bit of mental imbalance.

What if Raines, or possibly someone else, was so desperate for food that he'd resorted to illegally hunting small game within the confines of the park? It seemed an absurd notion in today's prepackaged, preprocessed world of convenient food sources. Absurd—unless you were starving.

But even the homeless like Raines didn't appear to be that desperate. The city helped. The state and the federal government helped. Churches, synagogues, and mosques helped. I read in an article once that more than six hundred food banks were open in the city. Why would someone resort to a primitive form of hunting in the middle of such a great metropolis in order to survive? It made me think about the park again, its sham wilderness, and all that it represented.

"What difference does all this make to you?" Raines interrupted my train of thought. "You a falconer yourself?"

"That's right."

"Not in New York, though. I never saw you at any of the meets."

"No. In Virginia. You know there are some people around here who say they've been seeing a falconer flying a bird in the park," I told him.

"Yeah? No big deal. Probably just someone doing a demonstration or a show with the Park Conservancy."

"No, this is a little different. The witnesses say they've seen someone carrying an owl at night."

I watched him carefully for his reaction. He thought about it for a few moments before responding. "At night? A Great Horned?"

"Yeah. You wouldn't happen to know anything about it, would you?"

"Nope." He shook his head. "Don't know anything about it at all."

If what the old man had said was true, Raines was a much better pickpocket than a liar. We'd printed out a copy of the story of *The Book of the Mews.* "This ring any bells for you?" I pulled it out of my pocket, unfolded it, and handed it to him.

He looked it over, scratched his head, and began reading. "Some story," he said after a few moments and shrugged.

"You never heard of this before?"

"Of course. I always been into learning about the Civil War. Sometimes I can even see the cannons and the horsemen, the big plumes of smoke, men dying everywhere, swords flashing. Brothers even fighting one another. Slaves and Southern Belles. Those were some times." He shook his head and grinned.

"But you wouldn't be tempted to try to reenact this story on your own, like say, with an owl here in the park?"

"Not me, no sir."

I decided to try a different tack. "Where do you sleep at night this time of year, Pock?"

"Me? Oh, I don't know. Here and there."

"If someone were hunting with an owl in the park when it closes after dark, where do you suppose they'd go?"

He thought about it for a moment, eyeing me.

"Could be anywhere." He shrugged. "Lots of game, critters running around in here."

"Yeah, I've noticed."

"But hunting's illegal in this park."

"Sure it is. So is picking people's pockets."

"So?"

"I think you're lying when you say you don't know anything about this man with an owl in the park. Am I right?"

He gave a cheeky grin. Then his mood seemed to sour as he pointed a finger in my face. "Look, pal. I've been trying to be nice here, to answer your questions and help you out and all."

"Sure."

"I'm not doing anything wrong. I'm just getting by, like everybody else in the world."

"Okay."

"I'd like to move along now. I don't have anything more to say to you people."

He started to turn away, but Nicole stepped in front of him. "But you wouldn't want anything to happen to the owl, would you? Or whoever's flying it? We need to find out what's going on so we can help with the situation."

He hesitated.

"Just tell us one thing. Is the person with the owl kidnapping and killing people's pets?"

"What? No. I don't know what you're talking about."

"They're just hunting for food, then."

He scratched his chin. "Possibly."

"What about the shooting that happened last night?" I asked.

"What about it?"

"You heard about it?"

"Of course, it's all over the street."

"Cops found somebody's homemade falconry lure near the bodies."

"Christ," he said under his breath.

"What's that?"

"Nothing."

"You doing business with Los Miembros, Pock?"

"Me? No way. Not me."

"There're liable to be more people killed if we don't hurry up and figure out what's going on here."

"You don't think I know that?" He was clearly agitated now. His eyes darted back and forth, searching among the trees and rocks and bushes, as if they were seeing ghosts.

I tucked my business card in his jacket pocket. "Keep that. All right?"

"Whatever, man. I gotta go."

"Why don't you meet us here again tonight, after the fireworks when there aren't so many people around. We can talk about this further. Midnight work for you?"

He looked around again. "Maybe. I don't know. I gotta go." He set his chin, spun on his heels, and began walking away down the brick path.

"Midnight. We'll be here," I called after him.

He looked back but didn't answer. Nicole started to march

after him, but I held up my hand. "That's okay. Let him go," I said.

In the distance, the sound of jazz floated through the trees, mixing with the diesel rumble of a city bus.

14

Nicole returned to Grayland Tower to see if she could gather any more information from other apartment owners. Before joining her, I went to track down our client.

Columbia Presbyterian Hospital rises above the Hudson on Washington Heights within sight of the GW Bridge. I found Dr. Lonigan's modest office among a row of faculty spaces on the fifth floor of one of the outlying buildings.

Lonigan was speaking into her dictating machine. The door was open. I knocked on the frame.

"Working overtime. And on a major holiday, no less."

"Someone had to take call for today," she said, switching off her mike and setting it down on her desk. "I happened to come up in the rotation. Thought I'd catch up on one of my research papers while things are slow."

"We may have found our mysterious falconer," I said.

"Really?"

"It's not definite. He may not be the one. But we've spoken with him and he knows we're out here." I explained about our encounter with Raines.

"How's he linked to Watisi, though?" she asked when I was through.

"Remains to be seen. If he really is our guy, and if there is a link."

"A lot of 'ifs'."

"Yes. Darla told you about the shootings last night and what they found, right?"

"She did. And it concerns me. What do you think is going on?"

"Still not sure, exactly." I told her what we'd learned about Los Miembros and about *The Book of the Mews* and the theory that someone might be playing copycat.

"Interesting," she said.

"Something else our investigation has turned up."

"What is that?"

"You were arrested twice in Oregon almost twenty years ago."

The doctor glared at me for a moment. "I don't see what relevance any of that has to the current situation."

"Maybe none," I said. "I hope that's the case. But since, as an activist, you have been known to resort to extreme measures before, I'm worried that may also be the case now."

"That was a long time ago," she said. "We were fighting for what we believed in."

"You're still involved, though, aren't you? Darla told us there had been a protest."

"I support certain groups, yes. It has nothing to do with my accusations against Dominic Watisi."

"You're sure?"

"Absolutely."

I said nothing.

Lonigan, who still hadn't risen from her chair, tilted her head as she caught my eye. "Do you enjoy finding sport in watching one creature dismember another?"

I was taken aback by the abruptness of the question. "What are you talking about?"

"Hunting."

"That's not what it's about."

"What is it about then?"

I don't know why, but my first reaction was to smile. "That

all depends," I said.

"On what?"

"On the grace of the attack. On the swiftness and cunning of the quarry. On it being a fair fight."

"You make it sound almost poetic."

I shrugged. "For the animal it's more than poetic. It's survival. There is a lot of killing and a lot of death in the wild, whether we like or not. Predators are often more at risk than the prey."

"Like our famous red-tailed hawk, Pale Male, down in the park."

"Not exactly. That bird's got a million eyes looking out for him. Most hawks and falcons, if and when their time comes, die an anonymous death."

She pressed her bee-stung lips together, but said nothing.

"I'd like to hear more about your agenda in this whole thing," I said.

She said nothing.

I waited.

"Well," she said. "As I told you, it's no secret I'm an active supporter of a humane-based animal rights organization with headquarters here in the city. When the article appeared in the newspapers, somehow that fact was highlighted above most of the others."

"People want to sell newspapers," I said.

"I suppose. But the unfortunate consequence is that another group of individuals, primarily activist birdwatchers upset with domestic cats running loose . . . well, you know what they do."

"Kill small birds."

"Yes, some have been known to do that. And these bird people have somehow become convinced, based on absolutely no evidence whatsoever, that this owl was actually attacked by my cat and that I've concocted the whole story about my cat being missing."

The picture was becoming a little clearer. "So you thought you'd okay Darla bringing Nicole and me in to help placate the birdwatchers."

"That was part of the reason, yes."

"But now this looks like it may turn into something a whole lot more."

"Yes."

"Just so we're all on the same page here," I said.

"One more thing you should know," she said.

"I can't wait."

"We have a hearing scheduled tomorrow in housing court against Watisi."

"All right."

"Some protestors may show up."

"In the middle of what has become a murder investigation."

"I'm sorry."

"Sounds like the fun is just beginning," I said.

15

Back at Grayland Tower, Apartment 11C, another end unit a few floors below Dr. Lonigan's, belonged to a Mr. Mitchell Collins. At least, according to the list in my hand. Collins was the owner of one of the other missing pets, also a cat. With a couple of hours still to go before our appointment up in Harlem, Nicole had struck out so far. I pitched in to help. Collins' occupation was listed as international manufacturing consultant.

Ringing the bell, I couldn't help noticing the micro surveillance camera embedded in one of the wall sconces framing his apartment door. Apparently, Dominic Watisi wasn't the only one concerned with hyper-security at his residence. On the other hand, maybe it was routine for the likes of Grayland Tower. Protection for the paranoid.

After pushing the bell three times to no avail, I was just about to cross Collins off my list, when I saw a shadow move across the peephole from inside. Someone was home.

A deadbolt was thrown, the regular lock clicked, and the door swung open to reveal a tall, silver-haired man, trim for his age, with a runny nose and blood-soaked eyes.

"I'm sorry," he said. "I was sleeping and didn't hear the bell."

"Sorry to wake you, Mr. Collins."

"That's all right. What can I do for you?"

He was dressed in a slightly wrinkled oxford button-down and stylish corduroy trousers with pleats. An odd choice, I thought, for a sweltering summer evening, but in the air-conditioned sanctum of his apartment, perhaps not.

"My name's Frank Pavlicek. I'm a private investigator looking into the missing pets from the building. I was hoping to talk to you about your cat."

He looked me up and down for a moment. "Of course. Of course, come in."

He pulled the door open wider and stepped aside, allowing me to enter. I caught a whiff of something medicinal on his breath.

Collins' apartment was almost identical in layout to Lonigan's, but his décor couldn't have been more different. The place looked like a museum. From the entrance hall to the sitting room on our right, to as far as I could see down the hallway leading to the great room, the floors and walls were covered with thick oriental carpets and grass mats. Tapestries, wooden carvings, various types of weaponry including a spear, a shield and two blowguns, exotic African headdresses, paintings and photos of the Serengeti, and the like—all added to the display.

"You're a collector, I see."

"Yes," he said. "My curse, I'm afraid. The fewer historical artifacts there are left in the world, the more I seem to have to have them."

"African?"

"Yes, but that's just what you see here. It's why you caught me napping, too. My flight from Cameroon was delayed and didn't get into JFK until almost four A.M."

"Cameroon. That would be Sudan, wouldn't it?"

"Yes."

"A buying trip?"

He looked at a side table in the hall where an ebony statue of a slender naked woman with a basket on her stomach rested between a pair of ivory candlesticks. "Not for these types of items, I'm afraid. A client of mine, a tractor parts manufacturer with a factory there, has been having some labor negotiations difficulties. Things have grown rather testy, so I had to go over for a couple of days."

"Long trip for such a short time."

He shrugged. "It's what I do."

"From the news, it doesn't sound like the most stable place in the world. A lot of killing. The Janjaweed in Darfur."

"That's in the south of the country. I try not to involve myself in local politics."

He led me down the hall toward the great room, but turned right down another corridor that opened into a smaller room.

"I hope you don't mind if we talk in my office. I seem to spend most of my time here, and it's where Domino liked to spend most of her time, too."

"Domino?"

"My cat."

"Domino your only pet?"

"Yes. She's been missing now for a week and a half."

"So I understand. I'm sorry."

We entered the room, a light- and palm-filled atrium complete with a large desk, a desktop computer and two laptops, laser printer, and numerous engineering drawings.

"Please, have a seat," he said, beckoning to a leather side chair in front of the desk.

"Why so many computers?" I asked.

"I'm a tech-geek, I guess. I like to play with them in my spare time."

He sat in his own high-back chair behind the desk and flipped open an ornate silver box next to him beside the telephone. From it, he extracted a cigarette.

"You smoke?" he asked.

"No."

"Hope you don't mind if I do. Nasty habit. I cut way back for a while, but seem to have picked it back up again."

"It's your house."

He nodded and lifted a large wooden match from a compartment inside the box, striking it against the back of the desk and lighting his cigarette. He drew in a deep draught of smoke, leaned his head back, and exhaled toward the ceiling.

"So you're looking for the missing pets. Are you working for Korva Lonigan?"

"Yes," I said.

"I hope you can find Domino."

"How long have you owned her?"

"Domino? Oh, I don't know. I'd say it must be four, five years. She belonged to my ex-wife, until the woman decided to become allergic about the same time she was throwing me out of the house."

"So you ended up with the cat."

"Cold bargain, eh?"

"Was that when you moved in here?"

"That's right. About ten months ago, just after the building opened up again."

"And your wife, excuse me, I mean your ex-wife still lives in your old home?"

"Yes. Over in Saddlebrook."

"Any kids?"

"No. Just the two of us and the kitty."

"What made you decide to move into the city?"

He blew out another puff of smoke. "I wanted to be where the action is. I've always wanted to live in Manhattan, especially here on the park. Business is going well, despite the divorce. I'm single again. I could afford it." He shrugged.

"How'd you pick this particular building?"

"A realtor showed it to me when it was under renovation."

"Maybe Domino had trouble adjusting to her new environment, somehow found her way downstairs, and decided to strike out for greener pastures."

"Maybe, but I don't think so. My wife was the one who adored Domino, but at least I wasn't sneezing all over her every other second. She was safe here. I gave her her space. A cat needs space. You own one?"

"No."

"No pets of any kind?"

"I have a bird."

"Really?" He stamped out his cigarette looking interested. "What type of bird?"

"A hawk named Torch."

"A hawk. Hey, now that is cool."

"Yes," I said. "Tell me about what happened when you first noticed Domino was missing."

"If you're working for Dr. Lonigan, you're no doubt already aware of her theory regarding what happened to our pets."

"Yes."

"Have you ever owned an owl?"

"No, but I know people who do."

"Could someone have made one kill our pets?"

"First of all, if it's a wild bird, you don't really make a wild bird of prey do anything. You work with their natural instincts. They respond because of their hunger."

"All right then, assuming the owl was hungry enough. Theoretically, could it have killed my cat?"

"Yes."

"I was afraid you were going to say that."

"But before we start jumping to assumptions, which is what everybody seems to want to do around here, why don't you tell me exactly how you found out Domino was missing."

"I . . ." He looked down at hands. "It was all so idiotic."

I waited.

"I'd been out with some customers. Drinking. We'd hit quite a few bars in Midtown. I took a cab home. It was late." He laughed, shaking his head in a mocking sort of way. "It was my own stupidity, you see? For some reason I got it in my head that Domino needed a walk. He's an indoor cat with a litter box in New York City, but, as I say, I'd had a little too much too drink. And Domino has a leash, from when we used to live in New Jersey."

"So you took him outside."

"Yes."

"What time was this?"

"I don't remember, exactly. But it must have been well after two. The bar closed at two."

"Anybody see you?"

"Yes, the security guard downstairs, I think, although I wasn't really paying all that much attention."

"What happened then?"

"That's where it gets strange, you see. I'm not really sure what happened. I mean, I remember going out with Domino on her leash, but I don't remember coming back in with her. The next thing I remember I was back upstairs in bed in my apartment."

"Was that when you realized Domino was gone?"

"Yes." He nodded slowly. "I'm afraid it might have been all my fault."

"Had you heard of any other missing pets in the building before this happened?"

"No. I think mine might have been the first."

"And the guard didn't say anything when you walked back in without your cat? You don't remember doing or seeing anything else?"

"No. I'm sorry. Maybe I'm to blame for this whole mess.

Maybe I let my cat go when I shouldn't have and this owl caught him and got a taste for cat blood or whatever."

"Have you found any trace of Domino since she disappeared?"

"No. Not like some of the others. Nothing."

I looked over the list of apartment owners Darla had given us and compared it with the list of those involved in the lawsuit with Watisi.

"I see you're not involved in the dispute that some of the other owners are having with the developer."

"No," he said. "That is, not directly. I guess we all are, though, in a way. It affects all of our properties."

"Good point."

"Do you think my cat's dead, Mr. Pavlicek?"

"She could be."

He drew in a raggedy breath, as if he were struggling to get hold of his emotions.

"I'm sorry. You must have really cared for this cat."

He shook his head. "That's not it at all. Don't you see?"

"No, I'm sorry, I don't."

"This thing keeps hitting the papers like it has?"

"Yeah."

"Sooner or later my ex-wife is going to find out."

"You mean you haven't told her?"

He shook his head.

We stared at one another in silence for a moment.

"She's going to eviscerate me," he finally said.

16

"Oh, boy," I said.

"What?"

We were about to head out the door for our appointment with Damon Hicks' sister and brother. Nicole, deep in thought, was clicking away at her laptop on the kitchen table of our temporary apartment. I had just finished talking on my cell phone, which had purred as I was looking over her shoulder.

"That was Jackson Miller."

"I thought he wasn't going to get back to you for a couple of days," Nicole said.

"He said after he talked to me, curiosity got the better of him. He was able to track down a friend who's a dealer on Long Island, who e-mailed another dealer here in the city, who talked to another dealer who was able to document the existence of *The Book of the Mews.*"

"Awesome."

"It gets even better. Jackson is forwarding us an E-mail from the dealer who actually sold the book five years ago."

"Does he remember who he sold it to?"

"Oh yeah. He remembers. It was Dominic Watisi."

"You're kidding."

"Couldn't make that one up if I tried. Anyway, we've got documented evidence of the sale."

"Watisi's fingerprints are all over this now."

"Looks that way."

"What should we do now?"

I picked up the keys to Lonigan's Porsche that Nicole had left on the table. "We keep our appointment. We still need to try to find out what Cato Raines' role is in this and how that falconry lure ended up next to those two bodies last night. After that, we'll talk with Darla and Dr. Lonigan, hook up with Darla, and see if our falconer shows up tonight."

"What about going to the police, see if we can get them to serve a search warrant on Watisi?"

"It's still only circumstantial evidence," I said.

"But that's a pretty big circumstance."

"Yeah."

"What's bothering you?" she asked.

"I don't know. I'm just getting a funny feeling that there is more to this story than we're seeing."

"One step at a time, you've always told me."

"Sure. One step at a time."

We took the elevator downstairs. Jayani Miller was working the security desk again, this time by herself.

"You're back," I said as we passed by.

"Trying to keep myself awake." She smiled.

"You're missing the fireworks tonight."

"They don't do anything for me anyway."

We went across to the parking garage and found the Porsche in its usual slot. We climbed in and I was just about to turn over the engine when a tall, lanky young man with curly brown hair appeared beside the car and put his hand on the windshield. In it, he was holding some form of ID.

"What the—?" I locked the door, cranked the engine, and powered down the window a notch.

"You Frank Pavlicek?" the young man asked.

"Who wants to know?"

"Barry LaGrange, reporter with the *Post.* Can I ask you a few questions?"

"No comment," I said, and threw the car into reverse, preparing to back up.

"Wait a minute. Wait a minute."

"I said no comment. Now move, unless you want to get run over."

"For a guy who makes his living snooping around other people's lives, you sure aren't very forthcoming yourself."

"Comes with the territory."

"I'm just looking for more of a story here," he said. "Maybe we can help each other." He was passing a business card through the window.

I ignored it and started backing up.

"Hey!" he shouted.

The card dropped in my lap as the man leapt away from the fender swinging into his legs. I shifted into first, swung the wheel, and screeched past him.

"Great," I said. "As if we don't already have enough to worry about."

"I thought he was kind of cute," Nicole said.

I shook my head and by the time I shifted into third, heading further down the street, he was only a small figure in my rearview mirror, standing and staring at us with his hands on his hips.

It took nearly half an hour to drive the thirty blocks up to Lenox Terrace and find a place to park. The holiday evening celebration was just beginning and everybody seemed to be going somewhere. Rain was in the forecast, a chance of thundershowers, but that didn't seem to dampen anyone's spirits.

Marianne Hicks lived in a tastefully renovated brownstone across the street from some projects. There was a small back terrace off the alley and the smell of steaks grilling. You would have thought a party was in progress had it not been for the black ribbon hung across the door.

"You're right on time," the dead teen's sister said to Nicole as she opened the front door. "My brother's upstairs. I've told him you're coming."

"Marianne, this is my father, Frank."

Marianne Hicks was a startlingly attractive black woman of about thirty. She took my hand and shook it. "I'm very sorry to hear about your brother, Ms. Hicks," I said.

"Not half as sorry as we were that he ever let himself get mixed up with that gang. Please, come on in."

She led us into the living room, which was a long room modestly furnished with aging furniture.

"The funeral isn't until Tuesday," she went on. "But lots of people have been calling and coming by."

A pyramid of flower arrangements and cards took up most of one corner, and food and drinks were set out on trays. Heavy footsteps pounded down the stairwell in the hall.

A bespectacled black man of moderate build and wearing a dark tux came into the room.

"Stephen, these are the private investigators I was telling you about," his sister said.

Stephen Hicks shook both of our hands in turn. "Thank you for coming," he said. "I only wish it were under different circumstances. Sorry for the penguin suit."

His sister smiled. "Stephen's a limo driver, but he also sings baritone in his church choir. They're quite well known and they're doing a benefit concert tonight."

"We thought of asking them to cancel it," Stephen apologized, "but then, after talking with the pastor, we decided it was okay to go ahead."

"You have a few minutes to talk, though?" Nicole asked.

"Oh, it's okay. The concert doesn't start for another hour and a half."

We all took seats around the living room.

"I understand you two have an interest in the shooting last night," Stephen said.

"We do," I said.

"Marianne explained the situation to me. We've already been questioned by the police. Are you thinking this person you're looking for may be connected with whoever shot Damon?"

"Quite possibly."

"And you want to know how Damon came to be there."

"It might help."

The singer blew out a breath and cupped his hands together for a moment. "Damon had had problems since he was eleven or twelve," he said. "He lived with my father, who passed away two years ago. Since then, it's been hard to track him down."

"Marianne told me earlier that you and your sister weren't raised by your father," Nicole said.

"That's right. Our parents divorced when we were young. Mom's a nurse. Damon was the youngest. Our father was unemployed most of the time, but he managed to hang on to Damon."

"So after your father died, Damon hit the streets?"

"Pretty much. We tried to get him to come live here. He would have none of it."

"Was he in school?"

"If you can call it that. I doubt he was there very often."

"Where was he living?"

"We could never really get a fix on that. He seemed to move around a lot."

"But you knew he was involved with Los Miembros," I said.

Stephen nodded. "It was like they took over everything and became his family."

"Seems unusual, though, if you don't mind my saying. I mean, it appears you and your sister could have supported him financially."

"You're right," Marianne said. "Most of those kids come from nothing—abject poverty. But with Damon it was never about the money. It was all about power, and his mistaken ideas of being a man."

I hesitated. "You mind telling us what kind of things he was into?"

She looked at her brother, who looked at the floor. "He could have been a murderer himself, for all I know," Stephen said. "In fact, he probably was."

"Were they dealing drugs?"

"Sure. But I heard some other stuff a couple of months ago that caused me concern." He paused.

"Which was?"

"I heard Los Miembros—or at least whatever subgroup Damon was a part of—had gotten heavily involved in the sex trade. Another lawyer I know downtown said he prosecuted a case where one of them was convicted of running a prostitution ring and trafficking in women, a couple of which had come from overseas."

Marianne was shaking her head. "Our little brother. A slaver."

"The world really has turned upside down," Stephen said.

I didn't know what to say to that. I don't guess Nicole did, either. It was quiet in the room for a few moments.

"For what it's worth," I finally said, "NYPD thinks he and Mansuela were only peripheral players."

Stephen nodded. "That's what they told us, too. Not that it really makes much difference."

"I'm very sorry."

"He could have been such a leader, such an example, such a

great young man."

"Couldn't they all?" I said.

17

"Sounds like you've got some heavy duty stuff going on here, Franco," Darla Barnes said.

"Don't I know it."

"Maybe our kitty thing is just the tip of an iceberg."

"You think Lieutenant Marbush must be thinking the same thing by now?"

"Probably."

We were still in the apartment, even though it had been dark for over an hour. The plan called for Nicole to be staked out on the balcony of our apartment, armed with a low light camera, spotting scope, night vision goggles, and a good pair of binoculars, while Darla and I trolled through the park below. We had to wait for Darla.

We'd been able to see a little bit of the fireworks through the back windows of the apartment that faced the West Side.

"We thought you'd been abducted by aliens," Nicole said.

"Just about. That Halverson lady can talk your ear off. I left her a message this morning and thought I'd stop by to talk with her. Sorry I'm late."

"She's the one with the missing puppy, right?"

"Right. And the other one who found what looks like remains along with a feather."

"Those gone off to the lab, too?"

She nodded. "Roger."

"What?"

"The puppy's name was Roger. One of the little girls named it."

"You already talked to Mrs. Halverson before, though, didn't you?"

"Yeah, but I wanted to talk to her again after Jayani told us she was asking about the case down in the lobby. That woman talks to anybody and everybody."

"Find out anything new?"

"Not really. But now that you've told me about this book and the connection to Watisi, we're probably wasting our time canvassing the building. Maybe we'll be able to talk to Watisi after the hearing tomorrow."

"You're coming, then?"

"Wouldn't miss it. This is turning into my biggest case."

"You didn't happen to run into any reporters, did you?" I said.

"No, why?"

"There's a Channel 12 News van parked down on the curb in front."

"Maybe I should hide you two in a closet."

"It's been there a while now. They must be talking to someone else in the building." I also told her about our encounter with the reporter in the parking garage.

"Wonderful," she said. "Can't stop the power of the press. Let's hope whoever's down there doesn't spot us."

I went to the window again while Nicole helped Darla with the equipment. Down on the street, everything appeared quiet. A tall, skinny man exited the front of the building with quick, short steps. He was too far away for me to be able to decipher the look on his face, but he was definitely in a hurry. It was LaGrange, the reporter from the *Post*.

"There goes our friend from the *Daily Planet.*"

"Good," Darla said behind me. "Maybe that's one less thing

to worry about."

"I'm not so sure."

"Why's that?"

There was no mistaking the slender blonde who had left the building at LaGrange's side and whom the young man was now talking to.

"Our client just walked out the front door, too," I said.

Like any reasonably well-informed person, I read a lot. I tend to favor books over magazines and magazines over newspapers. Call it my suspicion of the "now factor," the pressure faced by those who must literally report what they think is "the news" overnight. Any literate adult on this planet knows that what happens in real life often tends to play out over time. It's the problem with photos, too. Still lifes that capture the perfect "moment" often result from tossing out a hundred or more other negatives that cumulatively might have told a more interesting story. The winning ballplayer holding the trophy might be struggling with a cocaine addiction. The smiling girl in her mother's arms could be cuddling up to her child abuser.

Certain people in everything from politics to business to religion have learned how to manipulate this weakness we have for wanting life made simple; how to parse words for the right quote, how to set up for the perfect photo-op, how to play the game.

I hoped our client wasn't becoming one of them.

Darla and I must have looked like a pair of washed up SWAT team members as we stepped out of the elevator and into the lobby.

On the street in front of the building Dr. Lonigan was gone, but in her place a bearded man hauling a TV video camera on his shoulder appeared as if on cue from around the corner of the building. He was followed by a teen with a dark goatee sporting a professional-grade digital camera who was followed by LaGrange.

"This is nuts," Jayani said as we approached the security desk. "We don't want any more publicity."

Darla sighed and looked at me.

"I was afraid of this," I said.

Jayani had been talking on the phone with someone else, but she hung up now. "Who are these people?"

"Backdrop."

"Huh?"

I didn't answer. Instead, I focused on LaGrange, who made eye contact with me from a distance and poked the cameraman in the shoulder urging him forward.

"I thought he was just print media," I said.

"Looks like it's time to the pay the piper." Darla made eyes at me.

"Ought to be a hoot."

"Very funny." She turned away from the guard and said under her breath, "Let's agree we don't say anything about the threats or the shooting or the links we've found to Watisi, all right?"

"You're preaching to the choir."

"If any of these people are doing their homework they may know enough already."

LaGrange and the cameraman were at the front door now preparing to enter.

"Okay," I said. "How about we just no-comment our way past them?"

"How's that going to look?"

"Probably better than anything I might say."

A squad car rolled to a stop outside. Two cops were inside and they switched on the whirling blue beacons. LaGrange and all the camera people paused and turned for a few seconds to take more pictures.

"Lovely," Darla said. "Why don't we just invite the mayor to join us while we're at it."

"Don't laugh. He might've been invited."

"Who do you really think tipped them all off we were coming out here."

"Prime suspect is our good doctor."

"Or it might've been anybody else we talked to—someone at the precinct even."

"Maybe."

The phone behind the security desk rang. Jayani said, "We gotta keep the street clear in front of here. My boss is not going to be happy about this."

"We're headed out, then they'll be gone," Darla said reassuringly.

Nicole's voice crackled over the walkie-talkie attached to my belt. "Dad? What's going on down there?"

I picked the handset off its clip and keyed the mike. "Just a little disturbance. We'll handle it. If you can get some good photos of the participants from up there, go for it."

"I'm on it," she said.

"Let's go," Darla said.

We headed through the revolving glass door. The two cops were now out of their car and speaking with one of the reporters.

"There they are!"

LaGrange whirled around and dragged his cameraman to face us as we exited the building.

"Hello again, Mr. Pavlicek."

I guess this guy didn't like being told no.

LaGrange's voice had changed, though. A conspiratorial half whisper that seemed custom designed to induce a response. I wasn't biting, though, and neither was Darla. She pushed past the two cameras as if they didn't exist.

"I'd like your comment on what's happening here, Ms.

Barnes," LaGrange said. "What's the nature of your investigation and who hired you?"

Darla glared at him the way she might a housefly. He knew damn well who had hired us.

We kept on walking and he fell into pace. Cameras were *whirring.*

"Did you know anything about the hearing tomorrow?" he persisted. "Have you heard there might be a protest?"

Darla said nothing.

Seeing he was getting nothing from her, LaGrange turned to me. "Mr. Pavlicek, what are you doing up here all the way from Virginia?"

Who else had he been talking to? But I didn't stop to give it any more thought.

LaGrange, with his apparent superhuman powers of deduction, must have sensed he was going to get nothing from us—at least for the time being. He turned and began speaking into the camera.

The two uniformed officers acted as though we were just extra security hired by the building. Thankfully, one of them also put a hand in the reporter's face.

"Back off, fellas," he said to the two with the cameras.

"Just trying to ask these people a few questions," LaGrange said evenly.

"And the people don't feel like talking." Darla already had her credentials out and was showing them to the officers.

The same officer turned back to LaGrange. "Like I said, I'm sorry, sir, but I'm going to have to ask you to back off," he said.

You had to give the reporter some credit. He knew trying to bait a cop in front of the cameras, while it might raise his stature some back in the newsroom, wouldn't get him very far when it came time to mine his inside sources from the boys in blue. "All right," he said.

He nodded and retreated reluctantly to the other side of the street with the camera people and attempted to regroup.

The officer, whose badge read *Mullins,* turned back to us.

"We got the word at roll call yesterday about you two, but you better watch your backs while you're out here chasing kitty hitter." He gestured toward the reporters. "Looks like you may have an audience."

Terrific. Surveillance by media. Just the way I'd normally have gone about it.

"Don't worry, we'll lose these idiots sooner or later," Darla said.

"Yeah? Well, sooner would be better so we can clear the street," Mullins said.

"Why don't I just threaten to shoot them?"

"Now there's an original thought, Ms. Barnes. That would definitely make the eleven P.M on channel six."

"I've got a better idea," I said.

"What's that?"

"We'll wait them out. Sooner or later they're all going to need to pee. And being the ex-cops and patient professional investigators that we are, we know how to hold it."

The cop looked at me and smiled. "Okay, but just remember, outside of provided restrooms human urination or defecation in a public park is against city statute."

"So what, you busting all the winos, teens, and the homeless now?"

Still smiling, he shook his head and waved us on.

18

The jogger's footsteps crunched a steady rhythm through the darkness on the 102nd Street Transverse. Playing rhythm section was the drone of distant building air conditioners, the din of crickets, grasshoppers, and katydids. It was twenty minutes to midnight and the hoped-for reunion with Cato Raines. What kind of idiot would be out here running in the park so late, even assuming the emergency phones were all working and the cop currently stationed at the booth on the quarter-mile connector was awake? Was it Raines?

The fireworks over the Hudson were now a distant memory. A brief thundershower had drenched the pavement a little earlier. The moon, which had made a dim and brief appearance after the rain, had almost disappeared again, fading behind another encroaching line of clouds. Did I expect the homeless falconer to show? Not really. But I thought his knowing we would be trolling through the park at this hour might force him into some sort of mistake. An hour and a half had passed since Darla and I had traipsed through the media gauntlet in front of Grayland Tower; at least an hour since we lost Barry LaGrange and his crew of picture takers, who obviously hadn't thought of bringing low-light camera equipment. My last radio check with Darla and Nicole, the former somewhere in the darkness and the latter keeping tabs on the scene from her balcony perch above, had been about fifteen minutes ago.

Through the night vision goggles, I could begin to make out

the running figure. Definitely not Raines—shorts, reflective sneakers, white tank top, a woman. She was tall and athletic looking, her long hair drawn back into a ponytail. She was pumping her arms with her head held back and to one side like some kind of wild, nocturnal mare.

The realization dawned on me all at once. It was none other than our client, Dr. Lonigan.

I flipped off the goggles and waited in the shadows, debating whether to alert her to my presence. There is a fleeting epiphany to such moments, like standing at the end of the diving board above the shimmering pool. In the end, I went with the indirect approach.

"You're out late," I said, stepping from the shadows so she could see that it was me.

"Oh." She pounded to a halt. "You gave me a start."

"May I ask what you're doing here?"

"Didn't Darla tell you? I like to run in the park."

"In the middle of the night? By yourself?"

"No. Not usually in the middle of the night. But I couldn't sleep and I was hoping I might run into you or Darla."

"It's a big park."

She flexed her arm and brushed a loose strand of hair back from in front of her face. "Guess you'll have to call me lucky then. Have you seen anything? Any sign of the man with the owl?"

I shook my head. "All's quiet on the falconer front."

"I heard you and Darla had to pass by a bunch of reporters earlier."

"Yes. What were you doing talking to them?"

"How did you—?"

I held up my hand.

"It doesn't matter. A reporter named LaGrange left a message for me at my apartment. He was waiting in the lobby when

I came back from the hospital. I told him I didn't want to talk about the matter any further."

"All right. But you should know that if this thing turns into some kind of public spectacle, the truth, whatever it is, may get lost."

"That's not what I want."

"You may not want it, but it can happen. And if it does, everyone gets burned."

"Is that what happened to you and your partner when you shot that teenager years ago?"

"More or less."

"And you're still bitter about it."

"I was, yeah, for quite a while."

"But you're not anymore."

"They teach you to change the subject like this and ask probing questions in medical school?"

I caught a hint of a smile in the darkness. She said nothing.

"You still haven't answered my question completely."

"What's that?"

"I can't help finding it suspicious that you're out here right now."

I would have liked to have heard her reply, but the walkie-talkie on my belt crackled softly.

"Frank."

It was Darla.

I picked the handset off its clip and keyed the SPEAK button. "Copy."

"I think I've got something. Looks like it could be our man."

Her voice came through with too much gain, but it was clear enough to understand her words. I looked at Dr. Lonigan, who stood riveted to her spot.

"Where are you?" I asked into the mike.

"On the south side of the Meer. Between the lake and the

Lasker Pool."

"I know right where it is," Lonigan said.

I pushed the button again. "Tell me what you see."

"It's pretty dark over here," Darla said. "But I see a small man with one of those mini flashlights by the water. Swinging something in the air shining a beam of light on it."

"Could be our guy."

"Oh, wait! Something big just swooped through the air in front of the light."

"Definitely our guy."

Lonigan turned and started running. "Come on," she called over her shoulder.

Come on, indeed.

In the dark, its scattered lamps glowing beneath oak and bald cypress, the Harlem Meer is a postcard quality swath of water. During the daytime, you can watch the swans and grebes drift around like tame pets. If someone with a well-trained falcon were stupid enough to hunt here, one of the grebes might make a tempting target. At night with an owl, you'd have to mount a pretty spectacular ambush.

Lonigan stopped next to the pool. I pounded to a halt next to her. We were both dripping with sweat in the humid air. I'd finished off my water bottle over an hour ago. There was no sign of Darla or the falconer. We stood to listen and catch our breath.

Nothing.

I keyed the walkie-talkie again and spoke more softly this time.

"Darla."

No reply. Several seconds passed.

"Darla, where are you?"

Still nothing.

I said into the hand piece, "Nicky, you there?"

"Yeah, Dad, it's me."

"You get Darla's position?"

"I think so. Looking at a map."

"Forget that." I was breathing easier now. "Just look out the balcony to your left about fifty, sixty degrees at the big body of water across the park."

A few seconds later, Nicole's voice returned, "Got it."

"See anything?"

"Not yet."

"Keep looking."

My legs and lungs were still burning, but I tried to ignore them.

Nicole came on again. "Dad?" she said.

"Yeah."

"I can't see a thing. Too many trees in the way."

"Right."

"I'm coming down there."

"Wait. Nicky." I keyed the mike again several times. "Nicky."

There was no response.

"Where is she?" Lonigan asked.

"She was on the balcony of our apartment. Supposed to be serving as a spotter."

I looked around and listened. Still no sign of Darla or Raines, if that was who she'd spotted.

"What now?" Lonigan asked.

I flipped my night vision goggles back down over my eyes. "Now. We take a good look around."

We walked at a cautious gait along the nearest pathway around the lake. I swept my head back and forth slowly, probing the darkness. It had been years, I thought, since I'd last ventured away from the well-lit thoroughfares in Central Park at night.

A trio of figures jumped out from behind the rocks along the shoreline ahead and began running away.

"There they go!" Lonigan whispered, her voice thin with excitement.

I took note of the spiked hair on one, the chains dangling, the heavy boots.

"Nope," I said. "Just some kids. Goths. Probably smoking weed or something."

Five minutes passed. Ten. Still no sign of Darla.

"You think something's happened to her?" Lonigan asked. She was still with me, moving as I moved.

I shook my head and shrugged. "Still a lot of park here. She could be anywhere."

A few seconds later, Nicole's voice came back on the radio over some static. "Dad. Dad, you there?"

I reached for my handset. "I'm here."

"I think I've spotted him."

"Who?"

"Raines. Or someone, at least, with a bird."

"What about Darla?"

Static. "Don't see her," she said.

"Where are you?"

"I'm not sure exactly."

"Somewhere around the Meer?"

"I think so." Static. "I ran up to 110th Street and cut across to come into the park from that end."

"Watch yourself," I said. "Wait for backup." I was trying to guess how far she was away and how long it would take for us to get there.

"Where are you, Dad?"

"Around the lake from you to your right. Can't say exactly how far."

"There's more of them," she said. Static. "I see Darla. I'm moving in."

More of whom? Where were they?

The shots that rang out then let me guess where. Sharp, staccato explosions echoed across the water. Like a string of firecrackers, followed by a chorus of larger caliber blasts.

I sprinted toward the sound with Lonigan on my heels. Hollered into my walkie-talkie, reaching for my gun.

19

"Not one of the brighter things I've ever done."

Darla Barnes grimaced as she held folded gauze against her lower leg to help stem the bleeding.

She had been lucky. A bullet had torn into her calf muscle, but—according to the paramedics and Dr. Lonigan's preliminary assessment—it had missed any vital arteries or nerves and was well back of the bone. She might be on crutches for a few weeks, but she would recover.

"I had him right there." She pointed to a spot down on the bank. "I must've been only about fifty feet away from him when he got away."

She was sitting on the rear deck of an ambulance while Lonigan and Nicole, who was unhurt, finished talking to the patrol officers and medical personnel who'd responded to the scene. Had Darla only been caught in the crossfire from some late-night Fourth of July revelers firing handguns? No one really believed it, although that was the story being fed to the media. With everyone on edge after the shootings in the park the night before, the cops weren't taking any chances.

My old friend looked me in the eyes. "Nicky saved my butt, Franco. If she hadn't shown up when she did, along with that other shooter, those two might've taken me out."

Those two were a pair of Latino males of average build, who'd appeared from out of the darkness to deliver some sort of muffled threats apparently aimed at the mysterious falconer.

When Darla made her move, they started shooting and the falconer ran. Nicole's intervention, along with the help of another unidentified shooter from somewhere across the water, forced the assailants to melt back into the bowels of the park as well.

"Yeah, well, I'm glad," I said. "But it wasn't because of me. I ordered her to stay away."

"She's a hardhead like her old man." Darla smiled through the pain.

The cops had already questioned Nicole before talking to me. I told them what little I knew: all of us had heard the shots. Afraid we wouldn't get there in time, Darla had gone after the falconer with no backup. The man with the owl, quite probably Cato Raines—although I didn't share that with the officers—along with the other person firing from across the lake, had simply vanished like smoke. As had the two who had started the gunplay.

"You both discharged your firearms," I said. "You think you hit either of the perps?"

"I know I didn't. Getting shot in the leg didn't help my aim."

"Nicole says she doesn't think she did, either, but the other shooter might have. That sounded like a decent-sized weapon they were firing. It was a lucky thing they didn't turn it on either of you."

"What do you think's going on, Franco?"

I shook my head.

"A gang war?"

"Maybe."

"But how are your falconer and all these missing pets mixed up in it?"

"You definitely saw a bird?"

"Had to be."

"Nicole says she saw it, too."

She looked over at the paramedics and Lonigan. "How did Dr. Lonigan end up out here with you?"

I lowered my voice and told her I'd run into Lonigan lower down in the park. "Are you absolutely sure you can trust this woman?" I asked.

"Her retainer check cleared, what else can I tell you?"

"You know about her record out in Oregon?"

"Oh, you found out about that, too, huh?" She shrugged. "Didn't seem like any big deal to me. Just a bunch of young tree huggers."

"Don't you think it's bizarre, though, to be running alone in the park at midnight?"

"Stupid, for sure."

"It was like she knew where I was and purposely came out looking for me."

She thought about that. "Maybe we ought to have a talk with her about her agenda."

I motioned toward the two officers questioning Dr. Lonigan. "What'd you tell the cops?"

"Same thing you probably did."

"You tell them we talked with Marbush?"

"Yeah."

"Think they'll be of any help?"

"Hopefully."

"Looks like you're going to be out of commission for a while."

She grimaced again, nodded.

"What did you plan to do if you caught the guy with the owl?"

"Pray he didn't try to sic the thing on me."

"Good plan," I said.

"What was the dude doing out here with the flashlight?"

"Sounds like he's got another lure. Sometimes you can also play games with birds, get them to fly by while you swing it like a matador. To do that, though, the bird needs to see the lure. An owl sees well in the dark, but he's probably got the bird conditioned to the flashlight. Or . . ."

"Or what?"

"The falconer was in an emergency situation. He knew he'd been spotted and needed to get his bird down in a hurry. You think he saw you?"

She shook her head. "No way. That's why I never got a good look at him. He never even turned in my direction."

"Which means he must have been worried about something or someone else."

"Yeah. The dudes who started shooting at him," she said.

Nicole had sauntered over to join the conversation. Turning so no one else could hear, she said, "I've got something interesting."

"You mean besides disobeying me when I tell you to stay put?"

She ignored me. "I shot some video."

"You what?" Darla glanced at the cops who were still busy talking with Lonigan.

"I brought along the low-light camcorder. I managed to get some footage of the falconer before all the shooting started."

Darla, looking impressed, raised eyebrows at me. "This girl brings the whole package."

"I just excused myself for a couple of minutes to use the public restroom by the boathouse and took a look at it," Nicole said. "I think it came out pretty well."

"What's it show?" I asked.

"Something strange. The glove on the hand holding the bird was not a normal falconer's glove, not like one I've ever seen anyway. It looked more like a hard cylinder, almost like a prosthesis or a heavy ace bandage."

"Really? That says a lot."

"Why?"

"Our falconer isn't from the US. At least he wasn't trained to handle birds of prey in North America."

"What do you mean?"

"What you saw is called a mangalah. Used in the Arab style of falconry. It's basically a cylindrical kind of cuff with no fingers."

"So we're looking for a Middle Easterner. Maybe not Raines after all."

"Or at least someone who was trained to handle birds Arab style."

"Do the Arabs hunt with owls?"

"Not generally."

"You all are freaking me out even more now," Darla said. "Something weird is definitely happening here."

One of the paramedics, a young woman, approached.

"Hate to break up your conference, people, but we do need to take Ms. Barnes to the hospital. Dr. Lonigan's going to accompany us."

"Okay," Darla said.

Just then, an unmarked police cruiser, magnetic beacon spinning on its roof, screeched to a halt at the curb. Lt. Marbush stepped out of the front passenger side and made a beeline toward us.

"Don't tell me," she said. "Dominic Watisi, in addition to hiring someone to steal kittens, has gotten himself caught up in a gangbanger's street fight."

"You tell us," I said.

Nicole and Dr. Lonigan came over, too. Everyone went through their stories again with the detective supervisor. I told her some of what we'd learned.

When all of us were through, the lieutenant looked at Darla.

"I'm glad you're okay," she said. "We'll get some crime scene people out here to look for ballistic evidence. Believe it or not, we really are investigating these killings. But you folks better stay out of the park after dark from now on, before one of you ends up like those two bodies last night."

"You don't need to worry about me," Darla said, smiling. "I ain't going anywhere with this leg."

Marbush looked over at Nicole and me. "How about you people?"

"We'll think about it," I said.

The lieutenant said, "You do that, Frank. The last thing I'd think you would want is your face splashed across the tabloids connected to a shooting once again."

The lieutenant climbed back into her car and closed the door. She was right. The paramedics and Dr. Lonigan loaded Darla into the back of the ambulance. I stood on the curb with Nicole and watched as both official vehicles pulled away.

20

But I guess I couldn't help myself.

At ten o'clock the next morning, I was standing with Nicole outside a courtroom waiting for a new salvo in the litigation of the dispute between the Grayland Tower apartment owners and Dominic Watisi. A preliminary hearing in the courtroom of the Honorable Carmichael Peabody, judge for the New York County Housing Court, was about to begin. Darla had spent the night at Mt. Sinai and wasn't scheduled to be released today, either. Which, in her present condition, was like caging an angry mountain lion.

"The proceedings will begin about twenty minutes late," a bored-looking bailiff cheerlessly informed the assembled masses.

"Great," Nicole said, her shoulders slumping with fatigue. "Just great."

She was still smarting from the tongue-lashing I'd given her on the way back to the apartment the night before. She had helped save Darla's life, after all, not to mention shooting the video footage, which was exactly as she'd described, by the way. But I had lit into her pretty hard about not following orders.

"Hey," I said. "Like I told you over breakfast, I'm sorry about chewing you out last night. I was as much to blame as you."

"That's not it, Dad. Someone out there tried to kill us—Darla and whoever was flying that owl anyway. Someone else was firing an M16, or whatever, and all we're doing is sitting in here waiting for a stupid court case."

"And waiting for Watisi to show or some more information to be revealed that might help us nail down his connection to our falconer in the park."

And for entertainment, we wouldn't even have to wait alone. I put the total at maybe fifty, sixty people. The same reporters and cameras from the night before were in attendance. But now they had more to work with. Two factions opposed one another, in fact, many of whom carried placards.

STOP THE SLAUGHTER OF INNOCENT PETS. SMALL ANIMALS HAVE RIGHTS. BIRDS HAVE RIGHTS, TOO. SAVE THE OWLS.

Each group was comprised of mostly women, but there were a small number of men as well. On the bird side a long-necked man with spectacles and a green backpack walked next to a turtle-bodied woman clad in ill-fitting shorts and clunky sandals. The cat-activist crowd included a braid-coiffed woman dressed in black with a bare midriff and belly button ring. She was speaking urgently with a young man dressed in a suit and tie.

While the opposing camps appeared peaceful for the moment, the three sheriff's deputies on duty at the metal detector watched them warily. Not to mention two of Marbush's plainclothes detectives, who had also shown up for the hearing and were doing their best to blend into the crowd.

"Hey," I said. "There's that reporter from the *Post* you thought was so cute. At least he's not hanging out with the guys with the cameras this morning." I'd also given Nicole the rundown on our encounter with the press the night before.

"You know what?" she said. "Why don't we go and talk to him? He looks like he's by himself. Maybe he's found out some stuff that can help."

I thought about it. It beat cooling our heels.

"I'll talk to him," I said.

"What about me?"

"You need to be here in case the hearing starts."

She bit her lip. "Okay. But be nice to him, Dad."

Right. So I was.

Unlike the night before, LaGrange was respectful and less confrontational. He seemed grateful for the chance to sit down and talk and bought me a cup of coffee at the fast-food restaurant just down the block from the courthouse.

"Look, Mr. Pavlicek, I've got a job to do and you've got a job to do. You're a peripheral player in this thing, I understand that. But I'm smelling there might be a big story here."

"Me, too," I said.

Realizing we wouldn't be able to take the Glocks into court, Nicole and I had left our handguns back at the apartment. The reporter, on the other hand, had arrived this morning with his full armamentarium: pen, paper, and tape recorder. Whoever said that the pen is mightier than the sword must have lived for a time in New York City.

"Okay then." He switched on his tape recorder.

"I'd rather you not do that," I said, indicating the machine.

"What? Tape you? I assure you, Mr. Pavlicek, it's for your protection as well as mine. This way we can be sure you won't be misquoted."

"That's what they all say."

"Why don't you start by telling me how you were hired?"

"I'll tell you what," I said. "Why don't we skip all that because you can probably piece all that together anyway. I'll tell you some things I know and you tell me some things you know. We can trade information and maybe that way we can both get what we want."

"Fair enough. So, tell me what you know."

"Uh-huh. You first."

He stared at me for a moment. "Okay. My understanding is that you're working for Dr. Lonigan, trying to substantiate the public charges she has made against Dominic Watisi regarding pets missing from Grayland Tower."

"Close enough."

"There was another shooting in the park last night and you and your partner were there."

I said nothing.

"You're not denying it."

I shrugged.

"What about Dominic Watisi?"

"Have you talked to him?" I asked.

He shook his head. "Just to his publicist and one or two of his employees."

"He denies involvement."

"To you, too, huh? Did you speak to him directly?"

"Yes."

He wrote something down.

"What do you know about the man?" I said.

LaGrange sighed and pushed a strand of curly dark hair off his forehead. "He's wealthy, obviously. He's incredibly secretive, which I'm sure you've figured out. Most of his hush-hush activity revolves around his finances and his development plans, but he also may be engaged in some off-the-books philanthropy."

"What do you mean?"

The reporter lowered his voice and said in a conspiratorial tone, "I talked to a former employee who told me Watisi has been helping finance illegals seeking asylum or setting up residence in the United States."

"Really."

"Yes, really."

"Not such a smart thing to do in today's climate."

"Exactly."

"Why hasn't this been in the paper yet?"

"I'm looking for corroboration," he said, looking at me hopefully.

"Sorry. Can't help you there. If it's true, what's Watisi get out of it? He running sweatshops or something?"

He shook his head. "I haven't been able to find anything at all of that nature. So far."

"The police know about this?"

"Not exactly. Watisi is careful to keep all of his activities in the realm of private charity work."

"Who does he work through?"

"His lawyer mostly, and a network of sympathetic clergy and social workers."

"Why don't you go talk to them?"

"No one else is talking. The most interesting hard facts I've been able to establish around this story are still about the building and the missing pets. How do you think he got the pets out, by the way?"

"Who?"

"This falconer, or whoever Watisi is supposed to have hired."

"Any number of ways, I suppose."

"I have a theory," he said.

"What's that?"

"You know all about the history of Grayland Tower, right?"

I nodded, vaguely, not wishing to admit my ignorance or that I was about two years behind in my reading of the *Sunday Times,* not to mention *Architectural Digest.*

"Back in the 1920s and 30s, there used to be a well-known restaurant on the ground floor. An old guy I talked to with the city, said that the cops used to think the foundation of the building was honeycombed with tunnels that were used during prohibition to smuggle in whiskey from somewhere in the park across the street."

"They ever find any tunnels?"

"Nope."

"But you think there might still be one."

"Maybe. You still haven't told me much, if anything, about what else you know about the shootings in the park."

"What do you know about Los Miembros?" I asked.

"Not much, unfortunately. Why, do you think the shootings are tied to your case?"

"Maybe."

He sat a little taller in his chair. "Oh, man. Maybe that's how Watisi is connected. Maybe some of the people he's helped finance are part of Los Miembros. Maybe he's hired them, too, like he's hired that falconer."

"You're jumping to a lot of conclusions and you're missing something," I said.

"What?"

"Two young men are dead and another person was almost killed last night. Seems like a little too much activity for a dispute over some apartments, don't you think?" I looked at my watch.

"Yeah, but—"

"I think we need to get back to the courtroom. We'll miss the hearing," I said.

Nicole and I took a seat in the back row of the courtroom. LaGrange, who'd smiled pleasantly at Nicole when I'd introduced them, sat in the front row, notepad and pen in hand. Judge Peabody made the protestors leave their signs outside and gaveled everyone into silence. For their part, Dr. Lonigan and a few of the other plaintiff apartment owners sat stoically beside their counsel, a businesslike brunette in a dark gray suit and black stockings.

Unfortunately, we were out of luck when it came to Watisi. I should have guessed. The wealthy developer apparently wasn't required to appear in person and had sent two middle-aged male attorneys in his stead.

"If Watisi isn't going to show, this may not be getting us anywhere," I whispered to Nicole. I'd already told her what I'd learned from the reporter.

Up front, the hearing appeared to have bogged down before it even started over some procedural motion or question. The judge had the opposing attorneys before his bench discussing an arcane section of the housing statutes in tones that were barely audible to the rest of us in the room.

This was the sort of thing that always drove me nuts about going to court. Half the time, the lawyers and judges would spar over puny conditions that only tangentially related to the matter at hand. They managed to create a mini-bureaucracy right there before your eyes.

My phone began to vibrate from inside my jacket pocket. I pulled it out and quietly and thankfully slipped out the door.

The call was from Marcia in Charlottesville.

"You okay?" she wanted to know when I answered. I made sure to stand far enough away from the TV camera crew that they wouldn't overhear what I said.

"Yeah, fine. Sorry I didn't call you last night. It turned into kind of a late evening."

"How's everything going?" she asked.

"Not so good."

"Why? What happened?"

"Darla was shot last night."

"What?"

"Took a bullet in the leg. She's going to be out of action for a while. But she's going to be okay."

"Does the client still want you to keep working?"

"I haven't talked to her yet. Things are a little crazy at the moment." I told her about the courtroom and the protestors. I glanced down the hall at the distant TV personnel. They were busy interviewing one of the activists who'd also stepped out of the courtroom, but thankfully no one was paying me any attention.

"Maybe you should just let the police handle the whole investigation."

"Can't," I said. "We're in too deep now. And besides, I think we may even have found our falconer."

"So he exists."

"Looks that way."

"I'm worried about you."

"We'll be all right."

"How's Nicole?"

I thought about the scene from the park the night before. "Proving herself more than worthy," I said.

"But if you're in some danger," she said.

"Don't worry, it'll be okay."

"I can get a ticket and fly up there this afternoon."

"I don't think that would be a good idea," I said. "Unless you want to go to work with me, too."

"Call me first thing tomorrow?" she said.

"Will do."

"I miss you."

"Miss you, too."

We said good-bye and hung up.

Just in time, too, because down the hall outside the courtroom, a minor jostle was beginning as people began to move out through the doors. Apparently, the hearing was already over. That quick.

I saw Nicole come out, followed by a whole posse of people—Barry LaGrange and a TV news reporter among them. A cameraman and the interviewer were scrambling to get quality shots and sound bites.

I had half a mind to duck for cover. The talk with LaGrange had gone okay, but the last thing I wanted was to see my face displayed on any City news program again.

No one could have anticipated what happened next.

A small round woman with long graying hair tripped and accidentally bumped into someone in the crowd in front of her.

"Hey!"

She lost her footing and began falling forward toward the wall, directly into the back of a goateed young man who was stooping over to pick up one of the signs propped there.

"What the—?"

The young man, apparently fearing he was under attack (the woman must have been with the opposition camp), swung his sign at the woman in a defensive reflex that had the same effect as tossing a piece of meat into a pit of hungry alligators.

The woman screamed. All brimstone broke loose. The man began beating her with the sign. Nicole, who was closest to the action, naturally rose to the poor woman's defense. I knew her Tae Kwan Do classes had been stimulating and educational for her, but I hadn't counted on seeing the results in live action in a courthouse.

Pretty soon, others had joined in the fray. Signs were swinging. Cries and shouts were ringing down the corridor. It was hard to tell which side was which. I felt obliged to join in, for no other reason than to help Nicole and protect the innocent old woman who'd been wrongly attacked.

I didn't see Dr. Lonigan, but I did spot Barry LaGrange out of the corner of my eye, notebook still in hand, attempting to shrink for cover behind a water fountain.

By the time the court deputies with the help of the two detectives had managed to end the altercation and the shouting died down, we'd all provided some outstanding footage for that night's telecast. Fortunately, no one was seriously injured. All declined to file charges. Not because they weren't hopping mad, but because they were fresh from the experience of witnessing the city's legal machinery in action, and no one was that crazy.

I could almost see the next day's headlines and the title for LaGrange's column being considered now:

PET PROTECTORS PUMMELED
ANIMAL INSTINCTS ERUPT
FUR FLIES OVER FELINES

Weep and take your pick.

Later, with Dr. Lonigan on the sidewalk outside, we sat on a bench licking our wounds.

"That had to be about the most idiotic thing I've ever been involved with in my life. Particularly with everything that's gone on."

"Just speculation," I said. "But how do you know one of those crazy people in there isn't behind this whole thing, for some reason?"

"Because many of those people I know personally. They would no more harm a cat than they would shoot Darla."

"Look," I said, "for better or worse, we've got a real situation here. We can't have distractions like what just happened in there and reporters running around sticking their noses into everything. I don't care if someone wants to use what you say happened to your cat to further their cause, as long as they don't try to get in my face about it. I'm not here to defend hunting or anything else. I'm here to do a job and that job is finding out what's going on with this guy, his bird in the park, and whoever's shooting people."

Amen to that.

Nicole screwed up her mouth. "Dr. Lonigan, I'm going to say

this and if you want to try to fire us over it, you go right ahead."

"Go ahead," Lonigan said.

"I don't exactly know how well you are connected to these animal rights people, but if you have any influence over them, you need to tell them to back off."

Lonigan narrowed her eyes. "What do you mean?"

"Just what my dad was trying to say a couple of days ago. These people might've read about this guy in the park with the owl or whatever and be trying to set up this scenario to claim there is illegal hunting so they can stir up trouble. Raise some money or whatever they're into."

"That's crazy. Why would anyone go to such great lengths to do that?"

"I don't know. All I'm saying is that you need to tell your animal friends to back off of our action."

Lonigan looked at us for a long moment. "All right," she finally said. "I'll make some calls."

"Thank you."

"What about Watisi?"

"He didn't show this morning, obviously," I said.

"Doesn't that tell you something?"

"Maybe, but if I had his kind of money, and could avoid dealing with the crowd we had in there this afternoon, I think I'd choose to hire the best lawyer I could find and put him or her between me and the circus, too. And now we find out he wasn't even required to show."

"Neither was I nor the rest of the apartment owners. But we wanted to look the judge in the face and let him know how strongly we felt about this situation."

"What, your faulty wiring or your missing pets?"

"Our missing pets, of course. And our faulty construction, too. And, well, the whole mess this situation has become."

"No housing judge in his right mind is going to touch this

case with a ten-foot pole. It looked like the judge was looking for an excuse to postpone. I had to take a phone call. Is that what went on in there?"

Lonigan's voice dropped an octave. "Pretty much. That's why I need you people or the police to come up with something more concrete that we can use against Watisi."

"All right," I said. "You're an oncologist, right?"

"Yes."

"Which means you're a specialist. You mostly get referrals from other doctors, clinics, whatever."

"Exactly."

"But let's say you're the family doctor out there. Sick kid walks into your exam room. What do you do? Start assuming right up front the kid's got cancer?"

"Of course I wouldn't."

"You'd have on open mind, right? You'd start ruling out possibilities."

"Okay, so you're doing the same thing as an investigator. Don't patronize me. I wasn't born yesterday."

"You're right," I said. "I'm sorry. All I'm trying to get you to see is that whoever shot Hicks and now Darla and whoever took your cat may not necessarily be the same people."

"Yes, but they could still all be working for Dominic Watisi."

"Have you heard anymore from the police?" I asked.

"No. Why?"

"I suspect another reason Watisi didn't show this morning is that it would have put him more on their radar screen."

"So you're still after him?"

"I'm after whoever looks guilty."

"Including your man who may be this falconer?"

"Including everyone."

"Good," she said. "With Darla incapacitated, you're all I've got left."

"Are we supposed to take that as a vote of confidence?" Nicole asked.

"Take it for what it's worth," Lonigan said.

We all sat in silence.

"Doesn't matter anyway," I said.

"What do you mean it doesn't matter?" Lonigan said. "I'm the one who hired Darla and she's the one who hired you."

I said nothing.

Nicole said, "What my dad's trying to tell you, Dr. Lonigan, is that he's going to find out who tried to kill Darla and me last night, whether you want to keep paying us or not."

"Why, because he's some kind of cowboy with an action-hero complex?"

Nicole glanced at me and smiled. "I've never heard it put quite that way before, but yeah."

21

I decided I needed to revisit the scene of the Meer shooting in daylight to see if anything struck me anew. I went alone. Nicole said she wanted to check online for more information about illegal immigrants in the city, Los Miembros, and any possible links she might find to Watisi.

Unbroken by last night's rain, the humidity was building once more. The sun was out, a hazy smudge overhead baking the ball fields and the North Meadow. People were out running and riding bikes, as usual, many of them dripping in sweat. Sailboats skimmed along the surface of the reservoir. The heat made the water look cool and inviting.

This time when I caught sight of him, the skinny kid in the baseball cap was jogging from 106th Street, straight out of Spanish Harlem into the park. His face was set in a grimace. It was a moment or two before I remembered him, the same kid I'd watched idly from the van a couple of days before. He wore the same blue jean shorts and yellow tee he'd been wearing three days before. What was he doing over here in the park?

"Yo, my friend, what's up?" I moved to intercept him on the grass and held out an arm to stop his progress. It was a spur of the moment decision, fueled as much by desperation as anything else.

He stopped, eyeing me with suspicion. "No friend of yours," he said, and tried to push around me.

I held out my arm, refusing to give ground. He was a rangy

kid, much stronger than he looked. It was hard to place his foreign-sounding accent, but one thing was sure; he hadn't picked it up around New York City.

"What you want?" His eyes grew small with suspicion.

"Just hang on a second. I'd like to ask you a couple of questions, if you don't mind."

As he looked me up and down again, the apparent irritation in his eyes took on a cast of fear.

"Don't worry. I'm not with immigration or the police."

"No government?"

"No government."

He seemed to relax a little. "What you want?" he asked again.

I began to appreciate just how thin he was. His arms were not only lean; they were tubes of skin and bone. And his forehead showed signs of temporal wasting. I found it hard to peg his age exactly.

"Just to talk," I said.

"Who are you?"

"My name's Frank Pavlicek. I'm from Virginia. I'm looking for some information. Hoping you can help me."

"You paying?"

Right down to business. You had to admire the brass on the kid.

"That depends," I said.

"You pervert?"

"No." I shook my head, noting his clipped English.

"Good. First you pay. Then we talk."

"All right." I reached into my jacket pocket and pulled a ten-dollar bill out of my wallet, hoping that would satisfy him.

It did. He motioned me toward a bench just inside the park across the street. The light was red down the block and traffic was stopped, so we jaywalked across to the bench.

"What you want?" he repeated the question as soon as we'd

both sat down. His face was a mask, the skin on his neck and cheeks pitted by scars.

"You live around here?" I asked.

"Yes."

"Whereabout?"

He thought it over for a moment. "Around. Up the Boulevard."

"You mean Martin Luther King Boulevard?"

"Yes."

"I saw you the other day over on Fred Douglas."

"I move around."

"You come into the park a lot?"

He shrugged. "Sometimes."

"How old are you?" I asked.

"Fifteen," he replied.

"You off school for the summer?"

His eyes darted around as if the question had come from another planet. "Yeah," he said, obviously lying.

He was probably an undocumented alien, maybe from somewhere in the Caribbean or possibly even Africa. From the wariness in his eyes, I guessed he was a recent arrival and probably holed up with his parents somewhere. They were working under the radar, maybe even housed by their employer, getting the lay of the land. They might attempt to enroll their son in school in the fall—they might not. I might have been missing some of the details, but I was pretty sure I had the outline right. I decided to skip asking about the parents for now. He might be more inclined to give me what I was after if I stuck to safer subjects.

"I'm looking for someone, someone in the park," I said.

"Yeah? Who?"

"A man who's been seen around here a few times after dark. Not much bigger than you actually."

"A white man like you?"

"No. I think he's dark-skinned."

"Lots of people around like that."

"Sure, but this one's different. He's probably carrying a bird."

The kid blinked. I'd struck some kind of a chord.

"What do you mean, a bird?"

"A bird. You know. Like the ones that fly in the sky. Like the ones in the park."

"And he's carrying it?" He was ducking and weaving now, but I could tell he knew something.

"Right."

He cupped his hand as if he were holding out an offering. "You mean a little bird."

"No. I'm talking about a big bird, like a hawk or an owl. You wear a special glove or hand piece to protect yourself from the talons and you carry the bird on the back of your fist."

His face took on a cloudy expression. "I don't know what you mean."

I decided to humor him. I had a picture in my wallet of me with my first hawk, Armistead, perched on my glove. I pulled it out and passed it over to him. "That's what I mean."

He stared at the picture. "This you?" he asked.

"Yes."

"With a hawk."

"Yes."

His eyes searched my face then went back to the picture.

"You ever seen an owl up close?" I asked.

He hesitated. "Sure. At the zoo."

"Have you ever seen anyone in the park, someone like yourself, carrying an owl, a big bird just like this?"

"Just walking around?" He shook his head. "No. Nothing like that."

"You sure?"

"I'm sure, man." He handed the picture back to me.

"What about the shooting in the park the other night that killed the two gangbangers?"

His eyes were a blank expanse. "What about it?"

"You see anything?"

"Nope."

"Hear anything?"

He slowly shook his head. "That all you wanted to ask me?"

"What about the two that were killed—Los Miembros, right?"

"That's what I heard."

"You hear any more about them?"

"Like what?"

"Like were they selling smack, were they murdered over drugs?"

"I don't think so," he said.

"You don't. Why not?"

"I don't know, man. I just heard they were into other stuff. Okay?"

"What's your name?"

He looked up and down the street, as if scanning the pavement for approaching trouble. "No name, man. Not unless you willing to pay more."

This fifteen-year-old understood inflation. Reluctantly I peeled another ten from my wallet and forked it over. He tucked it into his pocket with the first one.

"Okay, so what is it?" I asked.

"My name's Sammy."

"Sammy. You got a last name?"

"Sammy Yel Bak." He spelled it out for me.

I took out a pen and wrote it down. I also wrote my name and cell phone number on the back of the photo and gave it to him. "Well, Sammy, here you go," I said. "You remember anything, you call me. All right?"

"What you looking for?"

"I just want to talk with anyone who knows about a man with an owl or about the shooting," I said.

"Okay." He started to get up from the bench.

"I'm just trying to find out what's going on, Sammy. Remember, I'm not with the police or anything."

"Okay."

"You have any brothers or sisters, Sammy?" I figured siblings might be a safer topic than parents.

His gaze shifted away from me toward the park. "No, sir. Not anymore. I got to go."

"Sure."

He pushed my photo into his shorts pocket and stood up.

"One more question. How come both times when I've seen you, you've been running?" I asked.

He shrugged. "Got places to be," he said and slipped away down a brick walkway between two rows of bushes.

I spent a few more hours poking around the north end of the park, looking for any footprints, droppings, bits of feather or bones, or any signs our mysterious falconer might have left of his activity. I found nothing.

The drawn-out face of Sammy Yel Bak seemed to haunt my every thought, gnawing at me like a bad dream that wouldn't go away. I'd seen that kind of face before in pictures. It was a face that carried the look of real war.

Maybe we were looking for a ghost after all.

22

The security control room at Grayland Tower was located in the basement directly below the reception desk in the main lobby. The bank of video monitors watched by the guards was connected to a computer server and a small network running software that processed images from the building's fifty or more security cameras and monitored the structure's environmental controls, burglar alarm systems, broadband computer hubs, and other vital functions. The security cameras worked on a relay system, monitoring different sections of the building's twenty-seven stories at specific intervals.

It all amounted to a modestly elaborate, state-of-the-art data processing setup that was beyond my ability to figure out.

Fortunately, I'd brought Nicole.

"Tell me again what we're doing down here, Dad," she said.

"Hunting squirrels."

"Squirrels." She didn't look impressed.

"Yeah, you know. What happens when you're hunting squirrels and you walk into the woods with your red-tailed hawk following on?"

She recited what I'd taught her. "The squirrels freeze on tree trunks opposite you and try to make themselves invisible."

"Right. And I'm betting we might just find some squirrels inside this security video setup. Or if not, somewhere in this basement."

"You mean a tunnel like that reporter was talking about."

"Right."

"Can we be prosecuted for breaking in down here?"

"Probably. But we're still guests upstairs, at least until Dr. Lonigan decides to officially fire us."

"I'm betting if we do find a tunnel or something, we may just find more stuff Watisi is into."

She sat down in front of what appeared to be the main computer terminal. "What makes you think I'm going to be able to just magically figure out the passwords I need to access this complex digital system?"

"How about 'cause you're my daughter and just about the most intelligent young investigator and computer whiz on the planet?"

"I can run with that."

While Nicole went to work at one of the computer keyboards, I took the opportunity to scout out the sublevels of Grayland Tower. I say sublevels because there seemed to be more than one. An interconnecting labyrinth of passageways led down at least four stories, as far as I could tell. The tunnels served as conduits for all sorts of utility pipes and wires. Only one camera guarded this entire area. It was mounted on the main stairwell. I didn't even have to be a gymnast to fold my body over the railing and clamber down to the next level without entering its field of view.

The entire foundation of the building looked as though it had been overhauled during renovation and reconstruction. The exception was the northeast corner that interfaced with what looked like a section of steam grates and a narrow utility tunnel running under the street, the entrance to which was covered by a rusty grate surrounded by a layer of burnt orange clay. It was also protected by wired and monitored security fencing so a potential intruder couldn't pop a manhole cover and make his way into the building.

Intrigued, I was looking over all this construction when I heard Nicole's footsteps and whispered voice from the stairwell above.

"Dad. Dad, you down there?"

"Yeah," I said softly.

"I may have found something."

"Did you avoid the camera coming down the stairs?"

"Yeah, I saw it."

"Coming right up."

Back at the computer, I listened as Nicole patiently explained what it was she'd uncovered.

"It isn't much yet," she said. "But someone's put a back door in this network's basic operating system and possibly altered some video files."

"Which means?"

"I don't know what it means, exactly. But it's not the kind of thing anyone would do for routine network security or maintenance."

"Can you get into the affected files themselves?"

"Probably not. Even if I could, it might take me a few days or more to unravel all the pieces."

"Okay."

"Does this qualify as a squirrel?"

"Maybe."

"What do you want to do?" she asked.

"I'm thinking . . . Who would have access to this room and this equipment?"

"Security, of course. Possibly a maintenance person or janitor or someone else who worked in data processing for Watisi."

"What if one of those people let somebody else in?"

"It could happen, I suppose. But who would want to do that and why?"

"There's no way to trace the source of the tampering any sooner?"

"Not that I know of. But if you want to bring Jake into the process, he might have some ideas on how to speed up the process."

I thought it over. "Okay," I said. "Let's close up shop for now and leave this system the way we found it."

"No problemo."

"Can you cover your tracks?"

She flexed her fingers and tapped at the keys.

"Unless someone randomly decides to start dusting this keyboard for fingerprints or DNA, they'll never know I was here."

23

Nicole and I were seated in Lt. Marbush's office again at the precinct house in Central Park. Detectives Hickey and Martinez were also there, along with Marbush and another detective. The lieutenant wasn't in the mood for mincing words.

"You're trying to tell me our investigation into the Hicks slayings and Darla's wounding is definitely related to your client's fight with her landlord and some stupid cat?"

"You saw the lure at the murder scene the other night," I said.

"I saw a bloody stuffed animal."

"With a hunk of meat attached, don't forget."

"Don't remind me."

"There's something much larger happening here."

"Yeah, like the fact that your client, Dr. Lonigan, has had a long-standing grudge going against Dominic Watisi."

"What?"

"She didn't tell you people about that, did she? Lonigan and Watisi were on the same board of directors of a now defunct community development organization a few years ago. From all reports, they didn't get along then, either."

"Then why would Lonigan buy an expensive apartment from the man?"

"This is Manhattan," the lieutenant said. "It's prime real estate and Lonigan needed a place to live not too far from her work. My guess is the realtors handled the whole transaction.

Either that or Dr. Lonigan figured it was time to bury the hatchet."

"Why hasn't there been anything about this in the newspaper?" I'd read what I thought were all the articles by now, and Barry LaGrange sure hadn't mentioned or even hinted at such a prospect.

"My guess? Lonigan knows someone at the newspaper, and she didn't want her past relationship with Watisi revealed."

"But why wouldn't Watisi scream bloody murder in his own defense?"

She shrugged. "You'll have to ask him."

"What, exactly, did this community development organization do?"

"Helped find housing and provide other assistance for the underprivileged."

"Such as refugees and other newly arrived immigrants?"

"I know what you're thinking, Frank, but you can forget it. Watisi has already been thoroughly scrutinized by immigration authorities."

"I'm supposed to feel comforted by that."

"You're supposed to leave it alone. That's all."

"But there is definitely someone in the park with a bird."

She shrugged. "So call the State Department of Environmental Conservation or US Fish and Wildlife."

"What about the other shooter from the woods when Darla was hit, the one with the higher caliber weapon?" Nicole asked.

"We've already brought a guy in for questioning. Twenty-year-old Latino—some gun nut with ties to a rival gang who must've decided to shoot it out with Los Miembros. He's a strong candidate for the murders as well."

I looked out the window of Marbush's office. There was a maple tree behind the building, its dark green leaves sun speckled and waving in a puff of wind.

"So is Los Miembros trading in live warm bodies or what? We talked to someone who said one of the dead men was heavily into this."

"They're behind at least a couple of significant prostitution rings, we know that. A lot of their girls barely even speak English. They don't need to, for what they do." Her gaze was steady.

"That have anything to do with the motive behind the shootings?"

"Possibly. Or a hundred other things. Like I told you, this shooter we've got in custody was from the competition."

"So you think we're totally out in left field going after Watisi with our hired falconer theory?" I said.

"Wouldn't you?"

"You got anything else from ballistics to tie this guy to the shootings?"

"Not yet. Bullets were 7.62 x 39 mm assault rifle, Hollow Point, probably Russian."

"Nasty stuff."

"We've already executed a warrant and are trying to match the fragments to a rifle we pulled from the guy's apartment. It doesn't look like a match, but the gun he used the other night could be at the bottom of the East River somewhere," Marbush said.

"Without the gun or eyewitnesses, though, your case is still pretty circumstantial."

"Maybe. Look, forget about it, Frank," Marbush said. "You stick to your wildlife stuff. You want to go tracking down your birdman, have at it. If you make some connections and anything comes of it, give us a shout. I'll let you know if something more definite comes up from our end—and don't forget about what I told you last night. I heard about that little spectacle in housing court earlier." She stared at me.

“Darla’s convinced there is a link between the missing pets, what happened at the airport, and what’s going on in the park. She’s been living with this thing the longest,” Nicole said.

“Fair enough,” Marbush said. “But it looks like she also missed the Lonigan–Watisi connection from a few years back. I’m not saying either of you are bad detectives, Ms. Pavlicek. Just that you’re probably wrong.”

The lieutenant had a point. I didn’t think Darla had underestimated the urgency of the threats she’d received. Neither had I. But Darla was now hobbled and we were left with what was beginning to look like a crumbling case.

“All right,” I said.

“Look,” she said, “no matter what else happens, you’ve got me curious about the falconer guy. At roll call this morning and afternoon I’m instructing the officers on patrol in and around the park to keep an eye out for this idiot.”

“How about giving them my cell phone number, too,” I suggested. “If it’s after dark, it might be hard for them to tell what it is they’re looking at.”

“Okay,” she said. “And it should go without saying as far as you and your daughter are concerned, whatever you come up with, I’d like to be kept informed.”

“Got it.”

But I didn’t get it. Not really. As we left the precinct, the snickers and grins were gone. Warren Fitzhugh nodded gravely at me from his sergeant’s desk. I was beginning to feel the eyes of the hunter, the strange and paradoxical realization that as pursuers we might soon find ourselves being pursued; that I did not understand enough of the motivations of those involved to be able to properly respond to what would happen next.

24

"Why didn't you tell us you and Watisi had a history?" I asked our client.

Dr. Lonigan was at her easel, painting. She'd been working on a landscape she said, since coming home from work an hour earlier. She'd been so upset by the incident in housing court that morning, she said, that she'd left work early, right after seeing her patients.

"I didn't think it was relevant," she said.

"Not relevant? When you're out there making claims against the man quoted in the newspaper?"

"He's hiding something. He's always been hiding something."

"I may grant you that, but you're not exactly helping us do our jobs here."

"Sorry."

"You're sorry."

"Yes."

"What are you hiding, Dr. Lonigan?"

She pushed her brush in a wide stroke across the canvas. "Nothing. Just trying to help someone. Just trying to get to the bottom of all this. Same as you."

"Help someone?" This was a revelation. "Who might that be?"

Her eyes remained on her canvas. "Can't say."

"Lovely."

"I still would like you to keep working for me on this."

"You bet I will keep working on it," I said.

She turned to face me. "But not necessarily for me."

I said nothing.

She went back to her canvas. "Feel free to stay in the apartment and continue to use my car, if you'd like," she said.

Darla called me from her hospital bed.

"How come you guys haven't been by to bring me flowers?"

" 'Cause we're too busy out here trying to solve your case," I said. Actually, we'd been by twice but she'd been zonked both times and the docs didn't think she was ready to talk.

She chuckled under her breath. "You go, Franco." Her voice was still slightly slurred from whatever pain meds they'd given her.

I brought her up to speed on the information we'd gleaned in her absence and the NYPD's suspect when it came to the murders and her shooting. When I got to the part about the sign-swinging protestors at the courthouse, I could almost hear her shaking her head through the phone.

"You guys don't have to keep on with this, you know," she said.

"Are you kidding?" I said. "Someone's either got it all wrong or I'm missing a huge piece of the puzzle. And you lying in the hospital. I'm not about to walk from that."

"Didn't figure you would," she said.

I said nothing.

"I'm going to get some sleep now. You be careful out there, Frank. Take care of that daughter of yours. She's a diamond," she said. "You tell her I said so."

"She is that," I said. "And I will."

Darkness was still an hour away as Nicole drove us around the outside of Dominic Watisi's Westchester estate. We'd turned our backs on Lonigan's Porsche in favor of a nondescript Ford rental. Rush-hour traffic on the Major Deegan had delayed our arrival by at least an hour. I could only hope it would do the same for Watisi, who no doubt would be working late at his office in Harlem.

Before we ventured into Central Park again after our mystery falconer, I wanted to get a closer look at Watisi's castle. I had no idea what we were looking for, other than the fact that Watisi seemed so intent on protecting it. Maybe I was paranoid. Then again, maybe I wasn't paranoid enough.

The cameras dotting the spiked top of the estate's brick wall seemed to form an impregnable barrier. They were spread every thirty yards or so. We were probably on someone's video screen or tape right this moment. At the same time, I noticed something odd about several of the cameras.

"Stop the car right here," I said.

"What?" Nicole let her foot off the gas to slow down.

"Right here. Stop the car."

"But they'll have us on tape. Or they could be watching us right now."

"Maybe not."

She did as I said and braked us to a stop at the side of the road.

"Did you bring the stepladder I asked you to get?"

"In the trunk."

"Great," I said. "Here goes nothing."

I climbed out, she popped the trunk, and I pulled out the ladder.

"I hope you know what you're doing, Dad," she said.

"Me, too."

I stepped across the grass to the wall and leaned the ladder up against it. I climbed up and found myself nearly face to face with one of the cameras. It looked intimidating. I reached across, grabbed it by the lens, and began to pull on it.

"Are you nuts?" Nicole asked. "If whoever's in there wasn't watching us, they're definitely going to be now."

The camera swiveled on its base. It felt light as a feather. I twisted the lens—hard. It broke off in my hand.

I peered inside the casing. Nothing there.

"They're fakes," I said.

Nicole climbed out of the car and came over to the ladder.

"The cameras aren't real?"

"Nope. Not all of them anyway. Strictly used as deterrence. Sometimes, in order to save money, building owners will mix some fake cameras in with the real ones. I've been checking out these along the top of the wall. Some are real, but most aren't. My guess is whatever contractor Watisi used to put these cameras in messed up because we're smack dab in the middle of a row of fake ones."

"So there's a blind spot. We can walk right in."

"Hopefully."

"What about the ones back at Grayland Tower?"

"Oh, most of those were real enough, I think. But we're not exactly sitting in the middle of a high-crime area up here."

"What about further on inside?"

"Oh, I'm sure Watisi will have more real surveillance further on inside, including the human type."

"At least we can get in."

"It's a start," I said.

The road we were on looked empty enough. It curved downhill in front of us, but we hadn't passed a single other vehicle as we'd driven along it. Beautiful shade trees, maple and oak, blocked most of the sun here, making it less likely we'd be spotted once we scaled the wall. Only one way to find out for sure.

Nicole opened the trunk of the car and brought out her

backpack filled with camera equipment, in case we needed to document what was saw. The fact that we were going in armed meant that we were committing more than one felony. God help us if we were caught.

I went over the wall first, dropping into a nice thick stand of rhododendron, perfect for concealment. I waited for a minute or two. Nothing happened. So far so good. I whispered up to Nicole, who pulled up the ladder from the other side and leaned it down beside me on the inside of the wall, then climbed down next to me.

We waited some more. From where we stood, we could just make out the rooftops of what looked like the main residence or compound above the trees about a quarter mile downhill and to our right. My curiosity was immediately piqued, however, by a different set of structures, much closer to our location. Low-slung, barracks-type structures made of wood and corrugated metal, like large mobile homes or temporary housing.

"What do you make of those?" I said, pointing to them in the distance.

"Building project?" Nicole said.

"Doesn't look it. I don't see any construction equipment or the framework of any larger structure."

Nicole pulled her favorite camera from the bag, zoomed in with one of her telephoto lenses, and began snapping pictures. I grabbed a set of field glasses and scanned the area.

What looked like the shadow of a child's head moved inside the windows of one of the structures. A screen door opened and a brown-skinned woman pushed out through it, bearing a basket full of laundry. There was a clothesline to one side with sheets and pants and shirts hanging from it.

"People are living there," Nicole said.

"I see it."

"Hired help to run the estate?"

"Maybe, but you could house a pretty big workforce in all those buildings."

As I swept around the scene, more and more people became visible. A group of children playing on a swing set. Old men of indeterminate ethnic origin seated in the shadows, some of them smoking cigarettes or pipes.

"Looks like some kind of refugee camp, doesn't it?"

"Yeah, it does, doesn't it. Let's see if we can get a closer look."

We started to move along the base of the wall, using the rhododendron as cover. We hadn't made it very far, however, when trouble hit. The roar of an all-terrain vehicle seemed to rise up out of nowhere and a second or two later the four-wheeler itself popped over a rise between us and the main residence. There was a solo rider atop it, brandishing an automatic weapon. He hadn't spotted us yet—probably just patrolling—but he was about to. There was no avoiding that.

Worse, I recognized him as he drew closer. It was none other than my old buddy, the nameless stiff who'd been working as a bodyguard and driver down at Watisi's office in the city.

We had the jump on him. Only one thing to do.

"Let's try not to put ourselves in this type of jam in the future," I said to Nicole as I drew out my Glock and stood, pointing it directly at the approaching vehicle. Nicole followed suit.

No sooner had the driver caught sight of us emerging from the bushes than he slammed on his brakes about twenty feet in front of us and tried to reach for a walkie-talkie also strapped around his neck. But a quick gesture with my handgun made him think twice. He slowly raised his hands as the cloud of dust that had been trailing him drifted in front of him.

"You people are making a huge mistake," he said.

"Remains to be seen," I said.

He looked us over with the same appraising eyes he'd shown back at the office, but his cockiness seemed to evaporate in the face of a pair of gun barrels.

"Why don't you dismount that little pony of yours, take off that howitzer you're wearing, and set it down gently in the grass there beside you."

We waited while he did as I said. Then he started to reach for the key to turn off the engine.

"Ah, ah." I motioned with the gun again. "Leave it running."

He shrugged and stood to one side of the ATV with his hands still in the air.

"What are you people running here?" I raised my head in the direction of the distant barracks housing. "Some kind of illegal labor camp?"

"None of my business what the boss does with his money. He helps out a lot of people."

"I'm sure he does."

I thought about the situation. Nicole had taken enough pictures to provide plenty of documentary evidence of something suspicious, and who knew how many other yahoos like this Watisi had running around the place.

"I'll tell you what we're going to do, my good fellow," I said. "Not that you're going to be too happy about it."

Ten minutes later, we were safely back out on the highway, headed south toward the city, all our gear and camera equipment stowed in the trunk. I didn't know how long our young friend would remain gagged and tied securely to the bumper of his running vehicle, his ammunition gone and the batteries missing from his walkie-talkie. At least until someone missed him, that was for sure. Not to mention that we'd also relieved him of his fashionable dark trousers and purple jockey briefs, which Nicole had whistled at, and both of which we'd tossed in a Dumpster half a mile down the road from where we'd left him. I wasn't too worried about Watisi calling in the Westchester County or town cops to report a break-in at the estate, either. Not unless he wanted a lot more snooping investigators around besides us.

"That was awesome," Nicole said behind the wheel.

"It was stupid," I said. "We were lucky."

"You think Watisi is covering up some kind of huge international smuggling ring?"

"I think we've got some decent pictures of some activity that is bound to raise a lot of eyebrows," I said.

Nicole grinned. "Maybe it was stupid, but it was worth it," she said. "Just to see the look on that dork-head's face."

25

My cell phone bleeping in the darkness startled me into a heightened state of awareness. I'd fallen half asleep, camped in a cluster of trees near the Great Hill on the north end of the park, hoping for a miracle—that our falconer friend would show up again. My watch read one A.M.

Down the hill, out on the pond, it was nearly pitch black. Resting ducks and geese were visible in the dim glow cast by a distant street lamp. They might make tempting targets for an owl on the hunt. Not to mention a ready supply of field rats and other smaller night mammals moving through the grass and woods.

"Pavlicek," I said into the phone. My voice sounded hoarse, even to me.

"This the PI looking for the dude with the owl?"

"You got 'em."

"Joe Brodsky, Midtown North. Me and my partner think we spotted your guy, running into the woods down here by the Shakespeare Garden."

"Across from the history museum, isn't it?"

"Right. Think we've got him cornered, too. We chased him across the Seventy-Ninth Street Transverse and in behind Belvedere Castle. Already have two other units on the scene. Unless he's going to take a swim in the lake, he's not going to get by us. The lieutenant says to give you a call, maybe you can help talk to the guy."

"I'll be there as fast I can."

I scrambled to my feet and speed-dialed Nicole, who was cruising around the park in the rental car.

"Nicky, where are you?"

"On Fifth Avenue at Ninety-Sixth," she said, her voice sounding distant and hollow through the hands-free mike.

I was already running downhill toward the bridge and the North Meadow.

"Take the next street to the left, go around and head back uptown. Meet me at Fifth and a 104th in front of the Conservatory Garden. The police have our guy pinned by the castle on Seventy-Ninth."

"I'll be there," she said.

I clicked on my flashlight and sprinted through the dark.

Four or five minutes later, Nicole was pulling to a stop in front of me on the avenue.

"Go! Go!" I said, jumping in.

She hit the gas and we careened down the street.

Even running a couple of red lights, it took us another three or four minutes to reach the Transverse Road and cross the park to the castle. Four NYPD cruisers were now on the scene, their beacons strobing the night like a laser light show.

Brodsky met us at the curb. At least I figured it must be Brodsky from the way he was standing beside his cruiser as if he were waiting for someone.

"You Pavlicek?" he asked as we hurried out.

"That's me. This is my daughter, Nicole, who works with me."

Brodsky looked at Nicole with some interest. Sharp-looking guy with red hair, thick eyebrows. Apparently single. "Yeah, well, ah . . . Lt. Marbush is still en route. Like I said, we've got him cornered back in there."

He pointed to the side of the castle across from the amphitheater where a large construction crane towered over the landscape. Half the site was ringed by chain-link fence topped with concertina wire.

"Okay if we go in after him?" I had to be careful here. Didn't want to compromise the cooperation and access we were being given.

The patrolman rubbed the back of his neck. "I guess so. The lieutenant's coming in from New Jersey and she has to make it through the tunnel. But me and my partner are going with you."

"Sure."

His partner, a wiry-looking Italian named Halacini, moved in beside us carrying an oversized flashlight.

"This dude armed?" Brodsky asked. "I mean, besides the bird."

"He shouldn't be, but there's no telling for certain."

"Okay." He turned and spoke into his walkie-talkie.

"This is Brodsky. Hal and I are going in with the two PIs. Mag, you're in charge here. Watch our backs and let's not lose this idiot."

The air rang with mike clicks and static-filled replies.

"Watch for a big bird in the trees," I said. "Tell them, too. An owl, not making any noise."

"Yeah, okay." He pushed the button on his handpiece again. "And the PI says watch out for a big bird overhead, in a tree or something. Silent. Won't be making no noise."

Another officer, not realizing he was being overheard, said, "How the hell we supposed to do that?"

"What about night vision goggles?" Nicole asked, pulling a pair out of the backpack she was carrying.

"You got 'em, use 'em," Brodsky said. "We'll put you in the middle."

Nicole moved to my left with the officers flanking us. She

slipped the heavy glasses over her head. We formed a line, about five yards apart, and entered the construction site.

Sweat trickled down the back of my neck. The sky above was clear. A front had moved through a few hours before and the temperature had dropped. No wind. If this guy and his owl were hiding in here, we were in a perfect position to flush them from cover.

Our lights swept back and forth around Nicole. She took her time, moving her head slowly from side to side, like a boxer measuring her opponent.

We circled around the construction crane toward a hillside full of trees where the ground had been chewed up by machinery. A distant siren sounded—a fire engine on the way to some other calamity perhaps—and the rumble of an early-morning garbage truck mixed with the other noises of the city. But here in our section of the park, all was quiet save the crickets.

Nicole came to a halt. Her gaze fixed on a spot just ahead in the trees.

"I've got something," she said calmly.

"Where?" Brodsky's voice, sounding excited, came from a few feet beyond her, the arc of his light beginning to swing in her direction.

"It's okay," she said. "It's okay, don't worry. They're coming to us."

"What do you mean?"

"I mean they're walking right toward us. Not running. They see us, they're coming out, and it looks like they're just going to surrender."

"The guy with the bird?" I asked. "Is he carrying the owl?"

"Not exactly." Nicole kept her goggles focused on the middle distance.

"What do you mean?"

"Not he," she said. "She."

26

I trained my beam into the darkness of the hill, as did the two cops. Stepping calmly into the brightness came a small individual dressed in dark green pants and a blue hooded jacket.

There was indeed an owl on her fist, a sizeable Great Horned. Her homemade cuff looked to be styled after a mangalah, as we'd seen on Nicole's impromptu video. And there was no doubt she was a young woman, a girl actually.

She was dark skinned with deep brown eyes, and her hair hung down over her shoulders. She couldn't have been more than twelve or thirteen years old.

"I'll be damned," said Officer Halacini.

Nicole tore off her goggles and stared, openmouthed like the rest of us, at the wisp of a girl. As she approached, the hollowness of her cheeks made it clear she was malnourished. She appeared outwardly composed, but her eyes betrayed her fear.

"It's all right," Nicole called out. "We won't hurt you. We're here to help."

The girl said nothing. She kept moving. Her big bird attempted to bate momentarily, stretching its wings and lifting a giant talon, pulling against the jesses she held firmly between her fingers.

"Whoa," Brodsky said, his hand instinctively dropping to his sidearm, before the owl settled back to rest comfortably on her fist.

"It's all right," I said softly. "She's got hold of the bird by those straps on its ankles. The owl's not going anywhere unless she decides to let it."

"Yeah? Well, what's to stop her from flying that thing right at our heads?"

"Somehow, I don't think that's what this bird is trained for. And I don't think it's her intention, either. If it makes you feel any better, you're a lot bigger than an owl and you can use your baton."

Brodsky's hand dropped to his nightstick and remained there, but he didn't withdraw the stick.

"This is creepy," Halacini whispered. "Look at the eyes on that thing."

At night the eyes of Great Horned Owls are like vacuum lanterns gathering in the miniscule available light from the darkness. In our beams, the owl's eyes were mesmerizing. The bird looked directly at us, and almost seemed capable of hypnotizing its prey.

"You have a bird like this, too?" Brodsky asked.

"Not exactly," I said. "But I've flown hawks about as big. And I've been around some owls. Judging by the size, I'd guess this one's a female."

"Is that good or bad?"

"Depends. She's bigger and more powerful than a male. But not as quick."

"I'll keep that in mind."

"Would you guys mind shutting up before you scare her?" Nicole said.

The girl was still moving toward us.

"It's all right," Nicole urged, her voice soothing, coaxing. "We just want to help."

Owl and girl stopped about ten feet in front of us.

"Can you tell us what you're doing with the bird?"

She stared at Nicole and the rest of us, uncomprehending.

“Do you understand English?” Nicole asked.

The girl stared straight ahead.

“Great,” Brodsky said under his breath.

I tried my rudimentary Spanish with no luck. Nicole tried French. No go. Then the girl began speaking in a language I didn’t recognize.

“Any of you have any clue what she’s saying?” Brodsky asked.

“No,” I said. “But it sounds like Arabic.”

“Wonderful. Remind me to brush up on my Arabic when I get back to the precinct,” Brodsky said.

“What do we do now?” Nicole asked.

“Good question,” I said.

“She can’t hunt in the park, or whatever it is she’s doing, I know that much at least,” Brodsky said.

“Technically, at her age, she’s not even legally supposed to be handling a bird of prey,” I said. “But right now I think that’s the least of our worries. I think this girl was a witness to the murders in the park the other night.”

“No kidding.”

I was checking out this mysterious young falconer’s rigging, trying to figure out how I might convince her to transfer her owl to my hand on the falconer’s glove I had stowed in my backpack, or how I might be able to jury-rig a makeshift perch out of a good-sized tree branch. I also noticed there was no safety leash attached to the bird’s jesses and tied off to the girl’s glove, which meant she was intending to let the bird fly free or could do so at any moment.

I handed my flashlight to Nicole, knelt down and pulled the glove and a cord leash from the pack. I put on the glove and showed the leash to the girl.

She nodded and I nodded back. She adroitly plucked a leash made of braided leather from inside her jacket and began tying up the jesses and her glove with practiced skill.

"What's she doing?" Brodsky asked.

"Securing her bird. We don't want any accidents."

"I'm all for that."

I tried to signal that I wanted her to tie off her bird temporarily someplace for safekeeping. But it wasn't working.

"Let's see if we can get her to come back with us to the cars," Brodsky said.

"The owl, too," I said. "She doesn't look like she's ready to release it and we can't leave it out here tied to a perch."

"The bird might be freaked out by all the activity and the police cruisers," Nicole pointed out.

"You're right. Why don't you give the keys to the rental car to Officer Halacini here. He can pull the car down the drive out of sight of the patrol cars. We'll probably have better luck getting her to drive to the precinct with us. And we're better equipped to deal with anything that might come up with the bird."

"Roger that," Brodsky said. He turned to speak into his mike. "Brodsky again, here. We have our subject and are attempting to secure custody of the, uh, animal. Stand by."

"Standing by," came the replies.

The girl took a step back, her eyes growing alarmed at the static and the radio chatter.

"It's okay," Nicole said again. "Don't worry. Everything's going to be all right. We're your friends."

The girl looked at us warily.

"Friends," Nicole repeated.

Halacini, seemingly only too happy to get away from the big owl, took the keys to the rental car from Nicole and disappeared in the direction of the Transverse.

The girl said something in Arabic again. I was wishing Toronto were here.

"Well, I guess I've seen everything now," Brodsky said.

"Why don't we see if she'll walk with us," I said.

"What if she tries to bolt again?"

"With the bird tethered to her glove, I don't think she's about to. But if she does, you can go for the girl while I manage the owl."

"Right," he said without enthusiasm.

"Why don't you call the lieutenant and see what we can do about getting an Arabic-speaking translator."

He nodded and pulled out a cell phone. Punched in a number and began speaking softly with Marbush about the situation.

Meanwhile Nicole, with a combination of hand signals and soothing language, was attempting to communicate with the girl about coming along with us. The girl still seemed frightened. Maybe a little less so, but I was worried we might have trouble coaxing her to do as we asked.

We could always move to secure her by force. Cuff her and take control of the bird. But all of us sensed that would not be the right thing to do in this situation. It would only serve to alienate a potential cooperating witness who might help us unravel all that happened in the past few days.

I looked at the girl's free hand, ebony skin poking out from the sleeve of her sweatshirt. Where had she acquired the skills to handle a bird of prey in such a manner? What was she doing with the bird here and why now? Hunting?

I noticed a small falconer's bag slung around her shoulder and hanging from her waist. It was meant to contain bait food for the owl and was large enough to hold a bagged quarry. If she wasn't hunting, she sure was doing a good job pretending to be a hunter. She turned and looked at me examining her while Nicole went on talking.

The young falconer's expression told me she'd seen many kills before, that she knew how to handle herself, how to skin and take the meat from caught game.

"Come on. It'll be okay. Let's go," Nicole said.

I motioned for the girl to follow. She did as we asked.

At least she seemed compliant enough. We began walking slowly out of the construction area. Whatever happened now, I thought, at least we could solve the mystery of the falconer in the park. I had the feeling it was bound to be a strange and complicated story.

This young girl didn't seem like she could be responsible for threatening Darla or for the shootings. Had Watisi hired someone else? Cato Raines? My thoughts veered back and forth between the girl in the park and all the people we had talked to so far.

Halacini had pulled the rental car around the curve out of sight of the patrol vehicles. We spotted it as we emerged from the trees and began moving in that direction. The girl walked calmly along. Her bird, apparently accustomed to being around other people, perched on her glove just as calmly.

We had almost reached the car when I saw the flash of yellow from behind some bushes, the familiar red ball cap, the world-weary eyes.

Like everyone else, though, I was too slow to react. Sammy Yel Bak surfaced from his hiding spot, the Kalashnikov rifle he was pointing at us as steady in his youthful hands as if he'd fired and killed with it many times before.

The world seemed to stop for a moment. No one moved except Halacini, who leapt out of the car, his hand moving toward his sidearm. But when he saw the barrel of the AK-47 swing in his direction, he stopped and put his hands in the air.

"Everybody else, do that, too," Sammy said.

We all complied. I glanced at Nicole, whose eyes had grown huge. My first thought was terrorist, even though the kid seemed so young. My second thought, watching him react to the girl with the owl, was that a lot more was going on here than met the eye.

"Who the hell are you?" Brodsky asked the gunman.

"I've seen him on the street around here a couple of times. I talked to him yesterday. Gave him a photo and told him we were looking for the person with the owl."

"Now shut up," the young man said. "Everybody just shut up."

He motioned with the barrel of his gun to the girl with the owl. Obviously familiar with her rescuer, she moved out from between us and stepped with the bird to his side.

"That's a pretty dangerous toy you've got there, my friend. You sure you know how to fire it?" Brodsky was asking. He might've been bluffing, but I sensed he was genuinely testing the waters with this guy. Not a bad idea under the circumstances.

But Sammy was more than up for the challenge. The young man pulled one hand off the assault rifle keeping the other on the trigger and the barrel trained on us. His free hand was almost a blur as he whipped it behind his back, pulled a spare ammunition clip from his belt, reached back around to pop the clip out of the rifle and slam the fresh one into its place before any of us had a chance to do anything about it. Then he twirled the first ammunition clip in his fingers and neatly replaced it in his belt.

"Jesus," Brodsky said under his breath.

"I guess that answers that question," I said. "Where'd you learn how to do that, Sammy?"

"Not to worry, man," the boy said. "Not to worry."

I looked at him differently now than when I'd been talking to him on the street. The leanness in his frame, the tough sinewy muscles in his arms and legs. Sammy Yel Bak was more than just some other tough hanging around the neighborhood. He'd killed and seen his share of killing. Probably in some scorching desert city or steaming guerilla insurgency somewhere.

Without a family or someone else to fall back on, it would only be a matter of time until the gangbangers or the pimps or someone worse managed to recruit him for his talents, if they hadn't already.

Or maybe not. Some fierce anger burned behind his eyes, leading me to see beyond the hatred toward the hint of something noble.

"Look," I said. "We mean you or the girl no harm."

He held up us hand. "No talking." His eyes darted back and forth, settling on Nicole. "You." He motioned with the barrel of the gun. "You come, too."

"Wait a minute," I said, trying to keep the panic that was threatening to rise from within me in check. "This is getting out of hand. These are police officers you're threatening. You don't want to get in any deeper than you are already."

But the young gunman was undeterred. "You, you come," he repeated, looking at Nicole and threatening her with the rifle.

"I better go, Dad. We better do what he says." Nicole's voice was measured, resolute. I looked at my daughter.

"No way. No way," I said. It was one of the times in life your brain takes a backseat to instinct. I stepped between the barrel and Nicole. Sammy Yel Bak leapt quickly to intercept me.

This is it, I thought. *This is how it ends for me.*

But he jabbed me hard in the ribs with the thing without pulling the trigger. I might've tried to jujitsu the gun from his grasp, but he was too fast and too smart for that. The officers started to move, too, but his barrel was back on them in a heartbeat. Pain shot through my torso, bending me over, and for a moment I thought he might've put a round in me after all; until I realized there'd been no sound.

"Kid, you don't even begin to know all the trouble you're setting yourself up for," Brodsky said, his hands back in the air.

For a moment, I felt like a cop again. Sammy Yel Bak stepped back at the sound of the uniformed officer's voice. Was he calculating the impact of Brodsky's words? Or something else?

"It's okay, Dad." Nicole's voice came from behind me now. "I'll go with them. It'll be all right. I can take care of myself."

"That's not the point," I said. I straightened again and lifted my eyes to Sammy Yel Bak's. "No. Let me do it. Take me instead."

But Yel Bak was adamant. He shook his head and pointed toward Nicole. "Come. You, come."

She did as he instructed, letting her lips touch my cheek as she brushed by me. "I'm okay, Daddy," she whispered. "I'm going to be okay."

And then all three of them were in the rental car, moving rapidly away while we watched. Helpless. Brodsky was shouting something into his walkie-talkie. Nicole was at the wheel, only the back of her dark hair visible. The other two sat in back; Yel Bak, with the barrel of the Kalashnikov pointed at my daughter's ear; the eerie foreign-speaking girl sitting next to him, her owl propped at her side, its head turning almost completely around to look at us, its glowing eyes like amber circles playing tricks with the light.

27

Everyone was talking at once. No one, as far as I was concerned, seemed to be making any sense.

The clock on the wall read past ten A.M. Nicole had already been missing for more than nine hours. In a small conference room down the hall from Marbush's office, the lieutenant and I, along with a Captain Statinger, whom I vaguely remembered from my time on the force years before, and a representative from the mayor's office—a whispery, middle-aged woman with perm-controlled hair named Beverly Applegate—all sat around a table arguing about the young people with the owl and the AK-47 in the park.

Brodsky's entreaties on the radio had set into motion an immediate NYPD full-court press, of course. An all-out sweep of the area had yielded the stolen rental car, ten blocks away off of Columbus Avenue in the East Eighties, but that was all we had so far.

The car was in impound being checked for fingerprints and other evidence. Dominic Watisi was in a room down the hall with his attorney, being questioned by detectives regarding the dorms we'd seen at his estate and any possible links he might have to the young people in the park.

On our way into the building earlier, I noticed Barry LaGrange and a gaggle of other news types had set up a minor encampment outside the precinct house. They were no doubt enjoying the shade trees the park had to offer.

"I just don't understand why you're doing a whole ground search of the entire park," Beverly Applegate from the mayor's office was saying. "You've got a helicopter and men and dogs everywhere. You're going to frighten the tourists to death."

Captain Statinger, an austere-looking man nearing retirement, shot right back. "Look, Beverly, we've got two murders, a former officer wounded, and now a woman kidnapped. The officers have stated this bird girl was speaking Arabic and the young man was apparently well trained in handling the assault rifle he was carrying. For all we know, these events might even be terrorism related. That enough for you?"

"But I thought you already had the shooter from the other night."

"We thought we did," Marbush said. "Now it looks more likely this kid with the girl may have been the triggerman."

The political woman backed down. "I suppose you're right."

"What's happening with Watisi?" I asked.

The captain cleared his throat. "I'm sorry, Frank. We're talking to him down the hall, but he's stonewalling. And he's got a damn good attorney. Other than your story about this rare book, the buildings you say you saw on his private property, and Dr. Lonigan's unsubstantiated allegations, we still don't have anything solid to go on."

"What about illegal immigrants?" Marbush said. "These kids who have Frank's daughter appear to be in that category. Could one of Watisi's companies have something to do with this? Maybe they're hiring illegals under the table."

The captain shrugged. "The guy's in the real estate business and he owns a development company. He's not running a sweatshop down in the garment district as far as we've been able to tell."

"The sweatshops we're in the process of rooting out," Applegate intoned, no doubt spewing the party line from the mayor's office, although everyone in the room knew it was like trying to stop spammers on the Internet.

"Los Miembros are trafficking in prostitutes," I said. "Some of them are probably illegals."

"It's a possibility," Statinger said. "But how would the gang be connected to Watisi? We'll need time to check all this out."

"Time is what I don't have."

They ignored me.

"Maybe we should think about contacting the immigration service," Marbush said.

"Absolutely not," Applegate said.

"You know the city's policy. It's not the job of the NYPD to police immigration matters. You're investigating a crime, pure and simple. It's an abduction. The alleged perpetrator's immigration status should have nothing to do with the matter."

"But—" I tried to interject.

"We should be talking to the mayor . . ."

"The state attorney general . . ."

"The governor's office . . ."

They all went on like that for another couple of minutes. A discussion about sanctuary rules and executive orders and legal precedent, segueing into *blah, blah, blah.* So many memories, so many meetings over the years, especially while Jake and I were slowly ground through the legal machine. Finally, I couldn't take it any longer.

Bamm!

The thick table shuddered a little beneath my hand. "Look," I said.

Maybe I'd slammed my palm down a little too loudly. Everyone had stopped and was staring at me.

"I don't care if these people are from the moon. We're talking about my daughter here."

"Frank," Marbush said softly, "we're all sorry about your

daughter. Do you have anything additional to offer?"

I looked around the table at the assembled group. "Yes, as a matter of fact, I do. I think you should close down the whole park, immediately. Monitor all access going in or out—foot traffic, too."

"Are you kidding?" Applegate said.

Captain Statinger said, "You know how much manpower that would tie up, Pavlicek?"

"Something keeps drawing these people back to the park. That's where the girl with the bird's been sighted several times now. And I've personally seen the kid with the gun there. I think it's our best shot at catching them and getting Nicole back."

"Don't get me wrong. I understand how you feel. Your daughter was working with you on the job and if it was any of our kids . . ."

"But it isn't, is it?" I said.

The room fell into an uncomfortable silence. They weren't going to move on my recommendation. Not that I'd expected them to.

"I'm done here," I said, pushing up from the table and heading toward the exit.

"Don't go doing something stupid," the captain said. "The last thing we need right now is a vigilante parent."

His words bounced off my back like rubber daggers as I headed through the door.

Down the corridor, Sergeant Fitzhugh, carrying a thick manila folder, was helping two officers escort a trio of teenagers, white, angry and grunge-looking, toward another interview room down the corridor.

"Hey, Frank."

He stopped and waved the others on. The officers and the

teens continued down the corridor.

"How's it going in there?" Fitzhugh asked.

I shook my head.

"I heard about your daughter. Anything I can do?"

"Yeah, thanks. Put the word out at roll call for everyone working the park to be extra vigilant. They even see somebody looking cross-eyed, they need to check it out."

"You got it. I'm handing out the photos of your daughter you gave us, too. You think these turkeys that took off with her have gone to ground?"

"I don't know what they're up to. But I've got a feeling it's not what any of us are expecting."

"What makes you say that?"

"The kid with the Kalashnikov. Something in his face. He's fought someplace, I'm sure of it. Got to be overseas."

"So he isn't going to hesitate to kill. Makes him one dangerous little hombre, you ask me."

"Yeah, but it was more than that."

"What do you mean?"

"I got the feeling he was only trying to protect the girl with the owl."

He scratched his chin. "That would make him the extra shooter when Barnes was hit."

"Exactly."

"Okay. But what's the bird girl's story?"

"Unfortunately, we lost our best chance to find out."

"What are you going to do now?"

"I'm going to meet a plane at LaGuardia," I said.

28

After a phone call explaining my situation to a sympathetic representative, the car rental company agreed to provide me with a new vehicle. A pale Chevy compact this time, but by now I didn't care. I was just happy to be on the move, away from the precinct and everything that was going on down there.

I fell into a steady stream of cars crossing the Queensboro Bridge, took Queens Boulevard to the BQE, and headed up the Grand Central Parkway toward LaGuardia. Back across the river, the midmorning sun bathed the cityscape in gold. Another day in the great metropolis of smoke and commerce.

New York was never static. It was a constant stream of humanity flowing in and out, from anywhere and everywhere, like an ocean or a mountain forest after a fire, forever renewing itself from the ruins. That was something the 9/11 terrorists hadn't counted on. Was it happening again in the prefab woods of Central Park after dark? Nicole was finding out.

I found a space in the garage across from the terminals and walked across to meet the plane. Nothing else mattered right now, until I got her back.

Jake Toronto's flight was on time, a little early in fact. I caught up with him at the counter in baggage claim where he was discussing the need to have a thorough inspection of his checked-through weaponry with an anxious-looking airline agent and a TSA Security Officer.

Jake looked stronger and definitely more ready for action

than when he'd showed up back on my doorstep ten days before. His time overseas had taken a toll on him—that much was clear—but his eyes still blazed with the same certainty that caused others to take notice and step aside.

I walked up and bear-hugged him, clapping him on the back.

"About time you got here," he said. "Would you please explain to these people who I am and what I am not."

I handed over my ID and did my best, and eventually it did some good. The agent released Toronto's two big shipping containers into his custody and the TSA agent cleared out to watchdog duty somewhere else.

"How are you holding up?" Toronto asked in the car a few minutes later.

"Not so good," I said. "No sleep. I didn't think having something like this happen to Nicole would put me over the edge, but maybe it has."

He nodded. "Hey, you're human."

"Right."

"You got a plan?"

"Yes."

"Okay." He crossed his arms and leaned his head against the car window, closing his eyes.

"Speaking of sleep, how much have you had?"

"An hour just now on the plane. I had a lot of prep to do once I got your call."

I glanced at his weathered fatigue pants and battered leather jacket, the new lines that had begun to gather on his face. "It's good to have you back in the saddle, buddy."

"Feels good to be back."

We drove on in silence for a few minutes.

In the middle of the bridge on the way back into Manhattan he blurted, "So I hear we may be tangling with some remnants of Sudanese militias."

"What? You just got here," I said. "How do you know that?"

He opened his eyes and sat up straight again. "After I talked to you, I made a couple of phone calls."

"At three in the morning?"

He shrugged. "No one you'd know, trust me. But these people are connected to the street, especially in Harlem and around the north end of the park."

"Yeah, well maybe you'd better pass on this info to the NYPD."

"Don't worry. They'll find out soon enough, if they haven't already."

"No one said anything in the meeting at the precinct I just came from."

He shrugged. "You know how it goes in the belly of the beast."

"By the time they figure how they really want to attack this thing, it could be game over."

"So how do you plan to go after these people?"

"Two-pronged approach," I said. "First, we sit on Watisi."

"Okay. He dirty?"

"Somehow. He's definitely connected. The cops have figured that out by now, too. Problem is, he's lawyered up and it's going to take them too long to shake anything loose from him."

"Sure."

I looked at my watch. "He's probably still being questioned at the station house in Central Park with his attorney. My guess is they're going to have to let him go."

"Which is when we'll move in for another round of questioning."

"Yes, but we'll need to be careful. NYPD will have someone keeping tabs on him."

"A discreet round of questioning then," Toronto said.

Stepping out of the precinct in Central Park, Dominic Watisi was accompanied by his attorney, a fat, middle-aged gentleman with sagging cheeks, a receding hairline, and a two-thousand-dollar suit. They crossed the roadway to a parking lot where a dark blue limousine waited.

Through the binoculars I was able to pick out the NYPD surveillance, too. A guy sporting a full beard, muscle T-shirt, and a backpack was climbing onto a bicycle and either speaking softly to the other side of his schizophrenic personality or into a hidden microphone that went along with the earpiece he was wearing.

"Okay," I said. "We're on the move."

I fired up the Chevy, which we'd managed to tuck between a panel van and a city maintenance vehicle on the far side of the lot. Toronto stirred from another nap.

"All right then," he said. "Let's do it." Not a moment's hesitation in his voice, as if he'd been sleeping with one eye open.

"We've got a bicyclist on observation, probably in touch with a mobile unit a block or two away."

"Goodie."

"I'll stay well back of them. The limo should be easy enough to pick out. Probably headed back uptown to Watisi's office anyway. Once we get the indication they're headed that way, we'll cut across 125th Street and try to beat them there."

"How do we get out without being seen after we talk to him?"

"Somehow," I said.

"Good plan," he said.

It worked out almost as well as I had hoped. The limo was indeed headed back to Watisi's office and with a little fancy maneuvering we managed to arrive there, stash the car semi-legally between a Dumpster and a blocked-off section of street construction, and slip into the office reception area before the boss returned. A secretary, not Watisi's wife, looked up at us as we walked in.

"May I help you gentlemen?"

She was younger, about Nicole's age, brown skin, a diamond stud earring protruding garishly but not entirely unattractively from one side of her petite nose. I flashed my VA Investigator ID, hoping she wouldn't take the time to examine it, which she didn't.

"Internal Revenue," I said. "We're here to see Mr. Watisi."

"Oh. I'm sorry, but he isn't in at the moment."

"But he's expected back soon."

"I don't know, I—"

"We'll just wait in his office. We've been here before. His wife knows us."

"She does? Maybe that's okay then, although I'm not sure—"

"Listen, he's going to be here any minute with his lawyer. We just talked with them on the phone. They told us to wait inside and help ourselves to the club soda."

"Club soda?"

"Federal agents, miss. No drinking on the job."

"Okay."

If she said anything else, I didn't hear it because Toronto and I had already slipped through the door down the hall and into Watisi's office.

"Man with the clipboard," Toronto said.

"What's that?" I was busy making sure the door stayed closed behind us.

"Man with the clipboard. They say if you carry a clipboard, especially if you're Caucasian and look official enough, you can walk into almost any warehouse in America. You just demonstrated it again. I wonder what the federal prison term is for impersonating an IRS agent?"

"We haven't got much time." I took a look around. Everything was the same as I remembered it. "You think our kingpin developer keeps anything important in his office, like financial records or anything that might be of help to us?"

Toronto was scanning the room, too. "Best bet's the laptop," he said.

There was a black laptop computer perched on the developer's desk, its screen propped open but dark. I followed Toronto over to it.

"Probably in sleep mode," he said. He punched a couple of keys and the machine flickered to life.

"I'll watch the door," I said.

"What am I looking for?"

"Easy. Anything marked illegal employees, racketeering, extortion—that sort of thing," I said, slipping back to the closed door and putting my ear up to the wood.

"You are not a funny man."

"It's either that or lose it completely," I said.

He simply nodded.

The hallway was clear. The secretary must have gone back to her work. Either that or went to call for help.

Toronto worked the laptop, searching. After three or four minutes of admiring the rest of Watisi's office, I said, "Anything?"

"Maybe. We have a printer in here?"

I spotted one on the side table behind the desk.

"There." I pointed.

Toronto spun around in his chair and stood to lean over and pull a cable out from behind the printer. He snaked it across to the laptop and plugged it into the back of the computer. Turned it on and it began to spit out the pages.

"Just need one more minute."

I kept my ear to the door, straining to hear any sound. "That may be all we're going to get."

When Dominic Watisi burst into the room exactly two and a half minutes later, with his storm troopers and attorney in tow,

Toronto and I had already taken up stations on the couch in the seating area across from the desk. We acted as though we were making casual conversation and had been waiting there all along.

The laptop, printer, and cable, of course, had been set back in their original position. And unless Watisi was into fingerprinting on the spot or counting the number of blank sheets in his printer tray, we were going to be okay. The summary list of each of the companies in which he had an interest rested securely in my jacket pocket.

"You again." Watisi's eyes grew small and hard upon seeing me there. "What kind of ruse are you trying to pull with my secretary?"

"Really sorry about that," I said. "We had to get into the building quickly. Didn't want to run the risk of being seen."

"Seen? Seen by whom?"

"Who do you think? NYPD's keeping tabs on you."

"This is unacceptable," the lawyer said to his client.

"Mr. Watisi, we can take care of this." The security team this time included my old friend flanked by another young cretin, who looked equally narrow-eyed and hungry. Both had flinched and held back at the first sight of Toronto, but they seemed to have recovered from their initial trepidation.

"A horse that can't wait to leave the gate usually runs out of gas before the finish," Toronto said, staring at the security types but not stirring from his seat on the couch.

"What's that supposed to mean?"

Watisi held out his arm for the two bodyguards to back down.

"Who are these men?" the attorney asked.

"One of them," he said, indicating me, "is a private detective. The other one, I'm not so sure." He cast a curious eye on Toronto.

"Private detective? Did you hire him, Dominic?"

"No. He's the one whose daughter is missing. They're working with the other investigator, the woman who was shot."

"Is he the one who broke in to your estate up in Westchester?"

Watisi looked at me.

I shrugged.

The lawyer's eyes lasered into mine as he put on his game face. "Gentlemen, I'm afraid I'm going to have to ask you to leave these premises immediately. We'll be asking the police to file criminal charges against—"

Watisi held up his hand again. "It's all right, Harry. I believe we can deal with these men." He looked at me. "In fact, Mr. Pavlicek, I think you and I may have something in common."

"Oh?" I said. "What's that?"

The developer had been standing in the doorway with Harry, but now walked over and took the seat behind his big desk. We were about fifteen feet away from him. He motioned for his attorney to join us in one of the chairs in the sitting area. "We're both missing something," he said.

"Well, what do you know? But no fair, you already have a handle on my dilemma."

"Exactly. Children are the rarest of jewels."

This guy was either as full of hot air as a political spin doctor or up to something.

"You must know something about my daughter's disappearance then."

He shrugged and held up his hand again. "I wish I did. That might make all of our tasks a little easier."

The admission appeared genuine. I glanced at Toronto to see if he concurred, but my old buddy seemed to be more interested in picking something out from under his fingernail at the moment.

Watisi followed my gaze and glanced again at Toronto.

"But we all haven't been introduced. This is my lawyer, Harry

Smith," he said, indicating the balding man who now sat rigidly still opposite us. "And your new friend is?"

"Jake Toronto. He's my former partner."

"I see." He looked at Toronto. "And just what is it you do now, Mr. Toronto?"

Toronto looked up and bore into him with a slight smile. "I work for my friends," he said matter-of-factly.

"Of course. Let's hope we can all be friends," Watisi said.

"Just what exactly are you missing, Mr. Watisi?" I asked.

"Something not so precious as your daughter, Mr. Pavlicek. But something rare, and precious nonetheless. A book."

I stared at him for a moment. "*Book of the Mews,*" I said.

Toronto looked interested all of a sudden. "Say what?"

Watisi's face broke into a smile of admiration. "You're a thorough investigator."

"Actually you can chalk that one up to my daughter," I said.

"But you do know of this book."

"You bought it in a private sale a few years ago from a dealer here in Manhattan."

"Very good."

"Let's cut the crap here. What are you really hiding?" I said.

"Hiding?"

"Didn't you send someone to try to intimidate Darla Barnes at the airport? We saw the dormitories. We saw the security."

Watisi's brow furrowed. Smith, standing off to the side in the corner, crossed his arms and began to say something, but Watisi cut him off.

"What do you think I'm hiding, Mr. Pavlicek?"

"I haven't quite figured it out yet. Probably something to do with illegal immigrants and some plans that got out of hand."

Watisi looked incredulously at his lawyer. "Illegal immigrants? What in the world would I have to do with illegal immigrants?"

"You telling me you don't have some working for you at all

these buildings you own?"

"All documented and legal émigrés, if not citizens like myself. If any one of my employees is not, it's news to me."

I thought about that for a moment. I looked at the lawyer, who nodded.

"You believe these people who took your daughter are illegals?" Watisi asked.

"They aren't from around here, that's for sure."

"I don't know who they are."

"But what about the dorms we saw?"

Watisi seemed to be thinking something over for a moment before motioning to his attorney.

"No." Harry Smith's eyes grew wide as he stepped forward, speaking in low tones to his client. "I have to counsel against this, Dominic."

"Yes," Watisi said. "We have to trust some people sometimes, and this is one of those times."

Toronto looked at me, puzzled. I had no idea what they were talking about, either, but decided it was best to wait them out.

Smith stepped forward and spoke in a clear, even tone. Watisi looked away from him and us at his room full of books.

"Gentlemen, my client has asked me to inform you of something that heretofore has been kept under attorney–client privilege. I must demand, in no uncertain terms, that what you are about to hear remain strictly confidential."

"That's why it says 'private' on my card," I said. "Unless you're about to tell us you two are working on a serious criminal enterprise."

"No, of course not. Nothing of the sort." Smith looked at his client for one last opportunity to have his apparently imminent revelation stopped, but seeing none, pushed on. "Mr. Watisi has, for some time, been engaged in helping people who have recently come to this country. Mostly legally, but sometimes illegally."

"Okay." Now we were getting somewhere.

"His activities have been clandestine, mainly because he doesn't wish to be brought into any kind of spotlight over this. He has a network of people with whom he is in contact. Nothing on paper. No records of any kind. Each situation is different and sometimes discretion is required."

"Which is why this whole affair with the missing pets, the protests and the spectacle in the courtroom are bad for business."

"Yes," Smith said.

"And you've told the cops all of this."

"No. Otherwise, Mr. Watisi risks losing his anonymity in his efforts. He is only trying to help others enjoy the same kind of opportunity he himself has been able to take advantage of."

"So you folks are people smugglers," I said.

"Absolutely not. Mr. Watisi has had to fight against people like that from time to time. You have to understand, my client knows virtually nothing about the missing pets, the threat against Ms. Barnes at the airport, the shootings in the park, or, for that matter, the strange young people who unfortunately absconded with your daughter."

"Virtually nothing."

Dominic Watisi put down the volume on the history of the Revolutionary War he'd been examining. His eyes met mine as he turned. "The truth is," he said, "I am as interested as you gentlemen in finding out where these young people from the park are hiding. I'm afraid they may be fleeing from some individuals who mean them harm. I'm afraid they may not be alone."

"What are you talking about?"

"Several months ago a container ship from East Africa arrived somewhere here in the New York Metropolitan area. My sources tell me that it contained human cargo along with the actual cargo. This is nothing new, of course. It still goes on, although somewhat sporadically since the events of 9/11."

"Go on."

"I didn't report it to the police at that time, and still haven't, because I've had no specifics to give them, but I had recently been given at least a couple of tantalizing clues."

"Which are?"

"First, there were a number of smuggled African adults on board, but apparently a number of young women as well."

"Families?"

"No. Not families. These girls are orphans. And unlike most of the adults, they weren't paying extortion money for their safe passage."

I immediately flashed back to the image of the young girl bearing the owl on her cuff; the empty eyes, the hunger. "So they were brought in here to work."

"No, not exactly. These are teenage girls. They were told they would be working as nannies or in restaurants, but the truth, I'm afraid, is much darker."

"They were going to be pimped into prostitution," I said.

"Of course. What else?"

A lot was falling into place at once.

"What if those kids who took Nicole were just afraid?" said Toronto, who had probably seen enough in the past few months to fill a lifetime of such stories.

I thought back to the eyes of the young girl with the owl and Sammy Yel Bak's hand on the trigger of the Kalashnikov.

"That could be it."

"Yes," Watisi said. "That most definitely could be it."

"Do you know who's running the ring?"

"What I'm told is that it's an Hispanic street gang."

"Los Miembros," I said.

"Exactly. But something happened a few months ago."

"What's that?"

"Some of them managed to escape," he said.

"Jibes with what my contact told me," Toronto interjected. "But you've got some kind of Sudanese connection here, too."

"Yes," the developer said. "Someone's funneling these girls in, but I haven't been able to establish who."

"I've got a feeling he may be right under your nose," I said.

"What are you talking about?"

"In Grayland Tower, one of your apartment owners, Mitch Collins, travels back and forth to Sudan all the time."

"But he is a manufacturing consultant."

"I've got a feeling he knows something about this." I thought back to the computer equipment I'd seen in Collins' apartment. "Did you also know the video from your Grayland Tower security cameras is being tampered with?"

"What? No."

"We can get you the proof, if you need it."

"How's all this gonna help get Nicole back?" Toronto said. "I want to hear more about this book you all were talking about."

Watisi abruptly stood and walked past us toward the far end of the room. On the wall hung an inconspicuous plastic box, rectangular in shape and painted to match the background. I had assumed it was a thermostat, but Watisi produced a key from his pocket, pushed it into the side of the box and turned it to reveal a drop-down touchpad. I was half expecting a James Bond–type rotating bookcase or some such thing, but when he punched in a code, a nearly inaudible click sounded throughout the room. Watisi looked at the corner of the wall where a crack had suddenly appeared, revealing a door that wasn't visible earlier.

"Nice," Toronto said.

He and I followed Watisi through the doorway, trailed by the still-dour-looking attorney.

On the far side of the wall was a small room, the walls of which were lined by lavishly built bookcases made of mahogany with glass front doors. The cases were filled with numerous leather-bound volumes and other books with elaborate bindings. A dehumidifier, coupled with temperature and humidity gauges kept the place climate controlled.

"A decent collection," I said.

"Of course."

I'd had some dealings with book collectors in a university town like Charlottesville. Most, unless they were dealing in museum-quality first editions worth tens of thousands of dollars, declined to go to such great lengths to protect and preserve their collections. I'd even met one suspendered coot in a brick farm house who kept piles of old and rare books, some of which were quite valuable, stacked up like plates in his kitchen.

"You said you're missing *The Book of the Mews.* Does that mean it was stolen?"

"That's right. And it's the only copy in existence."

"It was taken from this room?"

He nodded. "Six months ago."

I was trying to imagine the setup. No windows or other visible entrances, unless Watisi had another magical trapdoor to spring on us.

"Someone had to know about this room and have a key and the code," I said.

"Precisely."

"Time out," Toronto said. "Time out. Would someone please catch me up on what's so important about this missing book?"

I did. That took about two or three minutes while Watisi and Smith cooled their heels, examining some of the other titles on display.

"You filed a police report?" I asked Watisi when we were through.

"Naturally." He placed the volume at which he'd been looking back on the shelf and closed the glass door.

"But it didn't get you very far."

"Naturally. It was the only book taken. If it had been the whole collection or more titles then . . . They probably suspect I misplaced it or something."

"No sign of forced entry?"

"None whatsoever."

"When did you first notice the book was missing?"

"I have the date written down. I check on the books in here nearly every day."

"How do you know you had the only copy of this title?"

"Because the dealer I bought it from bought it from the author's great granddaughter, now deceased. Excerpts have appeared in various places from time to time. She let a newspaper reporter photocopy some of the pages about twenty years ago, but I had the only complete original. A one of a kind. And although the printer used a cheap binding, I even managed to keep that preserved."

"Who else has a key to this room?"

"No one. I keep a copy in a safety deposit box and the only other one on my person."

Toronto had already been looking over the doorframe, examining the lock and electronic trigger mechanism as well.

"What do you think?" I asked him.

He shrugged. "Too easy. Just about any pro on the street could get in here with the right setup."

Watisi, apparently a little insulted, puffed up his shoulders and chest. "That's what the police said, too, but why would they take only this one book? It isn't even that well written. There are any number of other titles in here worth much more than *Book of the Mews.*"

"Whoever took it either wanted the information it contained or wanted to pass it on somehow."

Watisi's eyes began to dance. "Exactly what I've been thinking. And when this story about a falconer with an owl started surfacing and the lies about me began to be spread by these apartment owners who lost their pets, I began wondering if there might be a connection."

"You've told the NYPD all this."

"Some of it, yes. They say they're still investigating." He gave a slight roll of the eyes.

"Why didn't they mention it to me?"

"Because I asked them not to. I don't like my affairs being aired in public. That's how you end up with spectacles like that one outside the courtroom yesterday."

Hard to argue with the man there.

"There is something else I didn't tell the NYPD, however. Something that may help you find your daughter." Watisi looked at his lawyer.

"What's that?"

The developer's gaze dropped toward the floor. "As much as I hate to admit it, I think I realize now who may have stolen the book."

"Who would that be?"

"She's a low-level employee of mine with whom . . ." He shook his head in apparent disgust with himself. "With whom I'm ashamed to say I had a brief affair some time ago."

"Okay."

"She comes from a troubled past. After we broke things off, I found a job for her, but I'm afraid she may have taken up with one of the members of Los Miembros."

"Damon Hicks," I said.

"Yes. And worse, I may have instructed my people to not

look too closely at certain other activities she might be involved in for fear of extortion."

"Other activities such as people smuggling."

"Quite possibly." He folded his hands in front of his chin, as if praying for some form of penance.

"Who is it?"

"Who?" It was almost an afterthought and no real surprise to me. "Her name is Jayani Miller," he said.

29

On the way down to Grayland Tower, I dialed the Central Park Precinct and spoke with Lt. Marbush, who agreed to put out an APB on Jayani Miller and Mitch Collins to bring them both in for questioning, and to have a talk with the DA about Dominic Watisi. I also called Darla, whom Carl was driving home from the hospital, and filled her in.

"Whatever you got to do to get your daughter back, Franco," she said, her voice sounding a little less loopy than the day before. "I'm sorry for getting you into such a mess. If I had any idea it was going to turn out like this—"

"Forget it. If I was in your shoes, I'd have done the exact same thing."

"You don't think Miller's going to be at work?"

"Not anymore. Everything's started to hit the fan since Nicky's kidnapping. Miller has to know the heat's coming down on her."

"So why are you heading back to Grayland?"

"To see if we can roust Collins before the cops get there. And something else that reporter I was talking to said about tunnels. I never got to check it out thoroughly."

"It all seems to start and end with that building."

"Yeah, it does, doesn't it?"

"So what, you think those two kids who took Nicky are running from Miller, Collins, Los Miembros, and the like?"

"Something like that."

"And they can't go to the cops because they're illegal and they're scared. That would be better for Nicole then."

"Let's hope so. Unless—"

"Unless Miller, Collins, or someone else from Los Miembros finds them before you do. You got Jake there with you?"

"Sure do."

"You tell that man if I was there I'd give him a big kiss on his cheek. Tell him I said to get with the program and start kicking some butt if he has to."

"I'll pass on the message," I said.

I had barely hung up and tucked the phone back in my pocket when it began buzzing. I plucked it out and checked the display. Dr. Lonigan. I answered on the third ring.

"He's back," she said.

"Who's back?" I asked.

"Groucho," she said. "I can hardly believe it."

"What? What happened?"

"I don't know. I haven't the slightest idea. I came home from work for a little while a few minutes ago, and there he was in the doorway, standing waiting for me as if nothing had ever happened."

"Have you checked him out? Is he okay?"

"He looks as healthy as ever."

"Did you look around the apartment? Anything out of place or any sign of a break-in?"

"Not that I can see."

"Could he have been hiding somewhere there all along?"

"I don't see how that's possible. I . . . I really don't know what to say."

"What about the other pet owners?"

"I called everybody on the list before I called you. Of those I spoke to, no one else's pet has returned."

I said nothing, thinking things over.

"Frank, I know you must have a million other things on your mind at the moment."

"To put it mildly."

"I'm beginning to feel like such a fool over everything. Is there anything I can do?"

"Yes," I said. "Next time you hire a private investigator, be a little more honest with them up front."

"I . . . Like I said, I don't know what to say, I—"

"You knew Jayani Miller had had a relationship with Dominic Watisi, didn't you?"

She said nothing.

"You knew that and Watisi knew you did, and that's why he refused to talk to you about your lawsuit or your allegations regarding the pets."

"Someone did steal our pets, though."

"Yeah, they did. But it wasn't anyone working for Watisi to try to get back at you. And now two people are dead over part of it, and Nicole may be next."

"But why?"

"Who knows why? If you had been straight with us from the beginning about everything, we might've had the answer to that by now."

We were at Grayland Tower and braked to a stop in front.

"I am so, so sorry, Frank, I—"

"I've got to go," I told her and clicked off.

Toronto, who'd been listening to it all from across the seat, said, "So we find Nicky, blow town, and forget the check from the client."

"That sums it up."

He pulled on the handle to open his door.

As I suspected, Jayani Miller was not one of the guards working the security desk today. Two wide bodies were manning the desk instead.

"Where's Miller?" I asked.

"She called in sick this morning," the taller one of the two said.

"Must be something going around," Toronto said.

"Hey, you know you can't park in the front turnout like that."

"So tow us," I said.

"Or not," Toronto said, giving him the eye as we hustled to catch the elevator doors before they closed.

"Who are you two looking for?"

"Collins," I said. "11C."

"You're too late," the guard said. "He left fifteen minutes ago for Kennedy. He's headed overseas on another trip."

My phone buzzed again.

"Busy man," Toronto said.

Probably the doctor calling back. I was planning to ignore the call, but glancing at the display, I noticed it originated from a different local exchange.

"Is this the private investigator looking for the owl in Central Park?" a voice asked.

"Yeah. Who's this?"

"Pock. Remember me?"

"Raines."

"Yeah, Raines."

"What's going on?"

"You said you wanted info about who was flying that owl and what was happening with it."

"Yeah."

"And now your daughter's missing."

"That's right. You know something?"

"You come and meet me half an hour from now at the statue in the park, I'll tell you exactly where you can find her," he said.

★ ★ ★ ★ ★

I'm no sucker for symbolism. But Cato Raines' choice of a meeting spot couldn't have been more appropriate.

On the south side of Seventy-Second Street Drive in the park sits a large bronze sculpture. *The Falconer,* dating back to 1875, is the work of British sculptor George Blackall Simonds and depicts an Elizabethan falconer, raising on his gloved hand a falcon poised for release. The original sculpture of *The Falconer* was created in Trieste, Italy. Apparently, a wealthy nineteenth-century New York merchant named George Kemp saw it and admired it so much that he commissioned a full-scale replica for Central Park. It is a beautiful work of art, like much of the rest of the park—a romantic representation of the reality.

Raines was seated on the ground with his back leaning against the base of the statue in the shade, probably half asleep, most likely to get away from the heat and the noise from the road. Bushes were filling in the space where he sat opposite the traffic flowing by on the other side of the statue, so as to make him practically invisible to passersby. He was wearing the exact same outfit I'd seen him in a couple of days before, right down to the crazy suspenders he probably never changed.

It was Toronto who noticed we might have a problem as we approached from the woods away from the road.

"Something's wrong here," he said.

"What do you mean?"

"Look at the man's head."

Raines' head was clearly tilted at an abnormal angle, leaning back against the stone. As we drew closer, the cause became evident. Raines' eyes were still open, staring emptily into the middle distance. He had been shot through the right temple with a small-caliber bullet at close range. A trail of blood ran out from the wound and had stained the ground and the base of the statue. His dead hands were dirty and two of his fingertips were caked with orange clay.

"What a waste," Toronto sighed.

I shook my head, still looking over the body.

"There goes another hot lead."

"Maybe not," I said, pulling out my cell phone to dial 9-1-1. "I'm calling it in, but we can't stay here."

"Why not?" He was already scanning the immediate area, looking for any sign of the shooter.

"Because I've seen that color clay someplace before," I said.

30

"Tunnels. Great. I hate tunnels," Toronto said.

"Could be worse," I said. Our flashlight beams spread down the tunnel like swollen fingers reaching into the dark.

"How far do you think this goes?" he whispered.

We were in the bowels of Grayland Tower. I'd been right in tracing the clay from Raines' fingers to the construction around this utility tunnel.

"Hard to tell," I said. "But unless I've lost all sense of direction, I think we're headed straight toward the park."

"Under the street?"

"Yeah."

"What about the subway?"

"There are no subway tunnels running under Central Park."

"Really?"

"Really."

"Whoever built this building could have used this shaft to smuggle something inside the building that they didn't want anybody to see coming in the front door."

"Like maybe the liquor during Prohibition the reporter told me about."

"Mmmm." Toronto's light shone along the ceiling, illuminating a spidery network of brown piping and decayed wiring. "Or it might have just been used for service work. Old utility lines, that sort of thing."

"If it does connect up with the park, there's bound to be an exit somewhere. Possibly even a side room or foyer."

"You mean like where someone could be hiding Nicole or a bunch of smuggled kids."

"Exactly. My guess is either Jayani Miller or Los Miembros were using Raines as a go-between."

"For what?"

"To try to set up a scenario that would help them figure out where the girls and Sammy are hiding."

"You mean the falconry book."

"Yeah. Who knows what Raines' relationship was to Miller or the gang? But Miller passes the book to Raines after she finds out he may know something about the kids, hoping to goad him into bringing the kids out into the open somewhere so she can trap them. Raines was a survivalist type. He might've helped the kids trap the owl, taught the girl how to hunt with it."

"But I thought you said she looked like she was trained Arab style."

"That part I haven't figured out yet."

"I'm thinking we need to find a way to get down this tunnel and see what's at the other end," he said.

"The problem is, I don't think either you or I are going to be able to fit in there very easily to check it out."

I stepped up to the spot where the tunnel narrowed and approximated its girth with my hands. No way Toronto would fit with his wide shoulders. I might barely make it. But it would be like climbing down a blind cave with virtually no margin for error. I could easily get stuck. On the other hand, the girl with the owl and Sammy Yel Bak with his slender fingers curved around the trigger of the Kalashnikov, would have no problem. Neither would Nicole.

"The tunnel could open up again further in, and the other end might have a larger entrance," he said.

"Which we could confirm if we knew where it was. Or that

there even is such an entrance."

Toronto flipped out his cell phone. "No reception down here," he said. "I say we head back upstairs and call 9-1-1. Maybe they can get some sand rats or tunnel people in here to check this out."

He turned to go. I held out my hand to stop him.

"Hold on a second."

"Why?"

I had the unmistakable feeling I would find Nicole alive somewhere on the other side of this hole.

"We may not have time," I said.

"What do you mean?"

"Before Jayani and her people killed Raines, they may have forced him to tell them where the other entrance is in the park."

"If there is another entrance."

"Right."

"And if Nicky is even in there with these guys."

"Right."

"Lot of if's."

"Nicky's in there somewhere."

"How do you know?"

"I feel it."

While we were standing there with our thumbs in our mouths, the time for debate came abruptly to an end. From somewhere deep inside the tunnel echoed an ominous crack, followed in quick succession by another and then another. The unmistakable sound of a handgun going off.

"Gotta go." I dove toward the opening, reaching for my Glock.

"Here," Toronto said, snatching a small penlight from one of his pockets and shoving it at me. "At least use this. I'll get the cavalry."

I ducked my face below the lip of the opening and plunged ahead onto my stomach, leading with the dim light and my gun.

A wormhole for a coffin. Now wouldn't that be nice?

"Hey, Frank," Toronto said from behind me as I began wriggling down the narrow hole with barely an inch or two between my shoulders and the walls. "Keep your light down and your face to the stone. Makes it harder to see you coming."

What did he think this was, Tora Bora? I felt the tunnel begin to swallow me, its brick and stone supports chafing at my knees, elbows, shoulders, and forehead. The dim green phosphorescent glow of the penlight became my world. Face to the stone.

31

The passage through the narrow rock tube seemed to take five years. I squirmed forward inch by inch, the safety still on at the base of my Glock just in case. The last thing I needed was to deafen myself and possibly injure someone at the end of the tunnel ahead. It had to end somewhere. That gunfire hadn't come from the moon.

I focused on the rock face in front of my nose. I tried not to think about all the weight of the earth around me, the rocks and roots and trees, not to mention the hundreds of thousands of tons of steel, stone, and pavement that made up Midtown Manhattan. Instead, I concentrated on a memory of an outing with Torch earlier in the spring.

It was a warm March day, nearing the end of the season. The sun was out and a light breeze was blowing, but not enough to affect our hunting or cause Torch any trouble. In fact, the sky was completely clear and such an electric blue, it seemed to pulse with energy. Torch, following on as I negotiated my way through a variable grove of thicket and woods, soared from tree branch to tree branch, the only sound the faint deep note of his bells.

When a rabbit burst from the thicket, a large buck, Torch was all business, having stalked and sensed him long before I. His stoop was an eye blink of beauty, timed for the kill as he'd done hundreds of times before.

But this buck was no ordinary cottontail. He feinted and

dodged as expected, but he also managed to skillfully employ his cover—a rock outcropping, a jagged fur pine, and a dense rhododendron—in such a way as to cause Torch to pull tail fur but miss clutching the big rabbit's body with his talons. We chased and stalked him all over that wood it seemed, but he finally got away.

Half an hour later, Torch caught another rabbit, which made it a successful outing. But I couldn't forget the skill and the cunning of that big buck. Torch might not have been the baddest hunting hawk to ever come down the pike, but he was no slouch, either. The buck had proved a more than worthy foe.

This is what some of those sign-carrying fools at the courthouse who hated all kinds of hunting failed to understand, precisely because the vast majority of them had never actually picked up a rifle or a bow or, for that matter, flown a bird of prey at live quarry in the wild. Their minds were numbed to reality by Disneyfied visions of Bambi killers. The truth was more complex than that. The strong and the determined survived, hunter and prey alike. It was the height of human vanity to somehow believe man had completely evolved beyond all that.

Thinking back to the ludicrous scene with the dueling protestors kept me going. I focused on the green glow of the rock around me.

Soon, the air began to grow cooler. The walls of my tunnel remained as suffocating as ever, but I could sense a wider opening ahead.

I risked lifting my head slightly to look and there it was: a dim light filtered into the curving tunnel from up ahead. I was nearing the end of my torture, for better or worse.

I extinguished the penlight. With my arms extended out in front of me and no clearance to pull them back in to my sides, whoever was at the end of the passage and had fired those shots would be able to spot me coming if they focused on the tunnel.

I slowed my progress, too. There'd been no more shooting and I didn't want to risk making any noise. I still couldn't make out the end of the passage, but I guessed I was only about twenty or thirty feet from whatever awaited me there.

"You guys are friggin' idiots. I told you not to shoot anybody unless it was a last resort."

The voice was excited and out of breath.

"But look at the size of that rat. It just popped out of nowhere, man. Scared the bejesus out of me."

"I don't care about the goddamned rat. Where's your head at? We've got to figure out how to get all these bitches back to Jayani without looking like we're leading a parade up Malcolm X Boulevard."

"Sorry. What you want to do about Sammy and the white chick?"

"Jayani will take care of the white chick. As far as Sammy, I'm not going to spend any more time looking for him. Let him rot down here with the rats."

"That's nasty."

"Hey, that little bugger has practically blown this whole deal for us. He deserves it."

"What about the pets? Maybe we should lock them up down here and leave them for the rats, too?"

"Nah. We'll let the rest of 'em out, too. Someone will find them, or let 'em find their ways home if they can. Then maybe these crazy people upstairs will start forgetting about all this."

"How about the owl?"

"You want to carry that thing out of here?"

"Not me, man."

"Leave it tied down where it is. No reason to go near it."

"Hey, I know. We can feed the rat to it!"

"I said leave it be. We've got other things to worry about."

As they'd been busy talking, I'd managed to inch forward to

where the end of the hole became visible. All I could see through the opening, however, were the jittering patterns of a pair of flashlight beams being trained on a brick wall and an invisible ceiling overhead. I was probably still somewhere under the street but nearing the park.

"All right. Let's get going then," the second voice agreed.

The lights swirled about in tandem. A rusty hinge echoed through the chamber as they opened what appeared to be a door. The lights disappeared and the sound of their footsteps receded into the darkness.

Good timing. Deciding to forgo a light until I was through the tunnel and had a better idea what I was facing, I pulled myself forward until I poked out of the opening.

Fresh air. The atmosphere in this new chamber, while probably only marginally better than anywhere else in this subterranean area, felt like a cool breath of spring on my face after the rock shaft. But no sooner had I enjoyed the feeling than a bitter odor struck my nostrils. The rat, I guessed. I hoped I wouldn't be catapulting out of the opening and landing on the dead thing's carcass. There was no sound in this darkened room. But when I paused to listen more closely, I could make out an intermittent *whoosh* and rumble, muted, probably coming from the traffic several yards overhead.

I managed to find a small pebble and tossed it out the opening to gauge the distance to the floor. It was only a few feet down it seemed. Good thing, because I'd be scrambling out head first.

I made the maneuver—no easy feat while clutching the Glock—and a few seconds later found myself standing on solid ground again. I reached down and felt the surface of the floor. Like the wall, it appeared to be made of old bricks, built for who knows what purpose. I took a stance and raised the gun into a defensive position, switching on the green penlight again.

It was a storage room of some kind. A rack of old fifty-five gallon drums took up one wall. Stacks of empty boxes and empty food containers littered the floor. They had been the rat's hoped-for prize. The large rodent lay curled up in a pool of its blood in one corner.

An old wooden door hung partway open on the opposite wall. Beyond it, I could begin to make out a darkened passageway with narrower walls but a ceiling of similar height to the room in which I stood.

I had just begun to edge toward the doorway when I heard the muffled noise.

It sounded like the guttural grunts of some wild animal confined to a cage. In the eerie half-light of the chamber doorway, the sound could have come from some otherworldly dimension.

When I heard it a second time, however, I knew that these were human voices. Not just one or two, but several. I stepped through the door and began moving toward the source of the noise but stopped short when another door slammed shut somewhere further down the corridor.

I doused my light. I heard the sound of laughter and I could make out the bright beam from a large flashlight followed by a torso and a pair of legs rising into the darkness as if ascending a ladder.

Then a soft word was spoken, indecipherable. Abruptly, the light reversed course and began descending toward the floor again. Whoever was behind the beam, it was a safe bet they weren't exactly friendly. Before I knew it, the light had reached the bottom and had turned and was heading straight in my direction.

I barely had time to step gingerly behind the door before the powerful beam extended its long reach back into the chamber behind me. Footfalls on the brick approached, and a man breathed heavily. I squeezed the gun in my hand. But he obviously had no clue about my presence. There was no hesitation as he approached and moved right past me through the open door.

He stopped and began to fiddle with some piece of equipment, swearing under his breath, more out of aggravation at some petty annoyance than anything else. The beam, I could tell now, was trained into the room away from me.

Time to make a move.

I stepped around the door to see the silhouette of a man wearing a hooded sweatshirt bent over something in one corner of the darkness. The flashlight had been set on the floor beside him.

Two steps forward. Flip the safety on the Glock.

At the last second the man must have sensed my presence because he began to rise and turn in my direction. But it was too late. I swung the butt of the gun hard, felt the jolt as it crashed against the back of his skull.

He slumped heavily to the floor. I recognized him as one of the other guards from the building. I turned him over and searched him. He had been bent over a pouch full of marijuana, half its contents spilling onto the dry brick floor. He must have dropped it when he was in here earlier and realized his mistake as he was climbing up the ladder.

He had a nice Beretta Cougar with a full clip tucked into a hip rig under his sweatshirt which I helped myself to, the holster as well. Now I was heavily armed with the mini-Glock as backup.

There was no telling how long my friend here might be out, so I scrounged around the storeroom looking for something that might slow him down a little. I found exactly what I needed behind one of the big drums, a coiled length of black rubber gardening hose I was able to filet with my jackknife into strips that served nicely to bind his hands and feet.

The human sounds coming from the other end of the black tunnel appeared to have quieted, but I could still hear them as I picked up the flashlight and left the room again, leaving the guard bound in the darkness.

I would need to work fast. Jayani and whoever else might have been with this guy might begin to wonder where he was by now. The only good news being that having to crawl down the rungs of the ladder would make them a sitting duck for anyone taking aim on them, namely me.

Maybe sensing my presence, the voices seemed to be pulling me toward them again, like ancient sirens from the darkness.

Past the ladder at the end of the corridor a much larger and heavier wooden door stood closed. It was rough wood and coated in heavy and uneven black lacquer, caked with dust that nonetheless still managed to sparkle in the light from my beam. Large white letters on the door read *PROPERTY OF THE CITY OF NEW YORK* and *FDNY.*

The fire department. Maybe this place was used to access additional underground water lines or something. Whatever its original purpose, it didn't appear to have seen any use for years. Until now, that is.

I checked the readout on my digital phone. Still no signal down this deep. A two-way radio was all I needed to let Toronto know what I had discovered so he could direct help my way, but in our haste, that piece of equipment hadn't been on the requisition list.

The voices had stopped for the moment. Maybe they'd heard my footsteps and wondered if the guard or one of the others were coming back.

The heavy door had been secured from the outside with a freshly installed latch bolt. I unbolted the door and pulled it open, shining my light through the opening.

Human smells—urine, feces, fear even—washed over me.

There were most definitely people left in here in the dark. My beam caught a stick-like arm first. Then a hand, a torso, a face. More faces, four or five altogether. All of them bound and gagged with duct tape, their faces and clothes smudged with dirt, all of them African and female.

I shone the light back down the hall on the distant ladder to make sure no one was coming. Then I pushed through the door and into the room.

I started with the girl closest to the door. She was tall and thin, clad in nothing more than cutoff jeans and a T-shirt, the whites of her eyes wild with terror as she squinted into my beam.

"It's okay, it'll be okay," I said, patting the girl's arm as I began to undo the tape. She gave a sharp cry as the tape ripped away from her cheeks. "Shhh, it's all right. It'll be okay."

Pulling tape, trying to calm them, I moved down the line from one girl to the next. They were all terrified, emaciated and dehydrated. I wished I'd thought to bring along a bottle of water. All of them looked to be between ten and fourteen years old. None spoke any English.

When the last one was free I poked my light outside and checked the ladder again. Still no sign of anyone returning to check on the guard. I was closing the door and turning back to the frightened girls when it happened.

Something hard and cold poked into my ribs.

"Hole up there, bro." Sammy Yel Bak slid into the room like smoke behind the barrel of his AK-47. "Put your hands up."

"Where's my daughter?" I asked.

"She ain't here no more. They took her."

"Who took her?"

"Los Miembros. They took her and most of the rest of the girls, and after you knocked that fool on the head, now they be back any minute."

"Why'd you take my daughter?"

" 'Cause she look like I could trust her."

"Not me."

"No. Not then."

"I'm on your side," I said.

"I know," he said, flipping the safety on his rifle and letting the barrel drop to his side. "That's what your daughter told us. Now we all gotta move in a hurry." He motioned with his gun for me to move back into the room with the girls.

I did as he instructed. The refugees, rather than being more frightened, seemed to have calmed down considerably at the sight of him.

"C'mon, let's go."

He motioned to the group of girls, turned on his own small flashlight, and we all followed him to a back corner of the room where he shone his light on the low ceiling. There among the cobwebs overhead was a narrow line in the concrete. A trapdoor.

Sammy slung his gun over his shoulder. Three or four of the girls stepped forward holding out their hands to help boost him up. I lent a hand.

A couple of minutes later, we were all safely up through the opening, the door was closed and Sammy had bolted it shut from our side. Wherever we were, it was much cooler than below. The chamber was similar to the one we'd just left, except it was empty and connected to a much larger tunnel. Sammy and the girls began moving down the tunnel.

"Where are we going?" I asked.

"You'll see."

After fifty yards or so, the tunnel forked. We followed the left hand tunnel for another few yards until we entered another much larger chamber with posters and hand-painted pictures on the wall. Sammy bent over and lit a lamp. There were signs of habitation everywhere—water bottles, food wrappers, more lanterns, a ventless cookstove, portable CD players, even blankets and mattresses laid out on the floor.

"You people have been living down here," I said.

"That's it." Sammy turned and lifted a box from somewhere, began stuffing his pockets and a belt with ammunition for his rifle.

"How many?"

"Eighteen."

"How long have you been down here?"

"Few months." He shrugged.

"Months." I looked down the line of frightened eyes. The expressions on the girls' faces had shifted to one of wary curiosity.

"These girls have been smuggled in here to work as prostitutes by Los Miembros. You're protecting them."

He nodded. "They tell 'em they're going to be working in restaurants, in the kitchens or busing tables. Ain't true."

He said something to one of the taller girls in Arabic. The girl took his flashlight and disappeared back down the tunnel for the moment.

"How did they end up with you?"

"We're all the same. I just been here a lot longer."

"How come you didn't go to the police or ask someone for help?"

"We're illegal. We make it on our own."

"Where'd you learn to handle that gun?" I asked.

"War," he said simply.

"Sudan?"

He nodded. "Same place we all from."

"You kill those two gangbangers in the park the other night?"

He nodded again. "Had to. They had Faridah."

"She the girl with the owl?"

He nodded.

I looked around again at the room. "Lot of mouths to feed here."

"That's right. These girls here are the skinniest. Los Miembros must have figured these weren't worth the trouble."

"So they were planning to leave them here to die."

He said nothing.

"Where's the owl?"

"She's safe for now," he said. "Faridah knows where to find her."

"What have you guys been doing with that bird, hunting for meat?"

"Yes, sir. We got the idea from that book Jayani gave us. The girl, Faridah Abd al Mahir, she said her father had trained her how to handle the birds before he died."

That explained the Arab-style glove.

"So you were cooking down here?"

He nodded.

"You're lucky you didn't asphyxiate yourselves."

"You ever been hungry enough?" His gaze was steady.

"Where's Faridah now?"

"With your daughter and the rest of the girls. See, Jayani was the one. She'd tricked us, we knew. She'd been trying to figure out where we were."

"And she finally found you."

"Yes, sir."

"Did you know she was in bed with Los Miembros?"

"I do now."

"And the missing pets, how'd they figure into the plan?"

"I took 'em," he said. He gestured with his head and shone the light on a couple of cages, bags of cat food and kitty litter in the corner. "The girls needed something to keep them from going crazy down here. Jayani let me. I still trusted her, you see?"

"After the falconry thing didn't work, she was trying to use the pets as a way to figure out where you were hiding," I said.

"I guess so. Something like that."

"What about the feather and fur on the sidewalk?"

He shrugged. "I put 'em there so the owners would think their pets were gone."

"Do you know about Mitch Collins?"

"Who?"

The girl who had left returned bearing a small box and handed it to Sammy. "Look, mister, we got to get going, okay? You got guns. I saw you take one from that gangster. You go and take these girls with you. Keep them safe. Follow the other side of the tunnel we just passed. It'll lead you out into the park. The girls will show you."

"What about you?"

"I'm going after Jayani to get back Faridah and your daughter and the other girls."

"You know where she's taken them?"

"I know exactly where she's taken them."

"I want to know, too," I said.

32

Thunder rumbled in the darkness overhead. Drops began striking the canopy of leaves in the darkness of the park followed by a wave of heavy rain, more thunder. It was well after dark now. More than six hours had passed since I'd last seen Sammy Yel Bak. Lt. Marbush and I had agreed on a plan provided I went in with heavy backup. We were about a hundred yards north of the 97th Street Transverse, just inside the western edge of the park. West Drive was somewhere ahead in the darkness and the ball fields and the North Meadow. I moved quickly, any sounds I might be making obscured by the downpour. Toronto was about thirty feet to my left and behind me.

"Frank."

Marbush's voice crackled softly over the radio.

"Back at you," I whispered, hoping she could make me out.

"What's your ETA to contact?"

"Two to three minutes. Maybe less."

"Okay. Just to make you feel a little cozier, spotters on the buildings are having a hard time seeing anything and the chopper's out of play with the storm. All we've got are the troops on the ground."

"Roger that."

I motioned for Toronto to move up beside me. He scrambled forward, moving through the heavy foliage off the trail. Already we were both soaked to the bone.

"You're sure they're going to be in there now?" he asked.

"Got to be. Sammy says it's where Los Miembros meets to trade girls."

"Like a slave market, you mean."

"Something like that."

The Parks and Recreation storage facility was tucked neatly into the back of a hillside flanking the Drive. A pair of street-lights shone like lonely beacons up ahead. Only the dim roof of the building was visible from across the road.

"The owl girl going to be any help?" Toronto asked.

"Maybe. But she probably isn't going to want to take any chances without Sammy."

"If what you say about the kid is true, this girl Jayani and her pals may have bitten off more than they can chew when it comes to Sammy."

"Let's hope so. But he's only one against many."

"And you're sure you can trust the kid."

"Time to find out," I said.

We pushed on through the rain. The ground was uneven, the grass and the rocks slick with water. As if we weren't wet enough already, each bush or small tree branch we brushed past soaked us some more.

The temperature had taken a sudden drop as well. Steam rose from the beams of our small flashlights. I touched the stolen Beretta in my waistband to make sure it was still within easy reach. Marbush had been pretty accepting once she'd found out the truth about her shooting investigation and the missing pets fiasco. That, at least, gave me a warm feeling all over. The arrival of a pair of federal immigration agents to put the girls I'd managed to walk out of the tunnels in protective custody and escort them to the hospital proved less comforting.

I'm all in favor of protecting the homeland, securing our borders, you name it. The last thing I want is some jihadist surreptitiously bent on destruction showing up in my neighborhood. But when face to face with these illegals clearly bent on nothing more than their own survival—and making heroic efforts at it to boot—the platitudes tended to melt away like so much rainwater. Not my call, but I hoped they'd get a decent break, be offered asylum. I hoped their only memories of America and New York City wouldn't end up being Jayani and the Los Miembros sex slave ring, the upscale suburban clients of which no doubt would be shocked and horrified to know that the girls they were using for their own pleasure were not only underage but kidnap, rape, and imprisonment victims as well.

There were no cars on the Drive, closed at this hour. The rain blew in sheets in front of us and the sound of the occasional car *swish*ing by on the Transverse Road to our south only served to heighten the feeling of emptiness here.

Toronto and I switched off our lights, emerged from the overgrowth and crossed the pavement together like twin apparitions. A chain-link fence surrounded the storage structure. The gate was locked, but there was a hole the size of a taxicab in one side of the fence, so I'm not even sure why anyone bothered securing the gate.

We made our way through the opening and down a steep embankment to the broken-up pavement of the truck turnaround. The light from the street lamps reflected off the draining water and puddles, moving with the staccato beat of the rain pouring down. Even through the storm, the rich scent of oil and diesel fuel was redolent on the wind.

What were we doing here, I thought for a moment, chasing ghosts? But Jayani Miller was no ghost, and neither were Los Miembros, even if they did have a lot in common with the occasional slave traders who'd apparently roamed this section of Manhattan sixteen decades before.

As if on cue, the figure of Sammy Yel Bak emerged from the darkness of the open storage building, barely visible in the dim light. He was smoking a cigarette, the Kalashnikov held by a shoulder harness slung casually at his side. Something wasn't right.

He looked at us and said, "What you people want now? Can't you just leave it alone?" His voice was devoid of emotion. It didn't seem to fit the situation.

"I'm just after my daughter and I want to help you and the rest of the girls."

"Right. Everybody just wanna help. Help themselves to women. Help themselves to money."

"It's not like that, Sammy, and you know it. Not everyone is that way."

Sammy was silent for a moment. He took a final puff on his cigarette and tossed it into the rain. "Too late now anyway," he said.

"What do you mean?"

"They gone."

"Who's gone?"

"The girls." He coughed into his hand. "Los Miembros took them. Best you forget about them all now."

"Where's my daughter?"

"Dead." He shook his head. "All of us gonna be dead, sooner or later."

"Dead?" I fought at the note of panic welling up inside me. "Where is she?"

"I don't know, man," he said, slipping into his street accent. "How I supposed to know such things? Supposed to know everything, do you think? Sammy's supposed to know everything?"

Either he was drunk or drugged. Or was it something else? I studied his silhouette, the slope of his shoulders, and the fix of his gun.

"You seeing what I'm seeing?" I whispered to Toronto.

"Yeah . . . I see it."

"He's been shot."

I tapped Toronto on the shoulder and pointed to the shed. We hit the ground, guns drawn, as the first 9 mm rounds began striking the pavement around us.

We followed the tracers with return fire. Someone screamed and uttered an obscenity from deep within the storage shed. Sammy Yel Bak seemed oddly unaffected by it all, standing there with his Kalashnikov still hanging by its strap.

As if it was necessary or would do any good, I keyed in the radio handset and pulled it to my mouth.

"Code red. Code red. Shots fired in front of the storage shed."

Toronto crawled behind some storage barrels filled with sand and I followed and fired around them. Sammy was slumping to the ground. Maybe he'd been hit in the crossfire. Not that it would matter now.

The first SWAT team members scrambled across the pavement to our left, training their weapons into the black hole behind Sammy. A siren *whoop*ed close by as four other assault officers, rappelling down from the roof above, hit the ground outside the shed.

"Hold up! Hold up!" More obscenities erupted from inside the open-air shed. "You want to kill all these here women?"

The shed and the entire lot was flooded with light then as NYPD beams and laser finders bounced all around the inside walls.

"Hold up. Hold up, I said. It ain't worth all that." It was Jayani Miller, still in her security guard uniform, and three others, their weapons thrown to the ground, their hands high over their heads.

Toronto and I moved in as Sammy Yel Bak slumped to the ground. He was bleeding heavily from the abdomen, even the nose and mouth.

"We need an ambulance stat," I shouted.

"On the ground," the cop in charge blared through a bullhorn to the shooters. "Facedown on the ground with your hands behind your heads."

Miller and the others complied. Officers shone their lights and swarmed into the building. The brightness revealed a group of terrified young women, clumped into a mass at the back of the structure, apparently as frightened by the blazing police lights as they'd been by their captors and the shooting.

I searched the group of women while the cops secured the suspects. There were about a dozen girls altogether, in better condition than the ones I had brought out of the tunnel, as Sammy had said. Wild eyes in tears, dark skin, dressed in tattered jeans, shorts and T-shirts, all bound and gagged. And there, among them, with her hair a mess and her face bruised but looking very much alive, Nicole. Even with her bonds, she was hugging one of the group who was sobbing hysterically, the slight figure of the girl I had last seen with the owl.

I ran to them and put my arms around Nicole, pulling the gag from her face.

"Hey, Dad," she said softly.

"Hey yourself." I undid the rope around her hands and began helping untie the girl. "You okay?"

She nodded. "This is Faridah Abd al Mahir," she said.

"I know," I said. "Sammy told me. I found the other girls in the tunnel. He found me."

"He tried to help us, but they caught him and tortured him before they shot him. It was . . ." She wiped a tear from her cheek.

"He wasn't supposed to show here until we arrived." He still hadn't completely trusted me.

Paramedics arrived and quickly moved Sammy under cover. Faridah wanted to be near him so we approached within a few yards, but they had barely gone to work on Sammy when he went into cardiac arrest.

The rain poured down harder, beating like the sound of a locomotive on the roof of the shed. Toronto, Lt. Marbush, and even Darla—who had shown up on her crutches wearing an NYPD slicker—came over to be with us. Police, additional medical personnel, and immigration officers swirled around, making room for those working on Sammy's lifeless body.

Maybe if the entry wounds had been different. Maybe if they'd been in an operating room with a trauma surgeon. Maybe if they'd had just a few more minutes, been in some precious different place where the rain never fell, bullets never flew, and the night never closed around them like a curtain. They rushed Sammy into a waiting ambulance, and at one point in their fervor to save his life tore an emblem and a chain from his chest that Faridah rushed forward to take from them. I found myself whispering a prayer.

They did all they could.

33

On a cloudless morning three days later, Nicole, Darla, Toronto, an interpreter, and I accompanied Faridah Abd al Mahir in an ASPCA van as it drove her up to Nixon Deebee's farm with her Great Horned Owl in back. Faridah had not given the big female bird a name, which was probably just as well. Wildlife officials had agreed to allow her to transfer possession of the owl to Deebee, who would make sure she was well fed and fit before releasing her back into the wild.

Faridah, like the other girls, was a ward of the federal government now. As war refugees, their immigration status looked promising. If only Sammy Yel Bak had been so lucky. The waif-like girl sat quietly in the far back seat of the van between Nicole and the interpreter, her eyes an empty canvas, as she stared out at the passing scenery. Still dangling from her neck was the chain the paramedics had ripped from Sammy's neck. It had been a gift to Sammy from his father, Faridah had told us through the interpreter. It was a magic amulet, Sammy claimed, that had protected him from bullets countless times—a silver crusader's cross.

"Nice out here in the country," Darla said.

I nodded.

"It's nice that you're doing this . . . for the girl, I mean, and her bird."

I shrugged.

"No, I mean it. You and your daughter could have just walked away after I got shot, but you didn't. I won't forget that, Franco. And who would've believed this would have turned into such a crazy, wild thing with these kids."

I couldn't think of anything to say to that. Marcia had flown up to join us at the hotel in Midtown where we'd rented a couple of rooms. I had had several long talks with her and Nicole, whose bruises had begun to yellow and who seemed to be doing a little better. Mostly, we talked about Faridah and Sammy—by horror forced too soon from their childhood in another land—who'd somehow ended up thrown together in the underbelly of this city of their dreams, yet still managed to stand up against such impossible odds.

What had the young Christian Sammy, veteran of a real war with real weapons fought by children, seen in the slight Muslim girl and her band of fellow orphans? What had he seen in the *Book of the Mews* and their captured wild owl? Visions of chivalry? Arthurian or Al-Furusiyya knights in full armor, astride their mounts with banners waving, riding down Fifth Avenue? We would never know. What we did know was that Barry LaGrange's feature article in the *Post* two days before had forced the venue for Sammy Yel Bak's memorial service to be moved twice and brought out hordes of everyday New Yorkers to stand quietly behind the police lines in front of the big church on Malcolm X Boulevard. The lines of African-American, Pakistani, Indian, Bangladeshi, Sri Lankan, and even some Sudanese cab drivers in their cars backed up traffic for nearly an hour.

The cops were busy closing the rest of the matter, too. Cato Raines' ex-wife claimed his body and had him cremated without any kind of memorial. Jayani Miller, two other Grayland Tower guards, and a half dozen members of Los Miembros were all in custody facing numerous counts of abduction, rape, and murder. Mitchell Collins had been arrested at JFK while trying to flee the country. Dominic Watisi was not under arrest for anything yet. He was apparently coming clean with authorities and in true semi-celebrity fashion both his legal and propaganda teams were working full time both to try to keep him out of jail and to shore up any damage to his reputation.

We hadn't heard any more from Dr. Lonigan, but that changed when we pulled into the turnoff for Deebee's farm.

"Almost forgot," Darla said. She pulled a plain sealed envelope from her pocket and handed it to me.

"What's this?"

"A check for all the hours you put in plus expenses."

"Okay."

"Dr. Lonigan said you more than earned it."

"Amen to that."

"You know what else she said?"

"I can hardly wait."

"You remember Mitch Collins?"

"Yeah, they caught him."

"Right, and the cops are still trying to sort out his arrangement with Jayani and involvement with Los Miembros. But Lonigan says she was worried about him all along; she just didn't want to say anything. Guess he gave some big checks to her animal rights league or whatever."

"Beautiful."

Deebee was waiting for us as the van pulled into his driveway. We climbed out and he said he had a mew all prepared for the owl. The interpreter spoke with the ASPCA agent, and out of respect for Faridah, we all waited to allow her to don her glove and retrieve the owl from in back.

A few moments later, the young woman appeared from around the side of the van, walking calmly, the owl almost an extension of her arm.

"Nice to see a bird so relaxed around her falconer," Deebee said. He nodded with admiration and directed Faridah and the rest of us toward the barn and the mews.

The air was warm but much less humid this morning. A pair of butterflies played with one another over a sunflower in Deebee's garden. Even the dogs were relatively still and well behaved.

No one spoke as we entered the cool of the barn. We had reached the entrance to the stall prepared for the owl when the big bird riding on the girl's mangalah did something unexpected.

Tilting its head, the owl seemed to bow toward her handler. Faridah lowered her head and the bird gently grazed her hair with its beak.

"Hardly ever see that. Especially with an owl. This bird an imprint?" Deebee asked, a note of concern in his voice.

Proudly aloof, even trained birds of prey hardly ever offer such displays of attachment for their handlers. Imprinted birds, on the other hand, those raised and hand fed from birth by humans, develop such intense attachment to humans it would be tantamount to a death sentence to release one back to the wild.

"Oh, no," Nicole said. "We're sure of that. Sammy told me how they trapped her in the park and Faridah confirmed all the details. It wasn't too long ago, in fact. I thought they were very lucky to find her."

"They hunted with her?"

"Absolutely. Several times, in fact."

"Amazing."

The interpreter was translating softly for Faridah. The girl nodded to confirm Nicole's account, and in her face I read the deepest sadness, reaching back beyond her years to a slave on the underground railroad, to the protection she'd found in a young soldier, to ancestral nomads she had never known.

"One thing's for sure," Deebee said, looking at Faridah with a twinkle in his eye.

The girl looked up at the older man.

"You've gained yourself some kind of connection with this old owl, haven't you, little lady?"

Faridah smiled. We watched as she gently released the big bird's jesses and skillfully transferred the owl to its new perch.

"I guess you could call it an instinct for survival," Deebee said.

Wars may never end, I thought. Children may always die. But through it all, or in spite of it all, the city looms bright and never silent, its mist-laden spans made as if for hunting, its shadowed heights beckoning like baited lures, twirling in the darkness.

"I guess you could," I said.

ABOUT THE AUTHOR

Andy Straka is a native of upstate New York and a licensed falconer. Featured by *Publishers Weekly* as one of "ten rising stars" in crime fiction, he is the author of four previous novels. His debut Frank Pavlicek mystery, *A Witness Above,* garnered Shamus, Anthony, and Agatha Award nominations for Best First Novel in 2002. *A Killing Sky* received an Anthony Award nomination in 2003. *Cold Quarry* won the 2004 Shamus Award for best paperback original private eye novel.

Andy's inaugural non-series novel, *Record of Wrongs,* was labeled "a first-rate thriller" by *Mystery Scene* magazine in 2008. He lives with his family in Virginia.